q-13

THE BOOK OF REVENGE

NINE LIVES TRILOGY 3

WATERFORD CITY AND COUNTY WITHDRAWN LIBRARIES

E.R. MURRAY

MERCIER PRESS

IRISH PUBLISHER – IRISH STORY

LEABHARLANN
PHORT LÁIRGE

Bertrams	01/08/2018
UA	02344836

MERCIER PRESS
Cork
www.mercierpress.ie

© E. R. Murray, 2018

ISBN: 978 1 78117 576 7

10 9 8 7 6 5 4 3 2 1

This book is sold subject to the condition that it shall not, by way of trade or otherwise, be lent, resold, hired out or otherwise circulated without the publisher's prior consent in any form of binding or cover other than that in which it is published and without a similar condition including this condition being imposed on the subsequent purchaser.

No part of this publication may be reproduced or transmitted in any form or by any means, electronic or mechanical, including photocopying, recording or any information or retrieval system, without the prior permission of the publisher in writing.

All characters and events in this book are entirely fictional. Any resemblance to any person, living or dead, which may occur inadvertently is completely unintentional.

Printed and bound in the EU.

Prologue

'What do you mean my parents are alive?' asks Ebony, crossing to the open cottage window for some air.

As the breeze tumbles in, a sleek, black shape streaks across the bright sky, weaving through pillows of cloud. Ebony shivers, but it's only a crow. In the distance, the sea is calm and shimmering as the Oddley Cove fishermen prepare to haul in their nets, completely unaware of the battle that had raged through the night.

'It seems your parents' bodies were never found,' replies Mr O'Hara, 'because there were no bodies.'

'So where exactly are they?'

'In the past,' answers Mr O'Hara, rubbing one hand over the bristles of his thick, white moustache. 'Where no one would think to look.'

'But why?'

His face overcast, Mr O'Hara shrugs. 'I only received the information, not explanations.'

Despite the light streaming in, the cottage air is cool and heavy. Silence shrouds the room like a sickness. Ebony surveys the rest of the group, anger fizzing through her veins as Mulligan and Uncle Cornelius, Chiyoko and Old Joe watch closely. On the sofa, Icarus Bean brims with muted rage. Even Aunt Ruby is tight-lipped, her backlit hair glowing like polished jasper as she steadies herself with one hand on the kitchen table.

'What is he talking about?' Ebony asks, looking to her aunt. 'Grandpa told me all about my parents' accident.'

A confused frown crumples Aunt Ruby's forehead and she bites down on her lip. 'He can't have known–' she begins.

'My whole life,' interrupts Ebony, 'I've believed my parents were dead.'

'We all thought they were dead,' says Icarus, his fists balled as he glares at Mr O'Hara.

'The proof only just arrived,' says Mr O'Hara.

When he shows no sign of explaining further, Aunt Ruby pats the table with her palm. 'So where is it? This proof?' Her eyes glisten and her frown softens. Ebony's stomach flips – could O'Hara be speaking the truth?

Slowly, Mr O'Hara pulls a photograph from his inside jacket pocket. 'This was delivered by a King Vulture just before you returned,' he says, placing it on the kitchen table.

There is a collective gasp.

The photograph is dated 1871. It shows a solemn-faced Ivy and Rufus Smart looking stiffly at the camera, their eyes clearly swollen. Between them, perched at a strange angle on a red velvet chair decorated with studs, Ebony sees her own face, eyes tightly closed. Behind the group, a mirror reflects a fireplace that Ebony recognises immediately. There are several framed paintings on the wall and some of them are familiar.

4

'It's the living room of 23 Mercury Lane,' says Ebony. 'What does this prove?' Leaning in for a better look, she notices that Ivy and Rufus are slightly out of focus, while her past self is completely clear. The expressionless face and closed eyes are eerie. 'Is my past self sick?'

Winston pokes his head out of Ebony's sleeve and squeaks. An odd feeling stirs in Ebony's gut. Her throat dries, making it painful to swallow.

'She's dead,' replies O'Hara.

'She's … what?' gasps Ebony.

Chiyoko takes Ebony's hand and gives it a squeeze. Before Mr O'Hara can answer, his wife intervenes.

'This is a memento mori, a post-mortem image,' says Mrs O'Hara, gently. 'A photograph to honour the dead. Very common in Victorian times – often, the only photo a person would ever have taken.'

Ebony gives a small cough. 'You're kidding, right? It's gross.' And yet she cannot peel her eyes away.

'How is this proof that they're alive, O'Hara?' asks Icarus. 'This is nonsense. I'm leaving.'

'No, wait! He's right – look!' calls Ebony, spotting something strange.

As Ebony points, the others lean in, like a string of Mrs O'Hara's shadow puppets. One by one, they gasp.

'Rufus is wearing runners,' says Ebony, 'and Ivy has a digital wristwatch. Those things didn't exist back then. They're giving us clues. These people aren't past incarnations – they're my parents!'

'She's right,' says Aunt Ruby, a mix of joy and concern on her face. 'They're in Victorian times – but why? And how have they managed not to bump into their past selves?'

Ebony stares hard at the photograph. 'I don't know, but look at the mirror! There's a message instead of a picture in one of the frames it's reflecting.'

The block capitals reflect backwards, but Ebony can decipher the message easily. She reads it out loud.

'Help us. We're stuck.' Ebony looks at each of the others in turn, licking her dry lips as her heart skips. 'We must do as they ask. We've got to help them.'

THIRD BODY FOUND IN RIVER LIFFEY – POLICE SUSPECT MURDER

As another body is pulled from the Liffey, police have issued a warning for Dublin residents to be on their guard. This is the third body to be found with a black skull mark in the middle of its forehead. The man, aged between twenty-five and thirty, has not yet been identified. Playing down concerns about a mass murderer loose in the city, a police spokesperson has confirmed that they are treating all three deaths as suspicious and have urged any witnesses to come forward.

The night was clear and crisp as Ebony Smart huddled against the chimney pot on top of 23 Mercury Lane, newspaper in hand. Unable to sleep, her dreams filled with red pinprick eyes and Zach's cruel laughter, only the cool night air and open sky could give her some relief.

It was almost ten weeks since Mr O'Hara had revealed

the truth about her parents and Icarus Bean had used the Shadowlands to travel into the past to look for them, but there had been no word about his progress. The last few weeks in the city had been increasingly tense. Ambrose had been voted out of his position as judge of the Order of Nine Lives, placing O'Hara temporarily in charge. Ebony and her aunt had been scouring the archives, trying to figure out a way to defeat the Deus-Umbra without the Silent Peregrine, in case the demon returned. Although their investigations had been fruitless, Ebony felt better being occupied – when night fell all her worries resurfaced. She hid her restlessness by sitting on the rooftop; the last thing she wanted was to be sent back to West Cork.

Although Ebony had enjoyed being near Old Joe and her animals, hiding out in Oddley Cove with her aunt and Uncle Cornelius on Mr O'Hara's command had felt wrong. Especially when the O'Haras had returned to Dublin right away, seeking medical help for Seamus, who had failed to wake up after the battle. Mr O'Hara had been adamant that the countryside would be the safest place for her, their guardian, until they knew Ambrose's next move. But then the attacks started.

When one of the Order's men missed his usual night shift no one seemed overly concerned – until his body turned up in the River Liffey bearing the mark of the Shadow Walkers on his forehead. The police began asking questions – questions that could lead to the existence of the

Order being revealed – and so the Order's main security was placed on high alert. After the second body, the Order realised they were being targeted and Ebony, Aunt Ruby and Uncle Cornelius were recalled to Dublin. Mr O'Hara had decided that there was safety in numbers and all members were commanded to travel in pairs after dark. It was clear that Zach and Ambrose were behind the deaths, so utmost caution was exercised.

Ebony's instincts told her that it was only a matter of time before their enemies launched an all-out attack on the Order and she believed they needed to prepare for the worst. After all, she had foiled their plans for world domination not once, but twice, destroying the soul-swapping machine and accidentally killing Zach's mother in the process. She had no doubt that both Ambrose and Zach would be seeking revenge.

Her legs crossed and her eyes fixed on the stars above the Dublin city rooftops, Ebony set the newspaper down and pressed her back into the cool brick as she stroked her pet rat, Winston, who was curled up in her lap. Pulling a bronze rose from her pocket with her other hand, she twiddled it absentmindedly between forefinger and thumb. As guardian, the rose allowed her access to the Reflectory, the place where all the Order's souls rested before they were reincarnated.

'Time's racing by, Winston,' said Ebony. 'We're sitting targets, getting nowhere fast. O'Hara and my aunt mean well, but waiting for Ambrose to make a move or slip up and show us his whereabouts is not going to work. We should be hunting our enemies down.'

Sitting up on his haunches, Winston looked into Ebony's eyes, blinking slowly.

'As for Icarus – what if something has gone wrong? What if something terrible happens to my parents?' Winston's tail drooped and his fur flattened. Ebony tickled under his chin. 'I know I've got you, but I've only just found out they're still alive. I don't want to lose them again before we even get to meet.'

Lifting his right paw, his signal for no, to show he understood, Winston snuggled in close. Shutting her eyes, Ebony heaved a big sigh and tried to decide on her next move. When Icarus had gone into the Shadowlands to see if he could reach her parents, Ebony had offered to go too, but everyone – even Winston – voted for her to stay. At the time she had been secretly relieved. The Shadowlands were dangerous and filled with Ambrose's Shadow Walkers, each desperate to capture her for their master. But now, the waiting was unbearable. She had to overcome her fear and see if Icarus needed help. Working alone was out of the question; she had learned her lesson and knew that she needed the Order on her side.

'If only we knew what was delaying Icarus – he can't have just disappeared,' said Ebony. 'His absence weakens our position and it makes me uneasy. I need to go after him. Maybe I should try Mrs O'Hara? She can't travel in the

Shadowlands but she knows them in her own way. Any help is better than no help.'

Jumping up and down on the spot, Winston shook his head and thrust his right paw in the air, over and over. Placing the rose back in her pocket and scooping him up with two hands, Ebony lifted him up to eye level. He stopped his protest and blinked.

'I know you want to keep me safe, but Ambrose and Zach have to be stopped. They're killing people from the Order, and because I ruined their plans, it's only a matter of time until they come after me. We need to be ready for them. Icarus is one of our best men, but without knowing how to travel time in the Shadowlands, what can I do? If only I still had *The Book of Learning* to guide me.'

Ebony's thoughts took her back to the recent battle on the Shadow Walkers' ship, back to Ambrose ripping apart her beloved book and using its magic to bring the ship's dragon figurehead to life. The loss of the book still made her feel like part of her own self was missing.

A loud clanging noise from below jolted Ebony from her thoughts. Feeling her palm grow hot, Ebony inspected the skull-shaped mark left there by Ambrose so he could always locate her. The skull was no bigger than a pea, but the edges now looked red and swollen – they were almost glowing. She traced her fingers around the skull – the mark was pulsating like a nasty midge bite. And was it getting bigger?

'I don't like this,' she said.

Climbing to her feet, Ebony accidentally dislodged the newspaper. As she watched, the wind caught it and lifted it into the air like a kite, the pages rattling and separating. After setting Winston down, she carefully made her way down the sloping tiles to the roof's edge and peered into the street. The orange streetlights gave an eerie glow and shadows lurked everywhere. Scanning them for any sign of movement or a hint of danger, Ebony held her breath. Although her heart was pumping, everything seemed normal.

Another clang sounded in the street and this time Ebony was able to follow the noise to where a sack of recycling, left out for collection under a streetlight, had been torn open. A huge, bedraggled tortoiseshell cat with a crooked tail was wrestling with its contents, trying to hook an open food can with one paw.

'It's just a cat,' said Ebony, exhaling deeply. When Winston squealed, she added, 'Don't worry, he's down below in the street and no danger to you.'

As she turned to begin the climb back up to join Winston, she heard a cackle, followed by a crunch. Checking behind her, Ebony saw that the cat had now vanished. Only a clump of hair and the food can rolling along the pavement, leaving a trail of dark splotches, indicated it had been there at all. Winston squealed. When Ebony turned to look at him, he was pointing to the sky. Following the line of his paw, she saw a faraway flame shoot across the black night.

'A shooting star, Winston! Isn't it beautiful?'

But as he watched the ball of fire arc across the sky, Winston's fur bristled and he bared his teeth. His whiskers twitched and his tail stuck out poker straight. He pulled himself up to be as big and threatening as he could and hissed into the night air. Ebony scrambled back up the roof and lifted him with her unmarked hand. As the streak of colour died out, the pulsing in her other hand died away. On closer inspection, she saw that the swelling had gone – had she imagined it?

'It's just a dying star and a mangy old cat,' said Ebony. 'Nothing to be worried about.'

In her grasp, Winston trembled, his heart beating faster than a marching drum. Ebony cuddled him close and told herself it was because Winston didn't like heights. She should have left him in her room, snug and warm in his cage. In fact, she should probably be in bed too, trying to sleep, instead of gazing out over rooftops.

But deep down she knew something was wrong. Cats didn't cackle. And cats didn't make her hand throb.

Placing Winston in a side pocket of her trousers, Ebony walked carefully along the thin path running the length of the roof, back towards the skylight.

'We've got to use our time more effectively, Winston. I refuse to be an easy target,' she said, lowering her body through the skylight into the attic. 'This time, I will act first, with the Order of Nine Lives behind me. All I need to figure out is how to convince everyone to help.'

The next morning, Ebony was woken by the sound of raised voices. Hurriedly, she clambered out of bed and dressed. Snatching up Winston, she hid him in her sleeve before racing downstairs. As she sped into the kitchen, she almost collided with a red-faced Miss Malone. Aunt Ruby was towering over the big, blue-haired lady, her violet eyes sparking and her eyeballs looking like they were about to pop out. Miss Malone had her gaze fixed on an empty, bright-yellow saucer that she was spinning around in her cupped hands. There was none of the usual breakfast activity from the helicopters and dump trucks that lined the room and carried the food to the table; all was silent and still. Ebony's stomach rumbled.

'This is unthinkable!' spat Aunt Ruby. 'There is no reason to take such drastic action.'

'I am only relaying the message, Ruby.'

'What's going on?' asked Ebony.

But the two women were far too engrossed in their argument to reply. Looking around, Ebony spotted a sheet of paper screwed up on the floor – could that be the cause of their dispute? As she moved to pick it up, her aunt noticed and shot her a look that stopped her in her tracks.

'That's none of your business, Ebony. It's a private matter. Leave it where it is.'

Nodding agreement, Ebony angled her sleeve so that Winston could see the crumpled paper and discreetly pointed. Then she lowered her arm so he could climb down her leg. Understanding her wishes, Winston began his descent. Seconds later, he had the scrunched-up paper in his teeth and was dragging it along the floor towards his favourite hidey-hole behind the cooker. Ebony kept her fingers crossed as he made slow progress, hoping Aunt Ruby wouldn't notice him.

'And where exactly did Jeremiah get this intelligence?' asked Aunt Ruby.

'I've already told you, Mr O'Hara swore me to secrecy.'

'What intelligence?' asked Ebony, even though she was pretty certain it was pointless to ask.

She was right. The two ladies eyeballed each other, ignoring her. After a while, Ebony repeated her question.

This time, Aunt Ruby answered in a scornful voice, hands on hips. 'Headquarters has received some information about Icarus's past that makes them believe he may have been deceiving us all along and is actually an enemy of the Order.' She paused to shake her head. 'O'Hara thinks that his failure to return from his current mission is confirmation of his treachery. As a result, he wants to issue a warrant for my brother's arrest and incarceration if he does return.'

'Icarus – a traitor?' asked Ebony, gritting her teeth and feeling the heat rise in her face. 'He's saved my life countless times and always behaves in the Order's best interests. There's no way he's our enemy. He's one of our best and we have no chance against Ambrose without him!'

At the mention of Ambrose, Miss Malone shuddered.

'What information could Mr O'Hara have possibly received that would make him think such a thing?' asked Ebony.

Glancing at Aunt Ruby, Miss Malone tightened her lips and shook her head. 'We're not allowed to tell you.'

Aunt Ruby glared at Miss Malone. 'Forget it, Ebony – it's utter nonsense and not worth knowing. Our concern should lie with Icarus's safe return and the success of his mission.'

'I agree,' said Ebony, taking a seat next to Miss Malone and clenching her hands together on the table in front of her. Peering around her aunt, she saw that Winston had reached the cooker. She watched for a second as he reversed in, trying to pull the ball of paper after him into the space between the appliance and the wall. 'Has there been any news of his progress?'

'None,' replied Miss Malone quietly.

'So what if he's hurt and can't return?' asked Aunt Ruby.

Spinning the saucer in her hands, Miss Malone kept her gaze averted, shifting uncomfortably in her chair. Determined to get to the bottom of things – her uncle's honour and meeting her parents was at stake – Ebony continued with her questioning.

'What do you think, Miss Malone? Do you think Icarus is a traitor?'

Miss Malone cleared her throat. 'I'm in agreement with you and your aunt, Ebony. Icarus is one of our best. But I've never seen O'Hara so worried. He's been suspicious for some time – but this new information has him spooked. And when the Order finds out that Icarus is in fact–'

Aunt Ruby threw Miss Malone a silencing look. Miss Malone winced, then pressed her lips together. Sighing, Aunt Ruby rubbed at her temple with a thumb and forefinger.

'That Icarus is in fact what?' asked Ebony, surveying her aunt's face. 'What's happened exactly? Has he done something wrong?'

'He has not,' replied Aunt Ruby, 'and that is why we will not discuss it any further.'

Miss Malone looked at Aunt Ruby, then back to the yellow saucer.

Feeling her hands turn shaky, Ebony clenched them more tightly and took a deep breath before continuing. 'But does Mr O'Hara have the power to command an arrest without a vote?'

'Without a judge in place, yes,' said Aunt Ruby. 'But he should wait for Icarus to return and see what he has to report.'

'Can't you suggest that to him, Miss Malone?' asked Ebony. 'Surely it's a reasonable request.'

'Mr O'Hara is doing what he thinks is best for all concerned,' replied Miss Malone. 'Enemy activity is increasing and we need to exercise extreme caution. There was an attack in the Phoenix Park last night – we were almost another man down.'

'But if Icarus is arrested, what will happen to my parents?' Ebony fought the tears that threatened to spill. 'If he'd been successful, he would have returned by now. They might never receive the help they need! Mr O'Hara can't do that – it's not fair!'

'It's not about fairness, Ebony,' said Miss Malone. 'It's about securing the safety of the Order's future – about securing your future.'

'Then it's even more important that we help Icarus,' said Ebony. 'Would you stand up against Mr O'Hara and back Icarus if I needed you to? Mr O'Hara may be able to command an arrest, but he has to listen to our people. If we stand against him and demand a vote, he'll have to agree, won't he? You said yourself that you agree with us.'

Aunt Ruby smiled at her niece. 'I know you're thinking of your uncle, but don't do anything rash. Mr O'Hara may accept that you're our guardian, but you haven't yet earned his full respect. Let me speak to him tomorrow. He has called us – Uncle Cornelius and me – to a meeting. I'm sure he'll be reasonable.'

'That would be best,' agreed Miss Malone. 'As the intelligence came from his wife, it must be treated with care.'

Realising she had let part of the secret slip, Miss Malone started. The saucer clattered as it dropped from her hand

and spun on the table. She looked up warily. Aunt Ruby's mouth dropped open and she put one hand to her heart. 'Mrs O'Hara? Are you sure?'

Her violet eyes burned brightly. Ebony could tell that her aunt, despite sounding calm, was concentrating her energy on trying to stay composed; this new information had unnerved her. Miss Malone nodded.

Ruby said, 'This changes everything. Why didn't you tell me before? I trust Mrs O'Hara completely, so these findings may just be true. But if they are, poor Icarus ...' She stared off into the distance, clearly trying to make sense of the situation. Then, as though suddenly remembering that Ebony and Miss Malone were there, she continued, 'But regardless, Icarus is no traitor. I must make O'Hara realise that he is mistaken.'

As her aunt lapsed into silence again, Ebony checked on Winston's progress. She was just in time to see the final edge of the paper disappear behind the cooker. Certain it would contain the information she was seeking – the reason behind O'Hara's sudden decision – she relaxed a little and waited to see which way the conversation would turn.

'Miss Malone, I must apologise for my earlier outburst. I know you're just doing your job,' said Aunt Ruby, lacing her long, slender fingers together as though trying to tie them into knots. 'Tea, anybody?'

Ebony rolled her eyes – what good was tea? – but Miss Malone nodded, seemingly relieved. Winston popped his head out from behind the cooker, his whiskers twitching as he checked the surrounding area. Seeing that it was all clear, he made his way back across the kitchen. Ebony kept her eyes averted.

Snatching up her chestnut pipe, Aunt Ruby scraped a match, lit her tobacco and then the gas ring. She placed the kettle on the hob, then turned to Ebony and smiled. At that exact moment, Winston arrived back at Ebony's side.

'Glad you could join us, little man,' she said. The pipe bounced up and down in her mouth as she spoke. Then, without warning, she turned and threw the match down behind the cooker. There was a flash as the paper Winston had hidden ignited. There was a sizzle and a whoosh as stale fat caught fire and flames leapt up the back of the cooker, scorching the wall.

Winston squealed and scampered to the kitchen door, as far away from the flames as he could manage. Ebony jumped up, crying, 'What are you doing?'

Miss Malone was already on her feet, spraying the flames with the fire extinguisher from next to the cooker. The fire went out instantly, leaving a small wisp of smoke and the scent of a washed-out bonfire on a rainy night.

'Are you crazy?' shouted Ebony. 'You could have set the whole house on fire!'

'It was under control,' replied Aunt Ruby, exhaling a stream of pipe smoke, a smile playing on her lips. 'Which is more than I can say for you!'

Beside the cooker, Miss Malone was still gripping the fire extinguisher with both hands, looking rather shell-shocked. Checking on Winston, Ebony discovered that he had his back flattened against the kitchen door, and his eyes were big and watery. Anger rose inside her, cold and sharp.

'What do you expect when, after all we've been through, you're still withholding information from me? I'm the guardian: I demand to know what's going on with Icarus.'

In reply, Aunt Ruby drew herself up to full height, her hair flaring out behind her despite the fact they were indoors. Her eyes flashed and sparked and her skin turned deathly white. When she spoke, her voice was thunderous.

'O'Hara has asked me to keep it confidential until after we've spoken. Trust me, if I'm to remain in a position where I can help Icarus, that's what I must do.'

The anger in Ebony shifted and coiled, twisting her insides. She felt the vein in her forehead throb as she clenched her jaw. Balling her fists, her face grew hot with rage. On the floor, Winston ran towards his best friend as she launched into a tirade.

'Trust? That goes both ways you know,' she yelled. 'I have to get my parents back – what if they're linked to the destiny I have to fulfil to reach Ultimation? Or to our ability to defeat Zach and Ambrose? If there's something stopping their return, then it's my duty as guardian to fix it. But I can't do that if I don't know everything that's going on.'

'That note from O'Hara summoned me and Uncle Cornelius tomorrow morning, warned of Icarus's impending arrest and the reason why – which I've already told you I cannot share – and asked a personal favour regarding Seamus. Also, it was addressed to me and is, therefore, none of your business.'

Vaguely aware of something tugging at her trouser leg, Ebony kicked out. There was a squeal as Winston skidded across the floor. Grinding to a halt, he stared up at her, his nose scrunched and his ears flat. Although Ebony knew that she'd hurt her friend, it barely registered in her brain. Inside, her rage was a torrent, taking over her senses. She felt venom pumping in her veins and her brain throbbed. The world turned wobbly and green spots danced in front of her eyes, but no matter how much she rubbed, they wouldn't clear.

'Ebony? Are you OK?' asked Miss Malone.

'Let's open the windows for some air,' said Aunt Ruby, turning to tug at the catch of the one behind her.

Miss Malone headed for the second window, but when Winston gave a squeal, she looked back. 'W-where's Ebony gone?' she said in horror.

But Ebony could no longer hear the words. Her thoughts were jumbled and tumbling and the world around her was changing. Squeezing her eyes shut and focusing all her energy, she managed to clear her mind. When she opened her eyes, everything was sketch-like, all shadowy and tonal. Her aunt and Miss Malone were now green, shimmering shapes in a different world. Ebony's stomach knotted. She had slipped into the Shadowlands – but how? She hadn't willed herself there. Had her anger brought her? Or had someone pulled her in?

'Ebony?'

The bird-like voice made Ebony jump and it took a second for her to figure out what direction the sound had come from.

'Mrs O'Hara? Is that you?'

The words felt sticky in her mouth, an effect of the Shadowlands. It had been a while since Ebony had dared to venture inside and, as always, the place instantly began to suck the joy out of her.

'Yes. We don't have much time.'

A figure appeared before Ebony like a half-finished sketch; it was green and wavering, but clearly female. Ebony swallowed and concentrated on the image until a faint but recognisable outline of Mrs O'Hara formed.

'I'm sorry about using the Shadowlands, but I had to get to you quickly. I'm receiving a vision that you must see, and Icarus has uncovered a dark secret that may have catastrophic results.'

Ebony's heart raced. 'What secret? Tell me.'

'First, the vision. I know you want to rally the Order against our enemies, but if you act now, you will fail – and risk losing the support of my husband. You need to know Ambrose's plan in order to thwart his intentions and you also need the Order's support. Be patient. Now, close your eyes and let me show you what is happening. Keep them closed – otherwise we'll lose our connection.'

Not sure what to expect, Ebony did as she was told.

As soon as she shut her eyes, a tar-black room with a dying fire appeared. To the right, the wall was marked with a Shadow Walker skull. In front of the smouldering fire, the silhouetted figure of Ambrose knelt on a dusty floor, gazing into the cinders. In his hand, he held a large set of cast-iron tongs and, despite the heat from the fire, he was shivering. Beside him, Zach was also kneeling, his head bowed and his hands resting on the skin of a bongo drum. In front of them, just above their heads, Ebony could make out an array of paraphernalia on a ledge hewn out of the wall above the fire; it was like the altar she'd uncovered in the hidden room in her Hideout. On it were rocks inked with black skulls, cracked ceramic pots, a bird carcass picked clean of flesh and a framed photograph, its image blurred and indistinguishable behind the smoke-stained glass. And in the middle of the altar was a sheep's skull: charred and fissured, the rims of its eyeholes were black with soot and a strange blue glow emanated from within.

I wonder where they are, thought Ebony.

Grabbing the sheep's skull with the tongs, Ambrose shoved it into the middle of the embers. As the embers began to splutter and flare, the rims of the sheep's eye sockets glowed brighter, emitting smoke. The blue light inside burst out from the hearth like ghostly flames, sending sparks of cobalt shooting around the room. Zach ducked to avoid them, but Ambrose remained in place, heaving a deep sigh as tiny dots of blue, like mackerel scales, freckled his face. Hesitantly, Zach straightened to his original position. As a spark hit his chin, his skin sizzled.

In the hearth, flames crackled and sparked. Lifting the sheep's skull carefully back onto the ledge, Ambrose removed a small vial from his pocket and poured the contents over it. Ebony narrowed her eyes, but there was no label. The thick, amber liquid coated the crown of the smoking skull and quickly evaporated. After muttering a few words under his breath, Ambrose pushed a wedge of moss into one eye socket. The blue glow thinned to a single, sniper-like beam and Ambrose shifted position so the beam connected with his gaze at eye level.

'Can you hear me?' whispered Ambrose, his voice hoarse and rasping as he stared intently into the blue.

Zach looked away from the skull, as though too afraid to face it. Smoke began to plume from the left socket, and the moss burst into flames. Zach coughed as the putrid fumes filled the room, but Ambrose didn't react, even though they must have been choking him too. His gaze was transfixed on the skull. As the blue light wavered, Ambrose jerked his head around and gave Zach a cold smile. Zach's face dropped, but Ambrose didn't seem to care.

Reaching out his hand, Ambrose placed his fingertips on the sizzling hot skull. Once more, the blue glow brightened. Wincing, Ambrose refused to cry out as his flesh sizzled, fusing with the white-hot bone. Pain etched across his face, Ambrose gave a nod. Immediately, Zach lifted his hands and began beating the drum, the skin vibrating in deep and melancholic tones. The drum rang out, loud and haunting. Shadows danced on the walls as the fire leapt higher. In the centre of the hearth, the outline of a winged creature appeared for an instant. As Ambrose's eyes widened, Ebony felt her throat dry and her airways constrict.

'It's here!' cried Ambrose, his voice tinged with delight. 'The Deus-Umbra is listening.'

Zach hit the drum harder, until the noise filled the space.

'We need to speak with you,' said Ambrose, speaking into the flames where the figure had been. 'I know you are weak and recovering, but I promise, if you help us defeat Ebony Smart and the Order, I will make sure you have what you desire above all else.'

A cruel cackling sound filled the air. Ebony watched as the flames leapt up, glowing blue and violet. Zach beat the drum harder, wincing as his palms struck the drum, but seemingly unable to stop. His arm and neck muscles bulged and his head seemed to swell, the veins in his temples throbbing. Keeping his eyes on the fire's heart, he began to rock in time to the beat as though in a trance. The flames seemed to close in, reaching out for him.

'Speak to us, mighty Deus-Umbra,' yelled Ambrose, his face crazed.

The flames turned wild and thick black smoke billowed out, filling the room. Zach began to tremble and shudder, jerking this way and that as though an electric current was shocking his body. The drumming stopped and Zach leapt to his feet. His body was unsteady and he stumbled. Seemingly unable to control his movements, Zach's body lurched to one side.

'Zach! What are you doing? Why have you stopped?' cried Ambrose, turning around.

Wondering the same, Ebony's eyes searched every inch of the scene, her hand instinctively clasping the crescent-moon-shaped amulet she wore around her neck that allowed her access to the sky world.

Facing Zach, Ambrose closed his mouth and tensed his jaw. The colour in his face drained away as he stared into Zach's eyes.

Zach's eyes glowed red for an instant and then, deeper than an ocean trench and colder than ice, they turned completely black. When he opened his mouth to speak, his jaw seemed to grow and expand, large fangs dripping with saliva suddenly visible.

4

'And what is it you think I desire?' said an inhuman voice, like metal scraping against metal.

'To be worshipped as a god. Like the old times, when there was peace between you and our kind.'

'And what makes you think I need you, human? When I am strong enough, I will take what I need.'

Ambrose chuckled. 'You only know how to terrorise – how will you make people obey? Bring you gifts and food? If you just take what you want, they will fear you and try to kill you. You will know no rest. I, however, will make them fall to their knees and worship you.'

'You failed me last time.' The demon's voice sounded darker, rasping, more menacing. 'You may have raised me, but you failed to defeat our enemies and let them drive me into hiding. What makes you think this time will be different?'

A vein in Ambrose's forehead pulsated as he replied. 'Help me capture the guardian and I will have complete power. And then I will make sure that the people – not just the Order, but all the people in the world – will worship you once more.'

'The world?' screeched the demon. Zach's body shook.

'Why should I trust you?'

'I can help you recover, grow strong, without exposing your existence. Keep you safe. You don't understand the modern world; you can't achieve what you want alone. The world has weapons now you can't even imagine – they might even be strong enough to defeat a demon. You need me.'

Zach's body shuddered violently, sparks spewing from his mouth. After a moment, the sparks died down. 'I will think on it,' growled the demon. 'But if I decide to help you with Ebony Smart and you fail me again, or go back on your word, I will tear you limb from limb. I will massacre all that follow you. Now I must go. Someone else is listening.'

As the demon withdrew and Zach began to come round, his eyes locked on to Ambrose; for an instant his irises flashed red and a shadow passed over his face. But Ambrose didn't notice. Instead, he held up a thin, silver chain, letting it dangle between finger and thumb.

'It'll think on it … Tear me limb from limb indeed! When I send my Shadow Walkers to sneak up on it and secure this around its ankle, the demon won't have any option but to do what I tell it.'

Ebony leaned in. The chain looked like a simple anklet, but she knew it must contain powerful magic if it could control a demon.

'What is it?' asked Zach.

'Here, try.' Ambrose slipped the chain over Zach's wrist, then produced a small control from his pocket. It looked like a car key fob with a single button. When he clicked the button, Zach shook and jolted, his teeth rattling, the pain forcing a scream from his throat.

Ebony gasped. Ambrose clicked the button again to stop it and then, without warning, turned around and stared in her direction. The stench of burning filled the air and a blast of heat assaulted Ebony's face. She gasped, the crescent-moon amulet digging into her palm as she fought to keep her eyes closed.

'How nice of you to join us, Ebony Smart!' said Ambrose, his mouth twisted. 'Next time we meet, it'll be in person and as you have just seen, I'll have a very powerful demon at my command. This time, I'm taking your soul. There'll be no stopping me.'

This was it. They were coming for her.

Ebony's eyes shot open and the vision disappeared. Seeking out Mrs O'Hara, she found the woman's outline was beginning to fade.

'Wait! You can't leave – you have to tell me Icarus's secret!' cried Ebony.

As Mrs O'Hara began her reply, her already faint image flickered, her voice crackling and fading in and out. 'Icarus … true heritage … is his brother.' Her image stabilised once more. 'It has turned Icarus's heart black and it will determine your end.'

'My end? Am I going to fail? Am I going to die?'

'The final battle is near and your destinies are entwined. If either of you is to survive, you must help each other.'

'But how? I couldn't hear the secret properly!'

There was no further explanation. Mrs O'Hara's voice faded as her image shimmered and melted away. Without warning, Ebony was back in the kitchen of 23 Mercury Lane. A squeal alerted her that she was standing on Winston's tail. Stumbling backwards, her legs not quite ready for solid ground, her head rang with Mrs O'Hara's warning: *Your destinies are entwined. If either of you is to survive, you must help each other.*

'Where did you go?' asked Miss Malone, moving to Ebony's side and supporting her with an arm around her shoulders.

Taking a moment to gather her thoughts, Ebony rubbed at her face. Above her head, a slate-grey cloud lingered, a sign of the sadness that the Shadowlands instilled in the people who went there. Pulling away from Miss Malone, Ebony bent to pick up Winston. As she nuzzled him, whispering an apology, he turned his head away from her and huffed.

'The Shadowlands,' said Aunt Ruby, nodding at the cloud with a concerned look on her face. 'Where she was told explicitly not to go until Icarus returns and we know that it's safe.'

'I didn't mean to! It was Mrs O'Hara – she was having a vision that she needed to share with me and she pulled me in. Ambrose aims to totally control the demon. It's not fully recovered from our last battle, but Ambrose has agreed to help it in return for its support. It's only a matter of time before it regains its full strength. So time is of the essence. My parents contacted us now for a reason and we need as many of our kind as we can to fight Ambrose. How else are we going to kill him and Zach?'

Miss Malone looked aghast, her skin pale and her face crumpled. 'Kill? That's your intention? But they're part of the Order.'

'It's us or them,' said Ebony, gritting her teeth as heat rose in her face. 'And it's time to avenge my grandpa's murder.' She slammed her fist on the table. 'Where is Icarus? Why haven't we heard anything? I knew I should have gone with him.'

'Enough,' snapped Aunt Ruby. 'This is getting us nowhere.'

Ebony fought the urge to argue. She had to learn how to travel through time to rescue her parents and would need her aunt's help in persuading Mr O'Hara that it was necessary.

'I'm sorry,' she said, using her best apologetic voice. 'But I'm worried. Mrs O'Hara said Icarus's heart has turned black – something bad must have happened. We must find out what before Icarus is arrested.'

Aunt Ruby tapped her pipe against the edge of a lily-shaped ashtray, emptying its contents. Strands of charred tobacco spilled out, creating a crescent-moon shape. Instinctively, Ebony touched the amulet around her neck again.

'I won't let that happen,' said Ruby. 'I'll talk to Jeremiah and make him see sense. In the meantime, we have other things to concern ourselves with – Seamus is on his way.'

'On his way? Has he come round?'

'No, but his doctors are starting to ask awkward questions. We can't risk the Order being revealed to ordinary folk. With Seamus removed from the hospital's care, they'll have less opportunity to pry.'

'So why is he coming here?' Although she knew she sounded mean, Ebony had a good reason for not wanting him around. Seamus would take time from their investigations and be a constant reminder of her guilt – if he hadn't helped her escape Zach and Ambrose using his shadow puppets, he wouldn't be in his current state.

'Mr O'Hara's always at work and Mrs O'Hara is being called upon to assist him more and more. I suggested that Seamus would be better off here because there's always some- one around.'

'That's true,' said Ebony, placing Winston on her shoulder and heading to the fridge. Guilt plucked at her stomach as she took out an apple and some slices of cheese, and she felt her resistance fade. 'He could have the room next to mine, like before.'

'That's very thoughtful, Ebony. Thank you.'

'It'll be good to have the surveillance team around too,' added Miss Malone. 'In case Ambrose returns.'

Ebony paused and glanced back, just in time to see Aunt Ruby glare at Miss Malone. 'Surveillance team?'

'Led by myself and Drinkwater – one of the men who helped you fight against Ambrose at Oddley Cove,' replied Miss Malone. 'We'll be stationed outside, guarding the house closely and making sure that everything is OK. With all the killings, Mr O'Hara felt it was important to take precautionary measures to ensure your safety. We're taking the first watch.'

Although she didn't want to feel like a prisoner in her own home, the thought comforted Ebony. But she needed some air so she could try to make sense of things. She couldn't afford to be scared. Taking out a freezer bag, Ebony dropped her apple and cheese inside, along with a packet of crackers. Shoving the food in one of her trouser pockets and stuffing Winston into her sleeve, she moved to the kitchen door.

'Can I go for a walk to clear my head?' she asked, pointing to the cloud above her.

'As it's daylight, it should be safe,' replied her aunt, 'but keep your wits about you. All the attacks so far may have happened at night but you can never be too careful.'

Ebony grabbed her jacket and headed out. She strode towards St Stephen's Green, her resolve hardening with every step: if their destinies were entwined, she would have to find out Icarus's secret.

The morning was already in full swing, making it too late to sneak into the Hideout in the park. The sun was out and the park was full, so Ebony decided to cut through it and walk the streets of Dublin to clear her mind. Back in Oddley Cove, the sound of waves always drowned out busy thoughts, but in the city she had to rely on the noise and bustle of others. Still, there was nothing like the gentle sway of water, so she headed towards the Liffey. Although bodies had been washing up in its waters, Zach and Ambrose were in hiding. If the vision Mrs O'Hara had shown her was to be believed, they needed time for their plan to work. She doubted they would attack her now, in the daytime, when there were so many people about.

As she left the bustle of the park behind, near the snorting horses and old-fashioned jaunting cars waiting for tourists, a busker could be heard strumming an acoustic guitar. The sound flooded her heart with warmth. Crossing over onto Grafton Street, Ebony paused. On the corner were three men dressed head to toe in black, their skin and clothes painted in a shiny black substance. They sat completely still, hands locked on their knees. On one of the men's shoulders sat a crow and, in front, a hat filled with coins glistened on the pavement.

Intrigued, Ebony watched for a moment. Onlookers laughed and pointed, taking photos as a little girl in a red coat approached with a coin. When she dropped the coin into the hat, one of the men reached a hand towards her. Laughing, the girl took hold of his hand, but as it gripped her so she couldn't pull away, her face fell. Looking back, she relaxed as her parents gave a round of applause. The crowd laughed and the crow lifted off – Ebony hadn't realised the bird was real. It landed on the little girl's head and she began to scream.

Immediately, the men jumped up to help her but that only scared her more and she lashed out. Rushing forward, her father scooped up the girl, whispering reassurances in her ear. The crow took off and flew straight at Ebony, its beak seemingly heading directly for her eyes. Holding her arms up, she covered her face, but the others were too busy calming the screaming girl to notice.

As the bird swooped and flapped past Ebony's ear, its wing feathers grazing her neck, she was certain she heard her name being whispered. Ebony froze. Again, she heard her name, more clearly this time, and her brain throbbed. Zach Stone's voice was cold and mocking, full of menace. Knowing he was usually close by when trying to access her mind, Ebony tried to scan around her. But the continuous flapping, feathers and claws snagging her hair, meant she couldn't open her eyes.

Reaching into her pocket, she grabbed the wedge of cheese from the freezer bag and threw it onto the ground. The crow chased after the cheese and, even though Zach's voice had died away, Ebony spun on her heels, checking all around her. The crowd was starting to disperse and the street performers were packing up. The girl in the red coat was being carried away, her head on her father's shoulder as she sobbed. There was no sign of Zach. Either he was gone or his power to read minds had increased.

Hurrying on, leaving Grafton Street behind, Ebony almost collided with a newspaper seller as she turned a corner. His noticeboard read:

HUNDREDS OF DUBLIN PETS DISAPPEAR

Covering her sleeve so Winston wouldn't see the headlines, a poster pinned to a lamp post caught her eye. It was a photograph of a tortoiseshell cat with a crooked tail. The word **MISSING** was printed above it and below, **€100 CASH REWARD**. Moving closer, Ebony frowned. If she wasn't mistaken, it was the huge cat she'd seen from the roof the night before.

Convincing herself that it was nothing but a coincidence – cats often looked similar and were bound to go missing in a busy city, especially inquisitive cats on the hunt for food – she pushed on. Spotting the murky waters of the Liffey up ahead, Ebony crossed O'Connell Bridge and headed for the wooden walkway to the left. On every lamp post were reward posters for missing dogs, cats, rabbits, pet birds and even a chipmunk. Hugging her sleeve close to her chest, feeling Winston's body heaving as he breathed, Ebony located an unoccupied bench. Thankful Winston was safe with her, she sat and stretched out her legs, letting the sun warm her face. She took the apple out of her pocket and, closing her eyes, bit into it, enjoying its sweetness on her tongue.

A loud yell broke the peace and Ebony sat up straight. A couple of bright-blue birds with zebra-like markings on their heads lifted from the railing in front of her and flew away, following the Liffey; they looked like exotic parakeets. Wondering if they were some of the missing pets, Ebony tried to remember whether she'd seen a poster for them, but another yell disturbed her thoughts. On the walkway, coming directly towards her, was a woman wearing yellow spotted pyjamas and carrying a lace parasol. Her gait was lumbering and her hair looked like fluffy pink candyfloss. She shouted something at a couple passing by, their hands joined, but they ignored her and hurried on. Before Ebony had a chance to look away, the woman pointed at her.

'You know about it, don't you?' she cried. 'You've seen it too!'

Checking around her, Ebony realised that the woman was definitely addressing her. Not sure what to do – would ignoring her make her angry? – Ebony smiled.

'How can you smile with that thing on the loose?' She stopped at Ebony's outstretched feet. 'Have you seen it?'

Stuffing her marked hand into her jacket pocket, Ebony heard the sound of feet tramping the wooden walkway behind her. Turning, she saw two policewomen heading in her direction. The woman also spotted them. Deciding to take the opportunity for a quick exit, Ebony got to her feet and shuffled away from the woman while her attention was diverted.

'Have you seen it too, ladies? The monster in the shadows? Red, piercing eyes and sharp, crooked claws. It took my dog, you know.'

Ebony stopped. The Deus-Umbra. It had to be. Listening in as the police reached the raving woman, Ebony held her breath.

'A monster in the shadows, you say, with red eyes,' said one of the policewomen, stifling a laugh. 'And it took your dog?'

'Yes. I hope he hasn't been harmed. Benji is his name. Have you seen Benji?'

'Another one off her rocker,' the policewoman said to her colleague under her breath. 'We'd better take her in.' Turning to the distraught woman, she said, 'If you come with us, we'll file a missing dog report at the station and help you find Benji.'

As they guided her away, one on either side, a shadow swooped overhead, darkening the world around Ebony for an instant as a cold wind ruffled her curls. The woman began to scream and Ebony looked up. A vast flock of birds was hurtling through the sky, following the Liffey towards the sea. Herring gulls, pigeons, crows, magpies, robins and a huge white bird that looked like a pelican: they were all mixed together, moving fast. In Ebony's experience, this was strange behaviour for birds. The only time she had ever seen anything like it was when the Silent Peregrine had called for back-up against the Deus-Umbra. It was as though something had unsettled them.

Hearing another voice yelling, Ebony zoned in. It was a man this time, but his words were similar. 'You've seen it, haven't you? The monster in the shadows?'

Without thinking twice, Ebony headed straight for him.

'Yes, I've seen it,' she said hastily, making sure no one was close enough to hear. 'Where did you see it? What was it doing?'

The man's eyes turned watery, rims reddening as he held back tears. 'It was in my garden. The brute snatched my cats and flew away.'

Before Ebony could ask anything else, he moved on, crying, 'Have you seen it, the monster in the shadows?' to every passer-by.

'Let's get out of here Winston, and quick!' said Ebony into her sleeve.

Feeling his little head nod, she turned towards home. Why was the Deus-Umbra stealing pets? Even though her palm didn't hurt, meaning there was no threat nearby, she raced back through the busiest streets, keeping her eyes peeled and her ears alert.

Ebony made it home just before noon. She had hoped Seamus would be settled in by then, but there was no sign that this was the case. Although she knew she would have to tell her aunt about the raving woman and missing pet posters, she wanted to try to make sense of it first. Not wanting to get caught up in Seamus's arrival, she shouted, 'I'm back!' from the hallway, then raced upstairs and hid in her room. Soon, there were rumblings and rattlings up and down the stairwell, followed by banging and clattering in the room next door. Several voices could be heard muttering and arguing, but Ebony purposely zoned out so she couldn't identify them.

At first, she stayed as quiet as she could, hoping that no one would disturb her as she tried to figure things out. The vision and the missing pets wouldn't leave her thoughts alone – but neither would the constant hammering. Hiding her head under the pillow and pulling it tight, Ebony had to fight to block out the noise. Her stomach rumbled hungrily, but she chose to ignore it. She would only get sucked into helping. Then, as her stomach rumbled again, realisation dawned.

In the vision, Ambrose had said the Deus-Umbra was

weak and needed to get stronger. And to get stronger, it needed food – food that was easy to catch and wouldn't put up much of a fight. She thought back to the tortoiseshell cat the night before and the clump of hair left behind when it disappeared.

'It's the only explanation,' she said out loud.

Ebony's stomach clenched as she realised how close the demon must have been last night and how lucky she was that it hadn't spotted her or Winston in the darkness. Sitting up, ready to explain her theory to Winston, she found that he was fast asleep at the foot of the bed. His body was rising and falling so peacefully she didn't have the heart to wake him. But then the hammering and voices stopped and the inevitable knock on her door came, making Winston jump into the air, hair standing on end.

'Who is it?' called Ebony, giving Winston a quick stroke to calm him.

When there was no reply, she opened the door a crack and peeped outside. Uncle Cornelius was waiting, leaning against the wall, looking weary. His hairy face was glistening with sweat and his long auburn locks stuck to one cheek in swirls. An old-fashioned bronze pocket watch dangled from his waistcoat, swinging from side to side hypnotically. As Ebony pulled the door wide open, Uncle Cornelius wiped a hand across his forehead and pointed towards the room next door. Then he beckoned for Ebony to follow him.

'You need my help?' asked Ebony.

Nodding, Uncle Cornelius grabbed her hand. Before she could protest, he yanked her into the next room and pointed to the bed, which was now hospital-style, with railings along the sides. It explained all the noise: there was no way the old or new bed could have made it up or down the staircase in one piece. Next to the bed was a small table, a monitor with several wires dangling from it and a chair for visitors. The monitor was whining continuously, a flat line running across its screen. Ebony's heart dropped; the last time she had heard that noise was when her grandpa had died.

She took Uncle Cornelius's arm and pulled him out of the room, onto the landing.

'OK, show me what you need me to do,' she said.

Uncle Cornelius pointed down the stairs and Ebony headed down. At the bottom, Seamus was slouched, still unconscious, in a wheelchair. He was attached to a drip. Ebony was surprised to find Miss Malone standing beside him in a nurse's outfit. She gave her a quizzical look.

'It was the only way we could get him here,' explained Miss Malone. 'Because the hospital can't diagnose what's wrong with him, they'd only let him leave with a qualified nurse.'

'And are you?' Aunt Ruby's voice floated into the hallway from outside the front door.

Sheepishly, Miss Malone pulled out some papers. 'With a little help from the Order, I am.'

Tutting, Ebony shook her head. 'Do you even know how to attach him to that machine up there?'

'Yes, I do, I've had some basic training. Now, help carry him upstairs in the wheelchair so I can get him settled.'

As Uncle Cornelius moved to one side, grabbing an armrest and a wheel, Miss Malone handed Ebony the drip, then moved to the other side. On three, they lifted, staggering with the weight, as Ebony followed holding the drip. When they were about halfway up the stairs, a thud sounded above and Uncle Cornelius jumped, almost dropping Seamus.

'It's the old house telling its stories again,' said Ebony, hoping she was right.

As soon as they reached Seamus's new room, Uncle Cornelius lifted him out of the wheelchair while Ebony held the drip high, making sure it didn't snag and pull out of his arm. As Ebony hung it on the special stand beside his bed, Miss Malone set to work attaching the monitor wires before securing the sides of the bed in an upright position. Seamus's face was peaceful and still as Ebony helped to pull the covers up and tuck him in. Winston scuttled in and hopped up onto the bed, settling himself on Seamus's chest as it rose and fell gently.

'All done?' asked Aunt Ruby from the doorway.

Turning, Ebony nodded.

Her aunt gave a gentle smile. 'He'll be OK, you'll see. This is the best place for him. And with our care, he'll recover. I'm sure of it.'

Another loud thud from above made everyone in the room jump. On the bed, Winston scrabbled under the pillow, leaving just his tail sticking out. No one spoke. Seconds later, there was a succession of slow, loud scratches, like nails being dragged along a blackboard.

'Did you hear that?' said Ebony. 'It's coming from the roof.'

Uncle Cornelius tilted his head, sniffed the air and gave a low growl. Heart pumping, Ebony moved towards the door that led up to the attic. Zach had tricked her once by pretending to be her grandpa on the roof – what if it was him?

'Not you, Ebony,' warned her aunt. 'You stay where you are.'

Despite her frustration, Ebony paused – after all, she wasn't even armed. As the scratching sounded again, followed by a strange cackle, Miss Malone pulled a gun from the pocket in her nurse's tunic and moved Ebony out of the way.

'Let me handle this,' she said, darting through the door. 'Everyone wait here, but be on your guard.'

Aunt Ruby nodded and followed her to the door leading to the attic, propping it open with her back as she also pulled out a gun. A strange, repetitive scuffing noise suddenly filled the air, followed by another cackle. Ebony felt her hand grow hot. *I know that sound*, she thought, but the heat from her hand made it difficult to concentrate. Checking the skull on her palm, Ebony found that, once again, the mark was swollen and glowing around the edges. She quickly jammed her hand in her pocket before anyone else noticed what was going on; it would only cause a distraction.

Signalling with a finger to her lips for the others to be quiet, Aunt Ruby tilted her head and they all listened intently.

The skylight creaked open and they could hear a series of light footsteps as Miss Malone made her way up to the top of the roof. On the bed, Seamus mumbled and stirred before falling quiet again. Beside Ebony, Uncle Cornelius rubbed one hairy hand over the other while Aunt Ruby placed one foot on the bottom stair, preparing to leap into action if necessary. As two shots rang out, causing Winston's tail to stick out straight as a pole, Uncle Cornelius gave a low growl and raced past Aunt Ruby, quickly disappearing. Ebony moved to follow, but her aunt put out an arm to stop her.

'Let Uncle Cornelius go. You don't have a weapon – although, from now on, I think you should have one with you at all times.'

They both looked at the ceiling, following the footsteps overhead, trying to decipher their exact location. Soon there were too many noises to be able to figure out what was happening, and they waited, breath held. Moments later, two sets of returning footsteps could be heard.

'Whatever it was, it must be gone,' said Ebony.

From upstairs, Miss Malone shouted, 'All clear. I saw a dark shape disappearing into the distance, so I fired two warning shots after it, just in case.'

'I heard that cackle a couple of nights ago,' said Ebony, moving to the window and peering out. 'I was up on the roof getting some air. I thought it was a stray cat but Winston wasn't convinced. He was obviously right.'

All eyes turned to Winston. As though sensing everyone's

stares, he shuffled out from under the pillow. Sitting on his back legs, he drew himself up and threw his front legs out like wings. Seamus's eyelids fluttered, but no one noticed – they were too busy watching Winston. Squeaking loudly, the rat began flapping his outstretched legs up and down.

'Shadow Walkers?' asked Miss Malone and Aunt Ruby looked to Ebony for guidance.

'No,' said Ebony. 'My hand would have hurt – but instead, it did this.'

She held up her palm to show the glowing skull and Miss Malone winced, taking a step back. Uncle Cornelius's lip curled up, another low growl escaping from his throat.

'What does it mean?' asked Miss Malone.

Sitting bolt upright in the bed, Seamus opened his eyes wide. Winston jumped several inches in the air and Miss Malone clamped her hand over her mouth as she screamed.

'The Deus-Umbra,' said Seamus, in a barely audible voice, looking around wildly.

Winston dropped his paws and nodded, left paw in the air.

'Seamus! You're awake,' cried Ebony, rushing to his side.

He looked her in the eye. 'Ebony? Where am I?'

'My house. Mercury Lane. You're quite safe.'

'No. The demon. It's coming for you.'

'Shh,' said Ebony, taking a damp cloth from Seamus's bedside table and wiping his sweaty brow. 'If it was the demon, it would have attacked. We're quite safe.'

'It *was* the demon. Ambrose is controlling it with some

kind of magical restraint. Right now he just wants to frighten you, but soon–'

Suddenly Seamus began to scream, waving his arms around as though fending off something big and dangerous, so Miss Malone and Uncle Cornelius took over. The wildcat held Seamus's hands while Miss Malone spoke to him in soothing tones. Aunt Ruby moved her niece away, an arm around her shoulders. Her jaw tightened, making her cheekbones sharpen.

As Seamus cried out, they both looked back to check on him. His skin was clammy and his eyes looked wild. Miss Malone administered an injection and, moments later, he began to calm down. Soon he was unconscious again.

Ebony sighed. 'Where could a demon hide in such a busy city?' she asked.

'I don't know, but that thing can clearly sneak up on us whenever Ambrose chooses,' replied Aunt Ruby. 'Whatever his ultimate plan is, Ambrose is buying time – he's toying with us, trying to frighten us by giving us a glimpse of his power.'

Miss Malone and Uncle Cornelius joined the others.

'I've given Seamus a sedative,' said Miss Malone. 'Should I call Mr O'Hara, let him and his wife know that he's woken up?'

'Let's wait a while, see if he comes round again,' said Aunt Ruby. 'I don't want to get their hopes up, just in case.' She turned to her niece. 'Let's get you armed, then we'll eat. It's been a long day but we've experienced worse. If Ambrose thinks he can scare us or wear us down, he's mistaken. Even if he does have the Deus-Umbra under his command.'

Dinner was a disastrous affair. Everyone sat in uncomfortable silence, lost in their own thoughts as Aunt Ruby attempted to cook. But the planned meal of bacon and cabbage was soon abandoned. Without enough water in the pan, coupled with Aunt Ruby's fickle attention span – every few minutes she ducked away to scribble in one of her invention journals – the cabbage boiled dry, pluming acrid smoke around the kitchen. Winston gave a little cough and Uncle Cornelius jumped to his feet to waft clean air in with the door. The cold draught from the long, dark hallway helped a little, but not much.

Flustered, Aunt Ruby reached into the oven and pulled out the huge bacon joint; the meat was pale and juicy. Uncle Cornelius's eyes lit up. Aunt Ruby had forgotten to light the oven and the meat was completely raw. Licking his lips, Uncle Cornelius lunged for the joint but Aunt Ruby snatched it away just in time and put it back in the fridge. Wiping her glistening forehead, she picked up the phone and ordered pizza.

Although she ordered one that everyone liked – extra pepperoni with pineapple – no one was much in the mood for eating when it arrived, except for Uncle Cornelius. Ebony and Miss Malone picked and poked at the toppings, Aunt Ruby managed a single slice and even Winston only tackled a crust. Slowly, Uncle Cornelius made his way through the two huge boxes. Picking up the last portion of pizza, he folded it over and stuffed it into his mouth in three giant bites. Miss Malone's face crumpled in disgust but Ebony couldn't help chuckling. After a moment, Aunt Ruby joined in. Tomato sauce and greasy pepperoni smudges adorning his hairy face, Uncle Cornelius gave everyone a big thumbs-up with a huge grin.

'Pets are going missing all over Dublin,' announced Ebony, deciding it was time to share what she knew. 'And I met people raving about seeing a monster in the shadows. One man saw it take his cats. I think that's how the Deus-Umbra is feeding itself and regaining its strength. Luckily, everyone else seemed to assume the people are crazy.'

Aunt Ruby sighed. 'They probably are after an encounter like that.'

'If Seamus is right and Ambrose now controls the Deus-Umbra, what if he unleashes it on us next? Properly, I mean – not just as a warning,' asked Ebony. Met with an uneasy silence, she continued, 'Surely it proves I should use the Shadowlands to go after Icarus.'

'It's too dangerous and you don't know what you're doing,' said Aunt Ruby.

'Mrs O'Hara could tell me what she knows.'

'It's not the same. She's a Shadow Custodian – you know that means she can't actually go into the Shadowlands. She doesn't have the same skills as Icarus. No.'

The air grew thick and tense as Aunt Ruby and Ebony glared at each other.

'Right,' said Miss Malone, checking Uncle Cornelius's dangling pocket watch and pushing back her chair, making everyone jump. 'I'd better report to HQ; my shift starts soon.'

'Shift?' asked Ebony.

'I told you, surveillance is beginning. I'm on duty tonight, with Drinkwater. Until noon tomorrow.'

'Isn't that slave labour?' asked Ebony, checking the time. 'That's more than twelve hours.'

Miss Malone shrugged. 'Look at us! We're as jumpy as frogs! I think it's for the best, don't you?'

As she rose, a knock at the door boomed, echoing around the house. Nervously, Winston leapt onto Ebony's shoulder and hid in her curls. Miss Malone accompanied Aunt Ruby to the front door, guns ready, but Ebony's heart pounded and she was too scared to follow – she had left the gun her aunt had given her upstairs in her rucksack.

'I hope I'm not losing my nerve, Winston,' she said, making a mental note to keep her gun with her at all times.

Moments later, Aunt Ruby returned. 'It was the extra monitors. I'm putting one on each floor of the house. They transmit information from Seamus's machine, so if anything goes wrong an alarm will sound and whoever is here will be able to hear it, no matter where they are.' Aunt Ruby listed the various alarms and their meanings, but Ebony was barely listening. The Deus-Umbra's cackle kept sounding in her head, along with Mrs O'Hara's warning. Making her excuses once her aunt's lecture finished, she headed up the stairs towards bed.

She hadn't got far when Aunt Ruby poked her head into the hallway. 'Chiyoko's coming to see Seamus in the morning, when myself and Uncle Cornelius report to O'Hara,' she said. 'Unless he wakes in the meantime, maybe we'll keep tonight's incident quiet for now?'

Although Ebony nodded agreement, her heart sank – she didn't like the thought of deceiving her friend but she understood her aunt's caution. Reaching her room, Ebony left the light switched off and peeped out of her window to see whether the surveillance was in place. As she expected, a black car was parked across the road in full view of the house. Two figures sat inside. Feeling a little safer, she closed the curtains and pushed her bedside cabinet in front of her bedroom door. Wanting to be completely alone, with just her rat and her thoughts for company, Ebony climbed into bed and hugged Winston close.

The following morning, September winds rattled around 23 Mercury Lane, making the floorboards creak and the old stone walls whisper. Ebony was propped up on her pillows, leafing through a book about the Mariana Trench, and beside her, Winston was snoozing. His fat body was snuggled into her leg and she stroked him with one finger, his soft fur familiar and warm against her skin. Next to him, Chiyoko was sprawled across the bed, also reading. It had taken a while for Ebony to coax her away from her tiny hand-held computer – she had brought the gadget from Japan and it was smaller than any Ebony had ever seen – but now she was engrossed. As the bedroom window rattled and a nearby door slammed, Ebony looked up from her book and brushed a stray curl from her eye.

'What was that?' she asked. 'Everyone else is out – except Mulligan.'

Chiyoko was so lost in a story of pirates and privateers from the south-west coast of Ireland that she hadn't heard a thing, so Ebony didn't bother adding that the wildcat only left the basement to feed or if there was a problem, even though it was on her mind. Hoping the sound was nothing to worry about – old houses were prone to strange noises – Ebony returned to her book. But unable to concentrate, she turned her attention to the window, where a pink-edged horse chestnut leaf was stuck to the glass. The low autumn sun lit the leaf from behind, giving it an ethereal glow. Ebony could see its complex threads of veins. Peering at it, she hoped there might be a message etched into its fibres, or perhaps a code to crack, a communication from Icarus Bean about her parents that would help to alleviate the painful waiting. But there was nothing. The leaf was simply a leaf. Ebony stared at the colours, letting them blur and swirl before her eyes.

An unexpected warmth in Ebony's palm pulled her from her daydream. Barely daring to look, she took a peek to see if the edges were glowing; sure enough, the skull's outline was red and angry. Was the Deus-Umbra nearby? Ebony's pulse raced, blood pumping in her ears. Standing up, she moved to the window – quietly, so as not to alarm Chiyoko – to see if security was still outside.

In the street, everything was still. Across the road, the Order of Nine Lives surveillance car was still parked in its spot. As the driver, Drinkwater, looked up from his newspaper, Ebony gave a half-hearted wave. He offered the slightest of nods and returned to his paper, muttering something to Miss Malone, who leaned forward and snuck a peek before returning to her watch.

Relieved that they were there, Ebony surveyed the street. A few crackling leaves and a stray crisp packet tumbled along the road. A cyclist pedalled by, swerving to miss the packet so it wouldn't tangle in her spokes. As Ebony watched the cyclist leave, she let out a huge sigh. Guilt ate at her for the second time that day – Seamus had not woken since Miss Malone had sedated him. *If Seamus hadn't used the puppets to save me, he wouldn't be ill – and it's not fair to keep what happened last night from his sister*. Pushing the thought away, she returned to the bed to cuddle Winston. The mark on her hand still glowing, Ebony took a deep breath and tried to calm her racing mind. *What did it mean?*

Putting down her book, Chiyoko watched Ebony for a

moment, her head tilted to one side. Winston snuggled in, happy to have some attention; his whiskers grazed Ebony's cheek and her heart lightened a little.

'Are you OK?' asked Chiyoko.

'Sure,' said Ebony flatly. 'It's just ...' Her eyes shifted to a calendar on her wall, a gift from Old Joe that was filled with photos of Oddley Cove. It didn't matter that he'd owned it first and written entries in the spaces from January to June; the pictures made her feel nearer to home. 'I thought we'd be closer to finding my parents by now. That Seamus would be better. That we'd be doing something useful against our enemies.'

Chiyoko nodded and her eyes glistened. 'I know,' she said in a quiet voice.

'It's strange,' continued Ebony. 'My whole life I was fine with my parents not being around. Their absence was a fact of life, something that just was. Even when Grandpa died ...' she paused and gulped, 'even then, I didn't think of them. But now,' her voice tapered to a whisper, 'it's all I can think about. My parents are alive and trapped in 1871 – how is that even possible? How have they avoided bumping into their past selves all this time?'

'I have a theory,' said Chiyoko with a cheeky grin. She reached into her pocket. 'If you let me check the archives on my computer, I'll be able to tell you.'

Ebony nodded, then waited for Chiyoko to fire up and do some searching, her eyes drawn to the window and the cloud-filled sky.

'Here we go,' said Chiyoko, showing Ebony her screen. It was an official death record. 'According to this, Victorian Rufus and Ivy Smart disappeared on 3 March and were officially pronounced missing a few weeks later. However, they made a miraculous reappearance on 13 April, the day you – I mean past you – died.'

'I remember reading about that when I first came to Dublin. So you think my parents purposely chose that date and took their place?'

'Yes. They stole their identities, sort of. Does that make sense?' asked Chiyoko.

'It's as good a theory as any. But it doesn't make me feel any better. We're still doing nothing to help them.'

'We've sent Icarus,' said Chiyoko, locking her computer and pocketing it before reaching over to rub her friend's arm. 'And you've been doing great work with your aunt.'

Winston nuzzled into Ebony's neck, but nothing made her feel any better. Instead, a strange idea formed in her mind – by wanting to find her parents, was she somehow being disloyal to her grandpa? She pushed the thought away, blinking several times in quick succession.

'Don't cry,' said Chiyoko. 'It'll work out. I'm sure you'll get to see your parents soon.'

'I just don't get it,' said Ebony. 'Our work has been pointless – we've found nothing. And why hasn't Icarus returned? Why is no one trying to find him?'

'Maybe they are but they're being cautious?' offered

Chiyoko, putting her book aside. 'They could be doing something in secret. With security on high alert, everyone is jittery. My father organised the Order's unanimous vote overthrowing Ambrose, so at least Ambrose can't control the final decrees any more – surely that's worth something?'

Ebony stared at the splayed pages of the book on her bed. She could just make out a bit of map showing the inlets of Roaring Water Bay, the seas of her childhood where she'd fished with her grandpa, believing her parents to be dead.

'That only helps souls that have used up their nine lives, not the rest of us. They're working in secret all right, coming up with ridiculous ideas like calling Icarus a traitor,' said Ebony, frowning. 'But after all we've been through? Finding out that I was the guardian, then having to convince the others in the Order that I'm worthy? Now that the Order accepts me, you'd have thought those closest to me would have stopped shutting me out.'

Chiyoko lowered her gaze and a slight blush tinged her cheeks. She shoved her straight, glossy fringe to one side with a brush of her hand and returned to her book, pretending to read, the cover upside down.

Ebony sighed. 'I'm sorry,' she said. 'I know it's not your fault. I'm not blaming you for your father's behaviour.'

Another slam sounded, making Winston leap onto the bed. This time, Chiyoko jumped up, a concerned look on her face.

'What was that?'

From outside the bedroom door, a low *dung, dung, dung,* began to pound.

'Is that drums?'

'You hear it too?' asked Ebony.

Chiyoko nodded. 'I heard something earlier, but I thought it was your water pipes rattling. This sounds like it's coming from out there.' She pointed towards the landing.

Standing on top of his cage, Winston bared his teeth.

'Let's go check on your brother.'

Together, Ebony and Chiyoko headed for the room next door, Winston following close behind. As Ebony took hold of the door handle, it felt as though a jolt of lightning shot through it into her flesh and a bright-red glow shone out from her palm, making her jump back. Chiyoko's eyes grew wide as she stared at the red glow.

'Your hand – what's wrong with it?'

Then, from inside Seamus's room, an inhuman scream rang out.

Chiyoko froze to the spot. Winston clambered onto Ebony's shoulder and patted at her face with his paw. Right away, Ebony's instincts kicked in: there was something wrong with Seamus – she had to help! Wrenching the bedroom door wide open, she raced into Seamus's room. Seamus was sitting bolt upright, his hair flying all around him. His eyes were closed and his mouth was twisted to one side, making a strange rasping noise as he fought to breathe. His face contorted in terror, he held his hands up in front of his body as though trying to protect himself. The wires attached to his hospital monitor swung violently, like eels trying to escape. The chair for visitors had been knocked over. It lay flat on its back, legs pointing towards the corner of the room. The strange noise rang out. *Dung. Dung. Dung.*

Ebony's blood ran cold. It was the noise she had heard in the vision when Ambrose had summoned the Deus-Umbra through Zach.

'Seamus, you're awake!' cried Chiyoko, running in, but her brother failed to react to her voice. 'Wh-what's wrong with him?' she asked Ebony, before turning to her brother. 'What do you see, Seamus?'

As Chiyoko moved towards the bed, Ebony shouted, 'Stay back!'

But Chiyoko was too distressed to listen. 'We have to help him!'

Hurrying towards her brother, Chiyoko reached the bed in three strides, but the second she was close enough, Seamus hit out, landing a hard punch on his sister's jaw. Chiyoko cried out and fell in a heap on the floor. Tears seeped from her eyes as she held her swelling face. Pulling herself across the floor, Chiyoko tucked in close to Ebony.

'What's happening?' she cried as Seamus roared. 'What's wrong with my brother?'

'Just stay down,' said Ebony, trying to figure out how to help.

'But what if Seamus dies?' asked Chiyoko.

She was silenced by another loud cry from her brother. Seamus was now standing on the bed, his body tilted forward at an unnatural angle as though held up by string, a strong wind gusting around him, making the wires dance and jangle. Seamus's body shook, then without warning, he turned in their direction and his eyes opened.

He had no irises or pupils – his eyes were completely black, just like Zach's had been.

Chiyoko stifled a scream and Ebony felt the pain in her hand intensify. Wind swirled around her, making her skin pucker and her blood turn icy. *Let this be over soon*, she thought.

Hearing a dark, menacing laugh, Ebony looked up. Smoke tendrils were curling into the air from the corner of Seamus's eye sockets. A demonic gargling escaped his throat.

'Seamus!' cried Chiyoko, her lips trembling and teeth chattering.

'Shh!' warned Ebony. But her words came too late.

Seamus lifted one hand, a single finger pointed towards the crouching girls. He juddered, eyes rolling upwards, as he cried out in a dark and distorted voice, 'I'm coming for you.'

The voice was like shadows and thunder and hatred all rolled into one. It sounded ice cold and bloodthirsty. Ebony's worst fears were realised: somehow, Ambrose was using the Deus-Umbra to possess Seamus.

Too frightened to speak, the girls stayed silent. On her shoulder, Ebony felt Winston shivering, but she couldn't console him; she didn't dare move. She fought to calm her racing heart – she had to stay strong. After Chiyoko's kidnapping last time, Ebony was determined to protect her friends as best as she could.

'I'm coming for you,' the demon repeated, louder and clearer this time.

Seamus's body jolted forward awkwardly; the demon within was trying to force him to move closer to the girls. But Seamus's body was too weak and his legs didn't move.

From somewhere deep inside Seamus came a bloodcurdling screech. Wind tore around the room, making the bedcovers billow and the curtains almost tear from their poles. Terrified,

Chiyoko crawled towards the door, but Ebony stayed put.

All of a sudden, an ear-splitting alarm sounded.

'What's that?' cried Chiyoko, slamming her hands over her ears.

'The monitors.'

There were different alarms for different eventualities; this one was louder than a low-flying jet. But Ebony hadn't been paying attention when her aunt had explained how they functioned – she hadn't expected anything to go wrong. Seamus cried out in his own voice, and at the same time, the demon roared.

'Is Seamus dying? Help him!' cried Chiyoko.

'Leave him alone, demon!' yelled Ebony, unsure how else to help.

She moved closer to the bed but couldn't attack the creature – she would only injure Seamus, not what was inside him. The demon cackled and Ebony saw a shudder run through Seamus's arm as she neared. In the next instant, his hand punched her in the chest, sending her flying. As she hit the floor, her side connected with the chair, knocking the wind from her as it crunched into her ribs. She lay on the floor, the screeching of the alarm searing into her brain. She had to turn the noise off – she couldn't think straight with its piercing racket.

Forcing herself to her feet, Ebony circled the bed and reached for the monitor, her eardrums splitting and her right side in agony. The demon turned Seamus's body to keep her in view, lashing out with tight fists. But this time Ebony was careful to keep her distance. As she checked over the machine, she finally spotted a Reset button and gave it a prod. As soon as she pressed it, the sound stopped. Her ears continued to ring in the silence.

Just as suddenly, the wind dropped and Seamus twisted and cried out, collapsing backwards onto the bed. The pain in Ebony's hand ceased and the glow died away. The Deus-Umbra was gone.

On the bed, Seamus was still, the wires in awkward tangles, flattened by his weight. Ebony gently tugged them free.

'Is he OK?' asked Chiyoko, as Ebony felt his forehead and cheeks. 'Is he hurt?'

Ebony lifted one of Seamus's hands and checked his pulse: it was racing. His breathing was ragged and rasping, instead of soft and rhythmic like earlier. 'I think he's all right,' she said.

Finally daring to straighten up, Chiyoko whimpered, 'What was that?'

'The Deus-Umbra,' said Ebony, feeling Winston judder on her shoulder. 'Ambrose was using the demon to send us a message – but it's gone now.'

As she spoke, images of the Deus-Umbra flooded Ebony's mind: its black, shifting form and pointed wings, the red eyes, the gaping fanged jaw, its terrible screeching and the stink of rotting flesh. She watched as Chiyoko shuddered, also reliving their capture.

'Let's see to your brother before we alert anyone.'

Chiyoko clambered to her feet and rushed to her brother's

side. Working together, they dragged Seamus's body up the bed, carefully resting his head back on the pillow.

'What do we do now?' asked Chiyoko.

'We'd better let everyone know,' said Ebony, gasping for breath. 'My aunt and Uncle Cornelius are at HQ right now – Drinkwater will take us there and Malone can mind Seamus.'

Trembling, Chiyoko nodded towards her brother. 'What if Ambrose does that again?'

Beside Seamus, Winston's tail quivered. Cowering, he hid his face behind his two front paws.

'We need help. This is more than we can handle alone.'

'But my father doesn't like being disturbed. He'll be angry with us.'

Ebony pointed to Seamus heaving and rasping on the bed. 'I'm not scared of your father – you saw what our enemies are capable of! And you heard what the demon said – he's coming for me. I'm not sitting around here waiting for him to attack. I'm going to act first – preferably with the Order's help.'

Chiyoko nodded her head in agreement. 'Then let's go!'

Without hesitating, Ebony raced back to her room, yanked on her shoes and grabbed her coat. Placing her gun in her trouser pocket and shouldering her rucksack, she collected Winston and bounded down the first flight of stairs.

'Come on!' she cried without stopping. 'For your brother's sake.'

Seconds later Ebony heard Chiyoko's footsteps clattering behind.

9

As Chiyoko hovered in the doorway, listening for further signs of trouble in the house, Ebony ran to the surveillance car and banged on the window.

'We need your help!' she yelled.

Instantly, Miss Malone and Drinkwater jumped out of the car.

'Drinkwater, we need a ride to headquarters.'

'Impossible,' he replied. His hair was black like Ebony's, only it was short and wiry and flecked with grey. 'We have orders to stay put until midday, when the next car arrives.'

Ebony sighed. He'd helped her row to the pirate ship when Ambrose had raised the Deus-Umbra and they were in immediate danger, but a lift was too much to ask?

'This is really important,' she tried. 'I need to see Mr O'Hara immediately. There was an incident inside.'

The colour drained from Miss Malone's face. 'An incident … on our watch? What kind of incident?'

'Something happened to Seamus and I must report it.'

'We can call it through.' Drinkwater gestured to his mobile.

'No. This needs to be conveyed in person. It's important.'

Drinkwater surveyed Ebony's face for a moment, an internal battle clearly visible. Frustrated, Ebony slammed her hand on the roof of the car.

'Sorry, Ebony, our orders are to watch the house and protect you and Seamus,' said Miss Malone. 'How are we meant to do that if you're separated?'

But before Ebony could respond, Drinkwater spoke up. 'Malone, I've seen this girl in action. If she thinks it's important, it must be.' He turned to Ebony. 'But we can't help you unless you tell us more.'

Ebony took a deep breath, choosing her words carefully. Although she had learned that withholding information didn't help anyone, she wanted guidance from Mr O'Hara and her aunt before sharing too much with other Order members. Things were already tense – she didn't want to risk unsettling people more than necessary.

'Do you both promise not to mention this to anyone unless we have Mr O'Hara's say so?'

Drinkwater and Miss Malone both nodded.

'Ambrose had the Deus-Umbra possess Seamus to communicate with us – and I want to know what Mr O'Hara and Aunt Ruby think we should do.'

Drinkwater didn't need any further convincing. 'OK. I'll take the heat for it. Malone will stay here and I'll whizz you over to headquarters – but I have to secure back-up for Malone first.'

On his mobile, Drinkwater announced their impending visit to the headquarters building in the giant glasshouse in the Botanic Gardens and ordered replacement security teams. 'You'd better send two cars, four guards,' he concluded, before hanging up. 'They'll be here within half an hour at the most. Should we wait?'

Miss Malone shook her head and flashed her gun. 'I'll be OK. This is urgent.'

'I'll take you via Glasnevin Cemetery on the other side of the Botanic Gardens, as a precaution,' said Drinkwater, addressing Ebony. 'No attacks have been reported there but there was some unusual activity along the HQ perimeter this morning. But don't worry, I'll escort you all the way.'

'Thank you,' said Ebony.

Ebony settled into the passenger seat. Picking up the newspaper, she read the headlines and the opening to the story:

DUBLINERS HALLUCINATE: CROWD PSYCHOSIS OR FAULTY DRUG?

Over the last few weeks, sightings of ghoulish, shadow-like figures have been reported by multiple people in the Dublin City area. Several people have been so affected by these 'hallucinations' that they have had to be committed for their own safety.

But she didn't get any further: Miss Malone reached in for the newspaper and tucked it under her arm. As Miss Malone crossed the street, Chiyoko clambered into the back of the car and slammed the door shut without saying a word. Noting her friend's creased brow and tight lips, Ebony adopted her gentlest voice. 'Try not to worry about Seamus – he's in good hands and back-up is on its way.'

Turning to Drinkwater, she said, 'Let's go.' Moments later they were racing through the city centre towards the cemetery.

Wind swirled around the hem of Ebony's trousers as she passed between the rows of ornate gravestones while heading towards the Order of Nine Lives headquarters. Up ahead, Drinkwater scanned their surroundings, his head swivelling like a bird of prey searching for food. Every now and again he paused, holding up his hand for the girls to be silent while he surveyed the area. Certain all was clear, he continued at a quick march, beckoning for the girls to follow. It didn't take long for Chiyoko to fall behind, but Ebony was too caught up in what she was going to say to Mr O'Hara to notice.

With Seamus's possession and the newspaper headline fresh in her mind, Ebony had one hand stuck in the pocket holding her gun, trying not to let her imagination or fear get the better of her. Ignoring the array of creepy angel faces staring down at her, she raced along the meandering pathways, trampling over the statues' long shadows stretching on the ground, vaguely aware of Chiyoko's feet sloshing through mounds of fallen leaves behind her, trying to keep up. Golden brown, fiery red and buttery yellow leaves covered Ebony's shoes, slowing her down as she prepared the words she was going to say. Usually, this was her favourite month and she liked to savour its beauty, but no matter how much she tried, Ebony couldn't delight in the autumnal hues. There was too much to worry about.

'Ebony, wait up!' called Chiyoko.

Drinkwater stopped so abruptly that Ebony crashed into him. As she stumbled, he caught her by the arms and righted her.

'I'll slow my pace,' he said. 'It's important we stay together.'

Turning to wait for her friend, Ebony caught sight of a half-decayed angel, its eyes sinking into its head and its jawbone withered and crumbling. Her mind jumping back to Seamus – his black eyes, the inhuman voice – she shuddered.

When Chiyoko caught up, they pushed on. Passing into the gardens in Drinkwater's shadow, she barely noticed the heady scent of damp flora and foliage. In her pocket, Winston was completely still, curled up asleep. Up ahead, headquarters finally appeared, sunlight glinting off its domed glass roof.

Although Ebony's legs felt shaky and her mind was racing, she was determined to show everyone how responsible she could be. Then Mr O'Hara would have no choice but to include her in his meetings – and would hopefully allow her to go into the Shadowlands in search of Icarus.

As Ebony neared the headquarters' doorway, she spied a heavily armed security guard and covered her pocket with one hand in case Winston decided to pop out his head. Not everyone was fond of rats. Without batting an eyelid, Drinkwater marched straight up to him.

'We're here to see O'Hara,' he announced.

The guard looked past Drinkwater at Ebony and Chiyoko. Instantly recognising them both, he checked a list on a clipboard in his hand, then stood pondering the situation. 'Mr O'Hara gave me strict instructions …' he said, pointing to the list but fidgeting uncomfortably under the gaze of his superior.

'I called through,' replied Drinkwater firmly, 'so he should be expecting us. If the message hasn't reached you yet, that's not my problem. But I will make sure someone answers for it. Let us pass.'

'You'll have to relinquish any weapons,' said the guard, eyeing Ebony's rucksack. 'I'll need to search that bag.'

Removing her rucksack, Ebony handed it over, keeping her hand over the pocket holding her gun.

Drinkwater lifted one eyebrow. 'I can have you demoted to cleaning the toilets immediately and permanently if this insolence continues. This girl is the guardian. Show some respect.'

Sheepishly, the man returned Ebony's rucksack without

even checking it and stepped aside. Ebony gave him a brief nod and did her best to look like she was calm and in control as the guard radioed through, even though her legs felt like they were about to give way. Once they were out of sight of security, Drinkwater paused.

'Are you prepared? O'Hara won't take the unexpected interruption lightly, so talk straight and talk fast.'

'I'm prepared,' said Ebony, fighting to keep her voice from wobbling.

'You're on your own from here,' he said. 'I've kept you safe so far, but you'll have to get Ruby to bring you home. I need to return to Mercury Lane to check that all's fine and make sure the men know the protocol. I've taken a chance bringing you here – I'll know soon enough whether O'Hara has a problem with my decision or not. Good luck.'

Ebony thanked Drinkwater and took a deep breath as he turned away. After a few steps he paused and called out, 'I hope you realise that you have my loyal support.'

Before she could reply, he was gone.

As Ebony turned in to the corridor filled with giant exotic plants that led to O'Hara's secret office, she took a deep breath and lifted Winston onto her shoulder in case he needed some air. He immediately scampered down her body onto the ground and began exploring the locality for tasty morsels of food. An ear-splitting yell from the security guard at the entrance rang out, followed by the clatter of several pairs of feet charging. Instinctively, Ebony pulled out her gun.

'Something's happened!' said Chiyoko, as they glanced back towards the noise.

A woman dressed all in black – the uniform of the security team – raced towards them from the direction of Mr O'Hara's office. She carried a huge gun in both hands, her stride fast and determined. Extra weapons secured around her waist clunked with every step. Ebony flattened herself against the wall, pulling Chiyoko with her, to let the woman pass.

'Shadow Walkers at the Glasnevin entrance,' barked the woman as she raced by. 'Stay inside until you get the all clear.'

'Shadow Walkers? Right now?' said Chiyoko. 'Do you think they were tracking you?'

'Maybe – but my hand's not hurting. I'm not quite sure exactly how this mark works, but it hurts when they're really close by,' replied Ebony. 'What I do know is we'd better hurry in case your father gets called away.'

As they headed down the corridor together, past vast fan-shaped leaves, Ebony looked for the hidden entrance to Mr O'Hara's office. Behind them the warning calls and hurried footsteps died away as more security raced outside. Winston ran up ahead, pausing now and again to check if he'd reached the right spot. Eventually, he stopped and pointed upwards. Ebony brushed the vines away and found the barely visible X chalked on the wall that marked the doorway.

'I thought they'd be waiting for us – the guard radioed through!' said Ebony, turning to Chiyoko. 'If I push out the stone, will you get us in?'

Chiyoko paused.

'You're an O'Hara so I need your palm; it's the only way to pass security. Without it, we're trapped out here.'

'I'm still not sure it's a good idea to interrupt my father. Wouldn't it be better to wait outside? Even Drinkwater seemed uncertain.'

'Drinkwater brought us here, didn't he? Anyway, I want to make sure that Seamus has the best possible protection – and when your father sees that I'm trusting him and no longer keeping secrets, hopefully he'll reciprocate and allow me to take a more active role as guardian.'

As Chiyoko moved to help, the wall came alive and a brick slid towards them. Someone was opening the door from the inside. The two girls jumped back. Winston clambered up Ebony's leg and dropped into her pocket, his two front paws hooked over the edge so he could see out. Chiyoko took another step backwards as the bricks around the hole began to sink inwards, forming a visible door shape, but then stood her ground. Winston lifted his nose high in the air and twitched his whiskers. There was a shuffling sound and footsteps, and a huge hand with thick knuckles appeared in the hole, palm facing upwards. A bleep sounded as a beam of red light scanned the palm, followed by an automated announcement: 'O'Hara'.

Before Ebony could take the deep breath she needed to steady her voice, Mr O'Hara yanked open the door and towered over her, his ice-white hair gleaming and his walrus moustache quivering.

'This had better be good,' he said, fixing his grey eyes on Ebony's. She felt Winston drop down out of view. Noticing his daughter feebly trying to hide behind a tropical plant, he glared at her. 'You should know better, Chiyoko.'

'This isn't her fault,' started Ebony, but Mr O'Hara held his meaty hand up flat in front of her face, inches from her nose.

'Enough. I'm extremely busy. Drinkwater had better have a good reason for allowing you to come here and disturb my work.'

Feeling her bravery melt away, Ebony couldn't find the words she'd planned. Despite all the rehearsing as she'd made her way across the cemetery and through the gardens, they slipped from her mind like petals in the wind. Winston fidgeted in her pocket. The weight of him helped Ebony regain her composure, but still the right words failed her.

'I demand … I mean, as guardian … surely I have the right to demand … or the right …' Her voice squeaked and Ebony felt her face grow hot.

Mr O'Hara looked at her, his impatience clear. It made her blood boil.

'It's S-Seamus …' stuttered Chiyoko, and even though her father's face softened, she was too nervous to continue.

'I know my aunt and Uncle Cornelius are with you,' Ebony said. 'They need to hear this too.'

'About Seamus?' said Mr O'Hara. 'Tell me!'

'He was possessed by the Deus-Umbra and gave us a message from Ambrose.'

His face dropping and his skin growing pale, Mr O'Hara rubbed at his moustache. He blew out a puff of air, making his white hair dance like reeds as he looked to his daughter. Tears glistened in Chiyoko's eyes as she nodded, too choked up to speak.

'Miss Malone is with him and Drinkwater called for extra back-up and is on his way back there now – but maybe you should bring Seamus here. With the Order's people all around him, he might be safer.'

O'Hara's facial muscles relaxed a fraction as he stepped aside, pushing the door wide open. 'You'd better come in.'

Inside O'Hara's hot and humid office there was more equipment than before. Extra computer screens showed video footage and lists of numbers that multiplied at top speed. Ebony guessed it was some sort of coding but had no idea what the numbers could possibly mean – though Chiyoko's eyes lit up when she saw them. Scanners and radar screens were dotted between a variety of carnivorous plants, including colourful sundews, pitchers big enough to devour small deer and yawning Venus flytraps. The walls were covered in vines sporting vicious thorns and unusual blossoms. They dripped with condensation. It took a moment for Ebony's eyes to adjust to the tropical heat and kaleidoscopic colour.

When her eyes had settled, she spotted her aunt perched in front of a monitor showing footage of what looked like a cloudy riverbed and its debris – tin cans, a discarded shopping trolley and a rotting shoe. Aunt Ruby was wearing chunky headphones, her waist-length hair glowing bright red under the fingers of light fighting their way through the immense foliage. She was too engrossed in her screen to look up but, next to her, Uncle Cornelius was fully alert. Glancing between Ebony and O'Hara, he rubbed his podgy, hairy hands over each other. Clambering out of Ebony's pocket, Winston climbed onto her shoulder, his nose twitching as he looked around. Taking a deep breath, Ebony prepared to explain all, but the words still wouldn't come.

Movement in the corner of Ebony's eye alerted her to a big white paper screen. In front of it, Mrs O'Hara was perched on a low stool, her mask in place as she manipulated a string of bird shadow puppets. Raven-black hair spilled down her back and a pink-silk chrysanthemum was wedged behind her ear. Her body snaked and twisted, the muscles on her shoulders flexing as she made the puppets dance. Ebony felt her own shoulders relax. A video camera had been placed behind the screen to record the show; Ebony could hear its hum and see the tiny red light glow as the camera swivelled in time with Mrs O'Hara's every move. She was concentrating so hard that she was completely oblivious to the girls' arrival until Chiyoko, spotting her, ran over and flung her arms around her. Jolted from her task, Mrs O'Hara stopped what she was doing. She removed her mask and placed her puppets on her lap, and she hugged her sobbing daughter.

'Whatever's the matter?' she asked.

As though suddenly sensing movement, Aunt Ruby spun around. Her face darkened when she spotted Ebony. She removed her headphones.

'Didn't I tell you to stay at home? Who's with Seamus?' she asked, concern passing over her features.

Ebony's stomach felt like it was filled with violent waves, her throat full of pebbles. Fidgeting with her hair, she accidentally caught a wedge of Winston's fur. He squealed and leapt from her grip onto Mr O'Hara's computer desk, making the giant man step backwards, his nose wrinkled.

'Well?' asked Aunt Ruby. 'Are you going to explain yourself?'

'Drinkwater and Malone are there,' Ebony began. 'Ambrose used the Deus-Umbra to communicate through Seamus.'

As Aunt Ruby gasped, Ebony hurriedly relayed what had

happened as precisely as she could. As the story unfolded, Chiyoko verified the incident with fresh tears and Aunt Ruby's frown deepened. Uncle Cornelius's lip curled in a snarl, his large teeth showing. Mr O'Hara listened intently – Ebony felt his eyes fixed on her the whole time. When she finished, Mr O'Hara picked up his phone and called for someone named Lewis. Moments later, footsteps could be heard outside. When Mr O'Hara opened the door, in stepped a man that Ebony recognised from the battle in Oddley Cove. She particularly remembered his excellent rowing skills. A scar ran across his lip – a souvenir of the battle. Lewis stood poker straight, waiting for his orders.

'We need to increase surveillance and security,' O'Hara said, turning to the man. 'Issue a warning, Lewis, that no one is to go anywhere alone – at any time, not just after dark. Make sure it reaches everybody.'

The man nodded and left, giving Ebony a small smile as he passed. Once he was out of earshot, Aunt Ruby turned to her niece. 'Is there anything else?'

'I want to go into the Shadowlands to try to find Icarus.'

Mr O'Hara sighed loudly and turned to Ebony. 'Are you crazy? You don't have half of Icarus's skill – it's too dangerous.'

'I want us to work together against our enemies before they get the upper hand,' protested Ebony. 'But first, I need Icarus.' It took all of Ebony's concentration not to look at Mrs O'Hara as she continued. She suspected that revealing details of their linked destinies would place her under suspicion in O'Hara's eyes. 'As he's one of our best men, we're going to need him to help flush out Ambrose and Zach. I thought that since I've been with him in the Shadowlands before, I should try to locate him.'

Ebony caught Mrs O'Hara's eye and felt her resolve strengthen as the woman nodded. She was on the right track – if only she could persuade Mr O'Hara.

'Flush out Ambrose and Zach? That's impossible,' replied Mr O'Hara, his face rigid and serious. 'We cannot attack when we don't know what our enemies are planning. And we have no idea where they are. Let them come to us.'

'I think they're here in the city. It makes sense if the Shadow Walkers and Deus-Umbra are here – and Seamus's possession shows that Ambrose, and his hold over the Deus-Umbra, is growing stronger. We have to think of the future. If I went into the Shadowlands, I might be able to find some answers.'

'No. In fact, I forbid you to go anywhere near the Shadowlands. I suppose you've heard from your aunt that I intend to arrest your uncle on his return?'

'Yes, but I don't know why and I was hoping we could persuade you otherwise.'

'Which is another reason why you're banned from the Shadowlands. We can't risk Icarus receiving any tip-offs. As for the reason … right now, the fewer people that know, the better. I'm sorry.'

Ebony glanced at her aunt; Ruby's cheeks coloured

slightly and she looked away. On the desk, Winston gave a loud squeak – but only Ebony and Aunt Ruby understood it as a stand against the arrest. Mr O'Hara took no notice.

'My wife and your aunt have both already tried to argue Icarus's case,' he said, his forehead crumpling. Ebony noticed the dark rings underneath his eyes. 'But I'm afraid it's out of the question. As you said yourself, Seamus's possession shows that Ambrose is getting bolder and stronger. My wife has foreseen a terrible future and we can't risk infiltration from the inside.'

'What makes you think Icarus would betray us?' asked Ebony.

'He is not who he seems, Ebony. That is all I'm saying until I have him safely in my custody – and get some answers.'

Although she knew in her heart that Icarus would never betray the Order, Ebony also knew that Mr O'Hara believed he was acting in their best interests. She turned to Mrs O'Hara, who gave her an encouraging smile. Her mother's arms resting around her shoulders, Chiyoko was now calm, her face streaked with dried tears.

'But what will the arrest entail?' asked Ebony.

'Some questioning, perhaps interrogation. Maybe a trial. Hopefully he will be able to prove his loyalty quickly, but we will take whatever time is needed. If he is a potential danger, then he needs to be contained.'

Frustration welling up inside her, Ebony fought to keep her voice from shaking. 'But isn't Icarus innocent until proven guilty? It sounds like you've judged him already. There are Shadow Walkers at the Glasnevin gate right now – it's only a matter of time before a new battle begins.'

At the mention of Shadow Walkers, Uncle Cornelius bared his teeth and hissed, his sharp claws glistening. Aunt Ruby placed one hand on his arm to calm him, while looking to Mr O'Hara for direction. He said nothing.

'And what if he's found guilty?' asked Aunt Ruby.

'Exile,' said Mr O'Hara.

Aunt Ruby shook her head, her face downcast.

'No!' cried Ebony, her voice rising in pitch and volume against her will. 'It almost ruined him last time. I refuse to believe that Icarus is dangerous.'

An unexpected rustling sounded from the corner. Everyone's eyes turned to a shivering vine, its giant leaves shaking as though caught in a violent storm. While Chiyoko buried her face against her mother's shoulder, Ebony and Ruby whipped out their guns and pointed them in the direction of the noise. Uncle Cornelius crept forward, his teeth bared, and Winston flattened his ears, his hair standing on end.

'Trust me, Ebony,' said Icarus Bean, stepping out of the shadows of the foliage, his matted hair sticking up and his face grey and thin, 'O'Hara is right to be concerned.'

11

As soon as O'Hara set eyes on Icarus, he grabbed the phone on his desk and called for backup.

'Uncle! You're back!' said Ebony, rushing forward, unable to contain her excitement. Hearing Mr O'Hara's voice turning disgruntled, Ebony realised he was going to have to wait for support: everyone was busy fighting off Shadow Walkers and Lewis was carrying out his recent orders. It would buy some time with Icarus. 'We're so glad to see you. Where are my parents? Are they OK? I'm dying to meet them.'

Taking a step back, Icarus looked towards Aunt Ruby, a dark expression on his face. Ebony could see his chest heaving. His grey eyes, watery and red-rimmed, reminded her of lakes under moonlight. They were full of sorrow. Hands in his pockets, he rocked backwards and forwards on the balls of his feet but gave no reply. Also silent, Aunt Ruby took out her pipe and lit it, chugging on the stem as she watched her brother carefully. Uncle Cornelius whimpered, hopping from foot to foot but staying by Aunt Ruby's side.

'Where are they?' pressed Ebony. 'You've been gone for ages! I thought something bad had happened.'

On O'Hara's computer desk, Winston waved his front paws in the air and squeaked. Ebony ignored him; she felt her breath growing ragged as she waited for her uncle to speak – when was she going to get some answers?

Finally, O'Hara broke the silence. 'My guess is that your parents aren't here,' he said. 'It seems that, despite being gone for such a long time, Icarus has failed to bring them back. Suspicious, don't you think?'

Ebony spotted a tinge of crimson rising in Icarus's sallow cheeks. He smelled damp and stale with a distinct tang of muck, like he'd been living in a bog for the duration of his absence.

'What happened?' cried Ebony. 'Are my parents hurt?'

'No. They just refused to come.'

'How very convenient,' said Mr O'Hara.

'But why?' asked Ebony. 'I don't get it.'

'Believe me, I tried, but they were completely uncooperative.'

Ebony bit her lip and racked her brain. 'So why did they bother sending the SOS? I thought they were stuck and needed our help to get back.'

His reply was low and faint and Ebony had to strain to catch his words. 'They're stuck in their work, not the past. It turns out they don't want to come back – they just wanted some equipment that they can't get in the nineteenth century and didn't want to run the risk of returning themselves.'

'Equipment?' asked Ebony.

His answer stung. Surely they wanted to see her? Yes, they had abandoned her, but as soon as she heard what had happened she became convinced that they must have had a good reason and there was a chance of reconciliation. Initially, the possibility had seemed attractive, but only now, when it seemed that it wasn't going to happen, did she realise just how much the idea had really meant to her. Swallowing, Ebony tried to push her emotions away.

'They wanted *The Book of Learning*, to be precise,' added Icarus, rubbing his eyes with thumb and forefinger. Ebony spied a black mark on his arm, poking out from under his sleeve. Noticing she was watching, Icarus tugged his sleeve down and clasped his hands behind his back. 'But, of course, that's impossible now.'

Disappointment coursed through Ebony's body. Her chance to help her parents had been lost the moment she let Ambrose get his hands on the book. If only she had protected it – maybe they would have come back then. Maybe she was the reason they were refusing to return.

'But did they send us any information about what they've been doing? Did they tell you why they went away? They've been missing for years – surely they must have had something useful to share?'

'Oh, they had information to share, all right,' said Icarus. Snorting, he shook his head and clenched his fists.

Aunt Ruby chugged on her pipe and blew a cloud of smoke in her brother's direction. 'What did they need *The*

Book of Learning for, exactly?' she asked.

She sounded on edge and Ebony watched her closely.

'Its regenerative power,' said Icarus, matter-of-factly. 'They've been working on some project that they started before they left. They were rather cagey about it.'

He stared at his sister and Ebony saw an unspoken message pass between them.

'What project?' asked Ebony, eyeing her aunt suspiciously.

'I don't know the details. They were working on something top secret before they left. But to still be working on it after all these years … it must be important. Surely their best course of action would be to return if they ever want to complete it!'

'Apparently they can't complete it, not without the book,' said Icarus.

'I'll go to them!' said Ebony. 'I'll persuade them to return. Mr O'Hara, you said yourself that it's disappointing – let me help.'

Mr O'Hara looked at Icarus. Icarus, in reply, looked away.

'And how do you plan to get to them, Ebony?' asked Mr O'Hara.

'Let Icarus teach me what he knows!' cried Ebony, pointing to her uncle. 'You have no right to withhold the secrets of time travel, or my parents, from me …'

Her voice trailed off as Aunt Ruby cleared her throat, signalling to Ebony that it was time to back down. But Ebony's blood was boiling and backing down wasn't an option.

'We need to act now,' she continued. 'Our enemies have the Deus-Umbra at their command; when they attack, we'll need all the help we can get.'

Mr O'Hara's computer bleeped, the sound of an email arriving. He twitched. Eyes swivelling to the screen, he clicked into the email and his eyes widened. On the computer desk, Winston waved his paws, trying to get Ebony's attention, but she was too focused on persuading O'Hara. Clicking the mouse again, O'Hara turned the speakers to mute and perched on the edge of the desk, his back to the screen and arms folded, knocking Winston onto the keyboard. Lights began to flash as something moved around on his screen but O'Hara's body obscured her view. *He's hiding the monitor but at least I have his attention*, thought Ebony. Beside O'Hara, Winston's tail poked out, flicking from side to side; it looked like O'Hara had squashed him. Under different circumstances, Ebony would have found it funny, but right now she had to concentrate on obtaining his permission to travel in the Shadowlands. With no judge in charge, the Order answered to him.

Taking a deep breath, she asked as calmly as she could, 'So what's our next move?'

'Whatever it is, you can count me out,' answered Icarus.

'Are you OK, brother?' asked Aunt Ruby, rising to her feet and approaching him. 'I want you to know that we have heard some information about you but we're paying it no heed. It is of no consequence.'

'No consequence? None of you have any idea how lucky you are. None of you. But you!' Pointing a finger towards Aunt Ruby accusingly, he continued, 'You should have told me. You had no right to keep my heritage from me.'

'What do you mean?' asked Aunt Ruby, her face white and taut. 'I had no idea.'

Recalling the fragmented message from Mrs O'Hara in the Shadowlands, Ebony tried to make sense of their words.

'I don't believe you!' yelled Icarus, turning and punching a monitor.

There was a loud crack as the screen shattered, fissures spreading across the glass like tributaries of a river. On his arm, Ebony saw a flash of black; whatever it was, it seemed to be moving. Icarus held his hand over his sleeve and turned to his sister, his eyes brimming with fire. Instinctively, Ebony stepped back. Aunt Ruby exchanged a look of concern with Mrs O'Hara before moving closer to her brother, her hands held out towards him. 'Icarus, please, this changes nothing.'

But Icarus shoved his sister away roughly. She yelped with surprise and retreated, but he advanced on her, his eyes flashing, as though oblivious to who she was. In a few steps, Aunt Ruby was backed up against her desk with nowhere to go. Unsure how else to intervene, Ebony slowly moved for her gun. But Uncle Cornelius reached out and stopped her. Catching her eye, he gave a small shake of the head, then pounced, landing between Icarus and Ruby with an almighty roar. As though waking from a trance, Icarus staggered back and glanced around him. Realising what he had been doing, he groaned pitifully. Turning away, he clasped his head in his hands, sobs tearing through his frame.

Ebony watched, her heart filling with despair. Something was very wrong. Icarus had been changed by his trip – that much was obvious – but how and why? Mrs O'Hara had warned her that Icarus's heart had turned dark, but what could he have found out that was so bad?

'Enough of this!' shouted O'Hara, looking flustered. His eyes flicked to the door, then his watch. 'Icarus, stop that at once.' But despite his extra height and bulk, he was clearly wary of the other man and kept his distance.

'Help him, someone,' pleaded Ebony, covering her ears to try to block out his mournful wailing.

Mrs O'Hara picked up her mask and put it on, the crooked mouth drooping downwards like a melting face, then gathered her string of bird puppets. Gracefully, she moved towards Icarus.

'Shh,' she whispered, taking slow steps. It was like she was floating. Reaching Icarus, Mrs O'Hara made the shadow birds dance and dive around his head. Next, she began to hum a melody that sounded like a small bird. Joining in, Uncle Cornelius moved to her side and began to sing his special song that usually calmed Aunt Ruby when one of her birth-moon rages took her over. Images of dragonflies and seahorses bubbled from his mouth along with the melody. Soothed by the music and images, Icarus stopped pulling at his hair.

Moving closer, Mrs O'Hara waved an arm in an arc in front of Icarus's face. Her yellow sleeve swooshed and swayed like a shifting dune.

Finally, Icarus relaxed. His shoulders and head slumped, and his breaths calmed to a slow rasp. Then his legs buckled and gave way. He collapsed onto a nearby chair. As Aunt Ruby and Uncle Cornelius rushed to help him, Icarus stared at the ground in front of him, looking defeated. It was as though his spirit had abandoned him.

'For his own good, we'd better lock him up,' said Mr O'Hara, staring at Icarus Bean like he was an alien life form.

'This trip – the Shadowlands, trying to convince my parents, whatever news he's received – it's affected him greatly, he's too weak,' said Ebony.

'You don't need to fight my battles,' said Icarus.

But Mrs O'Hara's advice rang in Ebony's ears. *Your destinies are entwined. If either of you is to survive, you must help each other.* 'Locking him up would only add to his distress,' she continued.

'We'll bring him back with us to Mercury Lane,' suggested Aunt Ruby. 'He needs rest and care.'

Rising to his full height, Mr O'Hara shook his head emphatically. 'After what Ebony told us about Seamus? No way.' He stabbed a finger in Icarus's direction. 'I made it quite clear that his arrest was imminent. Icarus is clearly not in control of himself – he's dangerous. Now, where are those guards?'

Ebony stared at the pitiful scene before her.

'He's hardly a threat now – look at him!' said Aunt Ruby, her eyes flashing.

But there was no convincing Mr O'Hara and he reached for his phone. Before he could dial, it rang. Pressing the handset to his ear, Mr O'Hara grunted in agreement before announcing, 'I'll be right there.' He grabbed his jacket and checked he had his gun, then headed for the door.

'The Shadow Walkers have retreated but the men need to report. I'll return with guards. Stay with Icarus and make sure he doesn't do himself or anyone else an injury. I'll be back very soon.' Pausing in the doorway, he glanced at Ebony and then Aunt Ruby, a warning look in his eye. 'And no funny business. I mean it.'

'What do we do now?' asked Ebony as Aunt Ruby tentatively slipped an arm around her brother's shoulders.

Icarus showed no signs of moving. Slumped in his chair, his face was blotchy and sodden. Quietly, Mrs O'Hara returned to her stool and began disassembling her puppets with Chiyoko's help. Uncle Cornelius looked around him, scratching his sideburns with his long, curved fingernails.

'Whatever was wrong, it has passed,' replied Aunt Ruby.

'But for how long?' asked Ebony. 'What if it happens again?'

'Is it the time of his birth moon?' asked Mrs O'Hara, returning her puppets to near the screen. 'We're all prone to strange behaviour when our birth moon's around. It gets more difficult to control as we grow older.'

Ebony thought back to the time that her aunt had attacked her with a whip, and she looked at Icarus. Her instinct told her this was not the same and she grew even more desperate to know what was going on.

'It's not the effect of his birth moon,' said Aunt Ruby, her voice not much more than a whisper. 'I've witnessed that on multiple occasions and this is nothing like his usual reaction. It's a reaction to the information he was given during his trip to the past.'

'Icarus, what happened when you met my parents?' asked Ebony, hoping he would tell her what the others were concealing.

Icarus looked up at Ebony. His eyes were deep pools of sadness and fear, forcing Ebony to look away.

'I'll explain later,' said Aunt Ruby, 'once I have Icarus's permission, but now is not the time.'

Ebony had no choice but to agree, but she still needed to know more.

'Can you tell us what you have foreseen, Mrs O'Hara?' she asked. 'Your husband said you have seen a terrible future – can you share it? Or did you see anything that could help us when the time comes?'

Mrs O'Hara returned the mask to her face and began selecting her puppets. 'Better still, I can try to show you. It doesn't always work, especially when I'm tired – but I'll give it a go.'

As Chiyoko gathered chairs from around the room, everyone sat down in front of the screen, with Winston taking a seat on Ebony's lap. Icarus remained in the corner, arms wrapped tightly around his body and mumbling incoherently, but he couldn't resist watching also. Her eyes fixed on the screen as Mrs O'Hara began to position her puppets, Ebony crossed her fingers – without *The Book of Learning*, she had no access to clues like before – maybe this was what she needed to rely on?

As Mrs O'Hara moved behind the screen, Ebony took a deep breath and watched intently. First, a single cloud appeared, scudding across the top of the screen. Then, a crowd of people popped up below, their linked heads wobbling as Mrs O'Hara moved their joined bodies. Next, a Shadow Walker slipped into view; Ebony could hardly believe how lifelike the Shadow Walker looked, down to its piercing red eyes. Even though Ebony knew LEDs or bulbs must be creating the effect, it still made her shudder. As though thinking the same, Winston hid in Ebony's sleeve. As he did a U-turn and popped out his head, the Shadow Walker lashed out and, as its victim slumped, the creature slung the body over its shoulder and skulked away. Suddenly, all the puppets dropped from view. Only the cloud remained, a river appearing below, carrying a floating body. The silhouette of a curved bridge gave the location away.

'The Liffey,' said Ebony quietly. 'The deaths will continue.'

As the scene changed again, the clouds multiplied and expanded until the top third of the screen was completely dark. The room turned cold and Aunt Ruby pulled the neck of her jumpsuit higher and tighter. Below the black sky, people began to appear, but they were slower moving, their heads downcast. At the edges of the scene, several Shadow Walkers appeared with whips that crackled and sparked with electricity, flickering across the screen like the tentacles of a jellyfish. Uncle Cornelius growled, fidgeting in his chair as though fighting the urge to jump out of his seat and attack, even though the scene wasn't real.

'Ambrose will use the Shadow Walkers to take over the city,' said Ebony to her aunt, eyes wide. 'I always assumed the battle would be kept within our kind.'

'So did I,' confessed Aunt Ruby. 'This is unthinkable. Ambrose is growing more powerful than I ever imagined – but also reckless.'

Mulling her aunt's words over, Ebony returned her concentration to the puppets.

Once again, the scene dropped away, replaced by new props and puppets. This time, there was a car on its side, a skyline of tumbling buildings and Shadow Walkers everywhere. The people were barely recognisable as human, their shoulders slumped and steps slow. Feeling Winston's heartbeat quicken, Ebony tried not to let her own fears surface. But a glance at Icarus, still hugging himself and mumbling, made her throat constrict and her blood run cold.

Focusing back on the puppet show, Ebony grimaced as the Shadow Walkers lashed out, murdering people at will. After a moment, the images grew blurry and difficult to make out, the colours melting into shades of grey. Feeling Winston slip from her sleeve and a powerful tug on her skin and bones, like she was being turned inside out, nausea flooded Ebony's stomach and she tried to look away. It was impossible. The screen had a grip on her and she couldn't escape it, no matter how hard she fought. This had happened to her before and she knew what was coming. The blurriness making her dizzy, Ebony closed her eyes.

When she opened them, the air was filled with screams and yells, the slate-grey air thick with dust and the glow of distant fires. She was inside the puppet show. Fiery pain shot through her palm and she fought to stay standing, gripping her wrist in agony. All around her, men, women and children rushed by, heads bowed, trying to stay away from the shadows. It didn't take long to figure out why: alone, in pairs and in groups, Shadow Walkers lashed out, striking people at will. They were in charge.

'Where's the Order?' asked Ebony out loud, forgetting herself.

As a particularly large Shadow Walker came towards her, Ebony dodged to the side and it lumbered past. Turning, she saw a tank about to mow her down, just a heartbeat away; N1NE L1VE5 was written across its front. She leapt out of the way just in time. Barely believing her good luck but feeling sick to the stomach, Ebony watched the tank leave. It had only gone a few metres when there was a clatter of hooves and a herd of what looked like oryx leapt over the tank, their elegant horns gleaming and their black and white tails flashing as they raced by at top speed. Ebony noticed a large dog on their heels; it had a furry Mohican between its big round ears and spots all over its body. As it ran, it made a strange, eerie call; it wasn't like any dog Ebony had ever come across – in fact, it looked like an African hunting dog. But that was impossible – what was going on? She rubbed her eyes, then surveyed the devastation around her.

Recognising the skyline and the crumbling walls along O'Connell Bridge, Ebony gasped – this was definitely Dublin, but not as she knew it. It was the Dublin of the future, if Ambrose was allowed to get his way. But what did the strange animals mean?

A crowd roared nearby. Ebony turned and followed the sound. Through the murky air, she spied a gathering across the water at the base of the O'Connell monument. But where was the Spire? There was a gap in the sky where its sharp silver spike should be. Squinting, she realised the Spire was still there, but that it had been lopped off a third of the way up. The top section had fallen to the left, smashing a trench through the GPO. Ebony noticed that the statues on that building's roof had been damaged; her favourite, the woman holding a key with a dog looking up at her, was gone.

Crossing O'Connell Bridge, she joined the back of the group. It was made up of thin, miserable-looking people, guarded by Shadow Walkers. A stage stood up ahead, but Ebony couldn't see it properly so she pushed her way through the crowd. As she neared it, she saw that the stage was in front of four winged angels, each completely black from head to toe to wing tip.

Suddenly Ambrose stepped onto the stage, positioning himself in front of the central angel. The Shadow Walkers prodded the crowd with long, sharp spears. On cue, the people cheered and clapped. Ebony could see their hearts weren't in it; in fact, the expressions on their faces suggested they had no heart for anything any more. She was reminded of Icarus, his broken demeanour and sad eyes. As that thought crossed her mind, another cheer rang out. Icarus from the future arrived on stage. At least, she thought it was Icarus: his body was thinner than ever and a black, vine-like mark curled and twisted up from his neck and along his jaw, branching out to fill half of his face. And his eyes looked cruel. Covering her mouth to stifle a gasp, Ebony stared, terrified of what might happen next, but unable to look away.

Ambrose lifted his arms to the sky and the people responded with yells and cheers, prompted by a few pokes from the Shadow Walkers, as another person arrived on stage, laughing cruelly. Ebony's mouth dropped open: it was Zach Stone – she would know his laugh anywhere – but he was barely recognisable. His eyes were completely black, his skin sallow and his hair thin and wispy – what had happened to him?

Then she saw her own future self dragged on stage by a Shadow Walker, wrapped in a snaking coil of thick chains, and her legs turned weak. The Shadow Walker handed the chain to Zach and he pulled so hard that her future self fell, hitting her cheek against Icarus's boot. Icarus kicked out and shuffled away, his head bowed. Ebony couldn't understand what she had just seen. Why was Icarus showing such open hostility towards her? Although terrified, she continued watching, hoping to see something that would help her to prevent this possible future.

Yanking the chain, dragging her future self along the wooden slats of the stage, Zach laughed aloud once more. The noise resounded around the crowd and Ebony watched as everyone around her shrank back.

'This man was a traitor,' announced Ambrose in a booming voice. 'He worked for the Order, your enslavers and deceivers for centuries.' He turned to Icarus. 'Do you deny it?'

As the crowd rumbled, Icarus shook his head. 'I do not deny it. It is true.'

'Do you renounce the Order?' continued Ambrose.

'What Order?' replied Icarus, a smile creeping across his lips. 'They are now crushed!'

His voice sounded different – cruel and inhuman. Ebony saw the mark spread further across his face. Beside him, her future self had managed to climb to her feet and was fighting to break free, but Zach held her tight.

'What shall we do with the girl?' asked Ambrose. 'She has kept the secrets of reincarnation for herself.'

Without a flicker of emotion, Icarus replied, 'Take her soul and then kill her.'

'Take her soul!' cried a voice from the crowd.

'Why should she have the power for herself?' cried another. 'Let us share in eternal life.'

'Kill her, kill her!' cried the crowd in unison.

Forgetting herself, Ebony yelled 'No!' at the top of her voice. 'It doesn't work like that! There can only be one hundred families!'

Realising her mistake, she ducked down. Checking around her, she was relieved to find that no one nearby had heard – all eyes were fixed on the stage as though hypnotised. But when Ebony looked back towards the stage, Ambrose was staring right at her, deep into her soul. Behind him, one of the angel statues began to move, its wings flapping back and forth. The angel's body started to grow and, as it lifted its head, Ebony recognised the fanged jaws even before the Deus-Umbra began to roar. The crowd shrank back as the demon sniffed the air.

'I'm glad you could join us, Ebony Smart,' said Ambrose.

Following Ambrose's gaze, Zach turned to face her also, his black eyes turning fiery red as the Deus-Umbra lifted into the air. The chained Ebony Smart on stage struggled, yelling in protest. The demon flapped to gain height, then circled the crowd. The terrified onlookers cowered, hoping he wouldn't select them or their loved ones as victims. Adults gripped their children close, trying to hide them under their clothing.

'You will pay for what you did to my mother,' shouted Zach. There was still a hint of Zach's voice, but it was laden with hate. 'Murderer.'

One by one, the crowd turned to face Ebony. Some looked angry, others looked confused – after all, how could she be on the stage and at the back of the crowd at the same time?

'I didn't kill her! I destroyed the soul-swapping machine,' Ebony yelled back. 'You're the murderer – and I will avenge my grandpa.'

Suddenly diving, jaws wide and saliva dripping from its fangs, the Deus-Umbra aimed straight for her. Around her, the crowd roared and Icarus pointed at her from the stage, leading the chant: 'Kill her! Kill her!'

Before Ebony knew what was happening, the scene dropped away and she felt her skin and bones wrench. Next, her body turned weightless and the world spun in hues of grey and black. Soon, colours returned, burning her eyes. She blinked away tears. The pain in her head and hand stopped and, when her eyes cleared, she was back in Mr O'Hara's office, flopped over in her seat. Panting and sweating, words tumbled uncontrollably out of her mouth: 'You're the murderer – I will avenge my grandpa; you're the murderer – I will avenge my grandpa.'

Feeling faint, Ebony tried to right herself and nearly slipped from the chair. Uncle Cornelius dropped to his knees beside her and took her face in his hands, staring into her eyes.

'I'm OK,' she said, staggering to her feet. Crossing to Icarus, she took him by the shoulders, trying to force him to make eye contact, but he turned his face away. Winston scurried after her and scrambled up her leg, dropping into the side pocket of her trousers.

'Whatever's going on, we'll get through it, won't we?'

'I can't promise that,' said Icarus, his voice throaty and gravelly.

'But you must! I don't know if you saw what I saw, but we have to stop it.'

'We saw,' said Aunt Ruby, the strain and worry in her voice confirming her words.

'The vision is only what might pass,' said Mrs O'Hara, frown lines creasing her forehead. 'There is still time to prevent this future from occurring.'

Desperate now, Ebony shook Icarus by the shoulders. 'I know you would never betray us. Uncle, please—'

'Go away!' he yelled, pushing her from him. 'Leave me alone! I am not your uncle. I was adopted into your family – I'm no relation.'

'What do you mean?'

Icarus lowered his head and groaned. Kneeling in front of her brother, Aunt Ruby took his hands in hers and stared up into his face. He resisted, turning away.

'I know that you're hurting, but you're my brother and always will be.'

'I almost attacked you,' said Icarus, spit forming in the corner of his mouth. Freeing his hands and dropping his head into his palms, Icarus shook violently. 'The blood within me runs dark and deep. O'Hara is right. I *am* dangerous.'

'No, brother, you're the same good and strong man as before. Your heritage is not your fault – do you think Ambrose knows?'

At the mention of Ambrose's name, Ebony felt her neck muscles and stomach tighten. What had he done to her uncle? And if he could get to Icarus like this, what chance did the rest of them have?

'Oh, he knows,' spat Icarus, his face darkening. 'He made sure to tell Ivy and Rufus before they ran. Why do you think they wouldn't come back with me? They have carried this secret a long time and their fear when they saw me was obvious. They don't trust me. And once the Order finds out, everyone will fear me. Even I'm afraid of the blood running through my veins.'

'Then we must not let Ambrose use this to his advantage,' said Aunt Ruby.

'You don't understand, Ruby. It's already too late,' said Icarus, suddenly sitting upright, making Aunt Ruby jump back. Yanking up his sleeve, he thrust his arm forward. 'Look! He already has me in his grip.'

As soon as she saw the flesh on his arm, Ebony recoiled. The skin on Icarus's forearm had turned yellowish, laced with a delicate inky line that traced along the central vein, branching out across two others. The longest started at the wrist and wound halfway to his elbow, thin and spidery and visibly pulsating. It was the mark from the vision. Uncle Cornelius tilted back his head and howled.

'No!' cried Aunt Ruby, so loudly that Mrs O'Hara shivered. 'How and when did this happen?'

'It happened after Rufus told me about my adoption. I didn't believe him, so I foolishly left the past to meet with Ambrose and find out the truth. The biggest mistake I ever made … But what does it matter? I'm no longer worthy to be around you or your family. He marked me so I'm linked to him; it's getting bigger every day and I can't beat it. I can already feel a change within. Why do you think I lost control and almost attacked you?'

'I'll help you!' said Aunt Ruby, her voice rising in pitch and desperation. 'We'll find a way to free you from his power. Just keep this hidden for as long as you can, do you hear me?'

From the corridor came the faint sound of marching feet.

'It's Mr O'Hara,' said Ebony. 'Quick, cover your arm.'

Icarus pulled down his sleeve. 'Let them take me, please. I have no fight left.'

'You'll get it back, I know you will. Together we can beat this, just like we've beaten everything else Ambrose has thrown at us,' said Ebony, only half-believing her own words.

The footsteps grew louder. A tear dripped from Uncle Cornelius's eye onto his hairy auburn cheek, glistening like a jewel. He wiped it away, then cleared his throat and straightened up. Unable to think of anything else to say, Ebony lifted Winston out of her pocket and hugged him close as the marching grew louder. The noise reverberated in her brain, making it ache. Closing her eyes, she breathed deeply to force it away. She felt like screaming.

Mr O'Hara arrived, four armed guards in tow, and pointed at Icarus.

Aunt Ruby, her eyes flashing with anger, said to the others, 'It's time to leave.' As she passed her brother, now flanked by a member of security on each side, she paused. Raising his chin with one finger, she said, 'You're my brother and I'll always believe in you.'

'Me too,' said Ebony.

Certain she saw a glimmer of hope in Icarus's eyes, Ebony returned Winston to her trouser pocket and followed her aunt and Uncle Cornelius out of the office, Chiyoko and Mrs O'Hara close behind. They hadn't gone far when Mr O'Hara called out, 'Wait!'

The men marched Icarus out of the office and down the corridor; his feet dragging and shoulders sagging, he didn't once look up. Ebony's gut twisted. Mr O'Hara watched them turn the corner before addressing the others. 'We can't bring Seamus here.'

'You're not serious!' said Ebony.

'He could bring the enemy directly into headquarters. We don't know Ambrose's power; we need to keep him away from here for as long as possible.'

Aunt Ruby and Uncle Cornelius exchanged glances. Chiyoko's scowl was as tight as a coiled spring.

'So do you want us to bring Chiyoko with us as well?' asked Ruby. 'Our surveillance will keep her safe.'

'I think that's the best solution,' said Mr O'Hara. He paused, looking Ruby in the eye, 'Keep Seamus safe too. Please.'

Ruby gave a small nod and O'Hara turned to his wife. 'I'll need your help, dear. There is much work to be done.'

Mrs O'Hara bowed to the others, then stepped back inside the office. Before anyone could say anything else, Mr O'Hara offered a hasty goodbye and sealed up the door. Only the brick wall remained.

'Let's get out of here,' said Chiyoko, head hung low as she led the way.

Fists balled by her sides, Ebony made a silent promise to help both Icarus and Seamus. The promise burned like fire in her blood, flaring with every step.

14

Once inside the car, Winston climbed out of Ebony's pocket and settled himself on her lap. Curled in a ball, he closed his eyes. Waiting until they were speeding through the city towards home, Ebony began quizzing her aunt.

'Did you really not know that Icarus was adopted?' she asked.

'No,' replied Aunt Ruby, swallowing hard. 'Not until O'Hara told me. I saw copies of the adoption papers this morning.'

'I've never seen him like this.'

'None of us has,' replied Aunt Ruby. 'He's had a shock.'

'He sounded really upset,' said Chiyoko

'I don't get it. Why is it affecting him so badly?' asked Ebony, screwing up her nose. 'I understand it's a shock – but the change in Icarus … It's like he's becoming a completely different person.'

Turning to face her niece in the back seat, Aunt Ruby's face looked grim. 'You do realise why, don't you? I know I said it was for Icarus to tell you, but you're a smart girl, Ebony – surely you've worked it out?'

Taking a moment, Ebony racked her brain. Slowly, realisation dawned: the mark, the sudden link between Icarus and Ambrose and Icarus's fear that Ambrose could control him – there could only be one reason for it.

Ebony cleared her throat, almost afraid to ask. 'Is he related to Ambrose?'

As Chiyoko gasped, Aunt Ruby caught Ebony's eye in the rear-view mirror. 'Their parents were killed when they were very young and they were split up. Now you understand why Mr O'Hara is so wary of him. It seems your parents are frightened too. Icarus is right; everyone will be afraid if they find out. Ambrose is, after all, trying to destroy us.'

'But that doesn't mean Icarus will help him!'

'We know that, but we have to convince the others.'

Leaning forward, Ebony gripped the back of her aunt's seat. 'So that mark on his skin – was it a tattoo?'

The car shook and swerved as Uncle Cornelius whimpered, momentarily losing control of the wheel. As he righted the car, Aunt Ruby gave a firm and abrupt reply. 'No.'

In the rear-view mirror, Ebony could see that her aunt's expression had darkened. Her eyes also looked watery – was Aunt Ruby going to cry?

'You panicked when you saw it – do you know what it is?'

'My husband, Connie, was afflicted with the same mark. Remember how I told you I was demoted to Travel and Transport? At the same time, my husband – along with your parents – were assigned to a secret project. And the mark appeared on his arm. I don't know what it meant, but it altered him.'

'So, wait – was he related to Ambrose too?'

'Yes, distantly,' replied Aunt Ruby. 'But not distantly enough to stop Ambrose asserting his influence over him. Luckily he was killed before Ambrose claimed complete power over him.' Aunt Ruby's face darkened. 'Connie was a good man, but by the time he died my husband was greatly changed. Whatever hold Ambrose had over him, whatever power that mark gave him, it ate Connie's soul from the inside out. That's why Icarus is so scared. In truth, I fear for him too. For now, he is safer in custody.'

'I bet that's why I found Connie's soul so damaged when I was inside the Reflectory. The sky world is trying to heal him before he passes through to Obliteration or Ultimation.'

'You'd be the best judge of that, Ebony,' said her aunt.

Inside, Ebony glowed.

Deciding to leave the matter there for now – at least she knew what Icarus's big secret was – Ebony focused her efforts on how she could help the Order by taking steps to prevent what she'd seen in the vision.

'The work you were doing with Mr O'Hara in his office – what were you looking for exactly?' Ebony asked her aunt, rubbing Winston on his neck. Enjoying the attention, Winston hunkered down. 'I thought I saw a riverbed.'

'You did – the Liffey, where the bodies have been turning up, in case there was some kind of underground lair – but in truth, we're not getting anywhere,' said Aunt Ruby with a sigh. 'The Order has been searching everywhere in the city for signs of enemy action, as well as Oddley Cove. Remember how, before the last battle, Mr O'Hara had been monitoring disappearing ships and it turned out to be *The Black Peregrine* and the Shadow Walkers? Well, he thinks that Ambrose might be using the attacks in the city as a decoy and that the real action will happen back there.'

'He could be right, but you don't sound convinced,' said Ebony, glancing at Chiyoko.

'I doubt they'll strike in the same place twice. You've seen Mrs O'Hara's visions. I believe Ambrose's intentions have changed. I have no doubt that he still wants the power of reincarnation, but I believe that he's coming at it from two angles now. He still needs your soul so he can control the Reflectory, but, from Mrs O'Hara's vision, it looks as if he has also put plans for world domination into action. To do that he'll attack the city: Dublin is the most populated area, so it makes sense to start here if you are trying to take over Ireland.'

'So what can we do?'

'I don't know – but whatever we decide, we have to be extra careful, especially after the whole Anti-Ebony Smart League business. That awful league may have been disbanded, but there's still some dissension among the Order and we don't want to spark it up again by upsetting Mr O'Hara.' Turning to Chiyoko, Aunt Ruby gave her an apologetic smile.

'Sorry, Chiyoko, I don't mean to be so blunt.'

Keeping her eyes towards the window, Chiyoko shrugged, her cheeks flaring scarlet. Ebony could see her chest heaving with quiet sighs.

'Do you think we'll be able to get Mr O'Hara on side?' asked Ebony.

'I hope so, but you know he finds it difficult to believe in anything without concrete evidence. He refuses to accept a future with Ambrose at the helm as a possibility – maybe he's in denial because, in truth, our numbers are small and without more knowledge of Ambrose's plans we have little hope of winning. If the Deus-Umbra really is under Ambrose's control, we have no way to defeat it – so no way to defeat him.'

Although desperate to do something of use, Ebony understood her aunt's caution. When O'Hara had returned from overseas just months before, he had turned the entire Order against her, accusing her of being a false guardian. Only when she revealed the Reflectory doorway and saved his daughter from the Deus-Umbra did he back down. He'd been supportive ever since to some extent, but Ebony knew he still viewed her as a little girl and believed that the grown-ups knew what was best for her; that she should do what she was told. She also knew that her aunt was right in suggesting it was best for her to stay on his good side. She couldn't afford to lose his support now, particularly as he was currently acting head of the Order.

'So what's our next move?' she asked.

'Mr O'Hara's method of waiting for more signs or another attack is too defensive. I think it's time to take matters into our own hands, go on the offensive and try to find Ambrose and Zach before they become too powerful.'

A blast of pain shot through her hand and Ebony's heart pumped so hard, she thought it might explode from her chest. Her aunt continued. 'Mr O'Hara means well, but his methods are too slow. I'm concerned for Icarus – for all of us. I've been formulating a plan–'

'Shadow Walker!' cried Chiyoko, interrupting their discussion.

All eyes swivelled to Chiyoko's window. On the pavement up ahead was a huge, red-eyed creature. It held a young boy by the neck, lifting him from the ground. A woman was attacking the Shadow Walker, beating it with her handbag and screaming at it to return her son.

'Sound the horn, Cornelius,' ordered Aunt Ruby.

As Uncle Cornelius responded, the horn blaring long and loud as they raced by, the Shadow Walker dropped the boy and turned to face the car. Quickly, the boy's mum grabbed his hand, hauled him to his feet and, together, they ran off. Ebony turned to watch out the back window, grasping her wrist to stem the pain. Angry at losing his victims, the Shadow Walker began to run after the car.

'It's coming,' Ebony called.

In a few steps, the Shadow Walker had caught up. There

was a loud *thump* as its fist smashed down on the roof. The noise made Ebony's ears ring. Winston leapt to the floor, while Chiyoko flung herself flat on the seat. The Shadow Walker attacked again, but this time Uncle Cornelius swerved and slammed on the brakes, before reversing in a donut shape, slamming into the creature and knocking it to the ground.

'We need to get Ebony to safety,' said Aunt Ruby.

Speeding off before the Shadow Walker could climb to its feet, Uncle Cornelius managed to create some distance between them and, after a few quick turns down random streets, seemed to lose the creature. He stepped on the accelerator, making the shops and houses whizz by, and soon they screeched to a stop outside 23 Mercury Lane. Immediately, one of the guards from the front surveillance car leapt out of his vehicle and, using the door as a shield, dropped to his knees, a gun trained on them.

Jumping out of the car before it had even stopped properly, Aunt Ruby raised her hands. 'It's us,' she called out and the gunman relaxed. Running over to him, Aunt Ruby spoke quickly, her voice a low hum as she gesticulated wildly. Then she turned, raced back at top speed and flung Ebony's door wide open.

'You two, go inside. We're going to go back to see if there are any more Shadow Walkers about. Don't worry, one of the surveillance teams will stay to watch the house. And Mulligan is in the basement. Any sign of trouble and you scream for help. Promise?'

'Promise,' agreed Ebony and Chiyoko in unison.

Uncle Cornelius escorted the pair to the doorstep and watched as Ebony undid the locks. As he ran back to the car, one surveillance car pulled out, waiting for Uncle Cornelius to take the lead. Ebony gave the other surveillance car a wave and the man inside saluted in return. Pushing her way inside 23 Mercury Lane, Ebony took hold of Chiyoko's hand, flicked on the lights and slammed the door firmly shut.

'Shall we wait upstairs or downstairs?' asked Ebony.

'Let's check on Seamus,' said Chiyoko.

Agreeing, Ebony freed Winston from her pocket. Together, the girls climbed the stairs, with Winston following quietly behind. As they passed Uncle Cornelius's study, Ebony noticed that the door was unlocked and ajar, dust motes dancing in the crack.

At the top of the stairs, the bedroom door was open. Miss Malone sat at Seamus's bedside, singing an out-of-tune lullaby. Seeing the girls, her cheeks reddened. Ebony noticed the dark circles under her eyes.

'Your shift finished hours ago!' said Ebony.

'After what happened, I didn't want to leave until you were back. He's stirred but hasn't woken. He has a bit of a fever, but other than that, there's been no change. Do you want me to stay a while?'

'No. You should go home and get some rest,' said Chiyoko.

When Ebony nodded agreement, Miss Malone held her hand to Seamus's forehead, then hurried away. Knowing Seamus was OK for the moment, Ebony waited until she heard the downstairs door slam behind Miss Malone, then she pulled Chiyoko back down to the study. A heavy, ivy-patterned key sat in the lock, twisted on its side. Ebony pushed the door open carefully; being there reminded her of when she'd found *The Book of Learning*.

As the door swung open, a whiff of dust, musty paper and old bones wafted out. Ebony pinched her nose as she entered, releasing it slowly to get used to the smell. The room was dark and dank until Chiyoko threw open the curtains, revealing desks filled with documents, letters, maps, photographs and ledgers as the early evening light streamed in. The place was a mess; it looked like there had been a struggle followed by a serious ransacking.

'What happened here?' whispered Chiyoko, surveying the chaos.

'It's Uncle Cornelius's natural filing system – only he's allowed in here, usually. Let's have a look around while we can!'

Spying the book cabinet, an idea struck Ebony. She might have lost *The Book of Learning* to the depths of the ocean, but what if there was another one? If the ancients had made one book with magical powers, might they have made more? If so, perhaps she could still help her parents.

Ebony headed straight for the bookshelves. The glinting metallic lettering on the leather-bound spines was calling her. Winston shuffled his whole body under reams of paper, looking for scraps. Meanwhile, Chiyoko stared up at the wall of fishing knots, sailing memorabilia and a stuffed marlin head in awe.

'This place is incredible!' said Chiyoko.

Ebony pointed to the binoculars facing the wall. 'See those? They showed me what happened to my grandpa. I think they show you the past. Try them!'

Enthralled, Chiyoko crept towards the binoculars. Standing in front of the bookshelves, Ebony checked on her companions. Winston was engrossed in a piece of mouldy cake, while Chiyoko was admiring the design around the edges of the binoculars. Behind the glass doors of the cabinet, the glinting spines sparkled and shone. Ebony closed her eyes, took a breath and opened them again, hoping that one book would appeal to her and turn out to be special, just like *The Book of Learning*. As she stared at the rows of spines, her fingers clutching the amulet around her neck, her eyes became unfocused and the books began to dance. They jiggled and bounced, their cases rattling on the shelves like gentle rain. Checking behind her once more, Ebony saw that the others were oblivious. It was as though the books were communicating with her. If she listened hard enough, would she understand their message?

Realising the cabinet doors were unlocked, she pulled one side open and reached for an extra thick spine, decorated with grooves in the shape of birds' feet. As soon as she touched it, the books stopped jostling. Opening the book to the first page, Ebony hardly dared breathe. She ran her finger over the page, willing something to happen.

A warm hand on her shoulder made her jump.

'There was only one *Book of Learning*,' said Aunt Ruby solemnly, handing over Winston. 'It's lost to the past, I'm afraid. You must find a new way now.'

'I thought you'd gone after the Shadow Walker!' said Ebony, eyeing her aunt warily.

'I was going to, but I decided to stay here and mind you two – Uncle Cornelius and one surveillance car will be enough for a quick scout. It looks like I made the right decision!'

Blushing, Ebony looked at her feet.

A strange cry from Chiyoko rang out, freezing Ebony's blood and making Aunt Ruby swivel round. Chiyoko was staring into the binoculars, her body shaking and her hands grasping the surround, her knuckles white. Aunt Ruby dashed to the girl's side and shook her by the shoulder, calling her name. There was no response.

'She's as rigid as a rock,' said Aunt Ruby. 'Help me!'

Slamming the book cabinet shut, Ebony raced to help. As Ruby unwrapped Chiyoko's fingers one at a time from the binoculars, Ebony tugged at the girl's waist. Her hands kept slipping off Chiyoko's silk dress, but after a few attempts, Chiyoko staggered back, gasping. She closed her eyes, tears streaming down her cheeks and her body trembling as she swallowed violent sobs. Aunt Ruby rubbed her hands with her own to warm them.

'What happened?' asked Ebony, feeling terrible – after all, she'd encouraged Chiyoko to take a look.

It took a while for Chiyoko to respond. 'I saw ... It was horrible ...'

'Take your time,' urged Aunt Ruby, tightening her grip.

'The D-Deus-U-Umbra was attacking Seamus, trying to take his puppets. But Seamus wouldn't let go and the demon went for his mask. Seamus refused to take it off; he put up a good fight. That monster – it looked like it was trying to pull my brother's face off. The vision stopped before I could see whether it succeeded.'

'It's OK,' said Aunt Ruby. 'My guess is that you're seeing what happened to Seamus in the last battle, things we don't yet know because Seamus is still unconscious.'

'But the demon was right there, fighting against us. How did it get to my brother when he was in the cottage, away from the battle? And my parents were with him.'

Ebony felt her face redden as guilt surged inside her. 'It must have found Seamus after the battle – maybe it was because Seamus had helped me? Maybe he drew its attention by using his skills as a Shadow Custodian, or by joining in the song using the conch?'

Aunt Ruby placed a hand on each girl's shoulder. 'But that's over – we're all safe and sound.'

'But we're not, are we?' asked Chiyoko, shrugging Aunt Ruby off. 'Seamus is sick and no one knows what's wrong with him and Shadow Walkers are popping up everywhere. How are we safe?'

'Your mother is coming tomorrow to see if she can help

Seamus,' said Aunt Ruby. 'And I know the Shadow Walkers are unpredictable, but I've done what I can. I've upped internal security on the house and surveillance has been doubled.'

Not looking convinced, Chiyoko shuddered. Guiding her towards Ebony, Aunt Ruby pointed to the stairs. 'She's in shock. Take her downstairs and give her some sweet tea. I'll check on Seamus, then join you.'

As Ebony helped Chiyoko out of the study, an idea hit. What was stopping her, once she'd learned how, from travelling through time to retrieve *The Book of Learning*? After all, she knew exactly when she'd lost it. There had to be a way! The idea alive in her mind, Ebony led Chiyoko to the kitchen as requested, only half-aware of her surroundings.

Her aunt was wrong: *The Book of Learning* didn't have to be lost.

'Are you feeling better?' asked Ebony, noticing that Chiyoko's grip on her mug of tea had loosened.

Chiyoko blew into the hot steam. 'Kind of, but not really. What if Seamus never gets well again? This is partly my father's fault. If he wasn't so stubborn, if he'd let Seamus learn from Mum without interfering, maybe my brother wouldn't be in this state.'

'And if I hadn't needed help …' added Ebony, her voice fading.

'Seamus didn't have to help you – he wanted to. I know you two didn't start off on the right foot, but even after all the pressure from Dad, he accepted you as guardian and wanted to protect you. If only my father had listened.' Chiyoko paused and heaved a big sigh. 'That mark on Icarus – do you think your aunt knows more about it than she's letting on?'

'Possibly. She probably thinks she's protecting me.'

'I'm so sick of adults thinking they know better than us,' added Chiyoko. 'I bet they're still keeping other stuff from us as well – all those hours in the office.'

'From what my aunt says, no progress has been made. The stuff your dad's been looking at is pointless.'

A frown spread across Chiyoko's face. 'The things he's showing your aunt, perhaps, but after all those years of working on his own and distrusting your aunt and Icarus, I wouldn't be surprised if he's still keeping some things secret, even after all we've been through. Especially now he thinks Icarus is working against us.'

'Like what?' asked Ebony, eyes wide.

'That's what we need to find out!'

The front door slammed and footsteps sounded in the hall, stopping the conversation. Chiyoko's body tensed, but hearing a cough, Ebony smiled. 'It's just Uncle Cornelius.'

As his footsteps padded up the stairs, Chiyoko sank deep into thought and Ebony's mind raced, trying to guess what her friend was planning. Minutes later, Aunt Ruby came in and switched on the light – Ebony hadn't realised how dark it had become – and eyed the girls carefully, her unlit pipe wedged in her mouth. Then Uncle Cornelius joined them, twitching his nose, his stomach rumbling. Ebony and Chiyoko watched him closely. Seemingly relaxed and licking his lips, he squashed himself back in his chair, his knife and fork poised expectantly.

'They didn't find anything and the full security detail is back outside,' said Aunt Ruby. 'Toast and jam, anyone?' Flicking open her silver lighter to light her pipe, she chugged on its stem as she waited for an answer.

'Yes, please!' said Chiyoko, her face brightening.

Winston somersaulted, but Ebony rolled her eyes. Uncle Cornelius jumped to his feet, retrieved a giant old bone that he'd hidden behind the kitchen bin and roared in protest. As he dropped to all fours with a look of disgust at Aunt Ruby, there was a sudden rumbling and the secret door under the sink sprang open. A huge head, all teeth and fur, filled the space, quickly followed by two gigantic swiping paws, their nails curved and sharp. His face scrunched up, Mulligan looked about him and, realising all was well, gave several loud roars. Noticing Chiyoko, he narrowed his eyes, sniffed the air, then backed away. Uncle Cornelius followed. Chiyoko eyed the swing door warily, her mouth hanging open, but Ebony just chuckled. Moments later, slices of hot toast with burnt, sometimes flaming, edges flew across the room and landed on the table.

'They're like missiles!' whispered Chiyoko, reaching up to snatch a slice from mid-air before it missed the table completely and ended up smashed against the kitchen door.

Winston pounced on the next one as it skidded across the table. Chiyoko already had her slice buttered and was dolloping on huge spoonfuls of plum jam that a mini electric dump truck – one of Aunt Ruby's creations – had just tipped onto the plastic tablecloth. This didn't deter Chiyoko: she was happy to scoop it up, the colour returning to her cheeks.

'This is the best dinner,' she said, her mouth stuffed with an extra fat crust. 'There's no way we'd be allowed this at home. We usually have ramen noodles or sushi.'

Ebony's stomach growled at the thought; her grandpa had regularly cut a slice of raw fish for eating when they were out on their little fishing boat. Ebony used to feel sick at the thought of it and she wouldn't even give it a try. But now she would give anything to take a piece of that raw fish from her grandpa's sharp fishing knife and pop it in her mouth, if only to see the smile it would bring to his face.

As a helicopter whizzed their way, carrying a second pot of slightly warmed butter, Ebony reached out and snatched it before it spilled on top of Winston. Oblivious, Winston tucked into a large splatter of jam that had landed just inches away from his nose.

'That's strange,' said Aunt Ruby in a loud, worried voice, making everyone stop in their tracks. Even Winston stopped nibbling. 'Did anyone touch this monitor?'

All eyes turned to where Aunt Ruby was standing. The monitor was flashing DISARMED. Ebony gulped and hid her glowing cheeks behind her slice of toast. 'I think it's my fault,' she said. 'I reset the one in Seamus's room after the whole possession thing, but I didn't think of checking the others.'

Aunt Ruby inspected the monitor more closely. 'No matter. Seamus seems to have recovered from his earlier incident.' Catching his sister's eye, she corrected herself. 'He's stable again, I mean. I'd better go check the other monitors.'

As Aunt Ruby set off on her rounds, Chiyoko leaned towards Ebony, a thoughtful look on her face. 'You know earlier when we were talking about my father keeping secrets? I'm sure he found something of interest when we were in his office. It looked like he was trying to hide whatever was on his computer screen from us.'

'I thought so too – but what good is that to us?' asked Ebony, frowning. 'We'll never get back in there!'

Chiyoko grinned and pulled her computer from her pocket, giving it a little wave. 'Our secret weapon. The file will be saved and I bet I can hack in to my dad's computer. If that doesn't work, your computer in the Hideout is linked to the Nine Lives system, right? I'm sure I could find the right files from there. Let's do some investigating.'

Winston, munching on his toast, thrust his left paw in the air, his signal for yes. Chiyoko's suggestion sent a shock of courage through Ebony's body. The time was right, she could feel it. A grin crept across her face. 'I'm in!'

They both jumped guiltily as Aunt Ruby rushed back into the kitchen. She was looking at her watch and didn't notice the nervous glance the two girls shared. 'Goodness me, look at the time! All the monitors have been reset, so we should be fine until morning. Do you two want your own rooms or to stay together?'

'Together,' said Ebony and Chiyoko at the same time, and then both giggled.

'Then you go and grab the first shower, Chiyoko. I've left a pair of Ebony's pyjamas on the bed for you.'

Slowly, Chiyoko got to her feet and left the kitchen. Ebony

could hear her feet thumping on the stairs as she raced up them, probably afraid of the big, dark house but too nervous or shy to admit it.

'By the way, Ebony, the plan I mentioned on the way back from headquarters,' said Aunt Ruby in a hushed voice, 'is to start your instruction right away. I think you're right – if anyone can convince your parents to return, it's you.'

'Instruction?'

'I will find a way for Icarus to show you what he knows about using the Shadowlands to travel in time.'

Ebony's pulse quickened at the thought; she knew she would have to be careful, but who else was going to go back in time and try to convince her parents to return?

'But he's under arrest – and he didn't seem very co-operative. Or in much of a position to help.'

Aunt Ruby bit her lip and gave a small nod. 'I'll help him through it. It's a rough patch. Regardless of blood, we're brother and sister. Nothing can destroy the bond between us. And I don't believe all that nonsense about bad blood – Ambrose's behaviour is dictated by choice, not what flows through his veins.'

But Ebony wasn't convinced. 'A rough patch? That thing on his arm ... He seemed so sad, so defeated. The way he attacked you – it's like he's out of control. I'm not sure even you'll get through to him, Aunt Ruby.' Then, realising how defeatist she sounded, she sat up in her chair and added, 'But at least I have you on my side.'

'I'm glad you've finally realised it,' replied her aunt. 'I've been working on restoring the Order and finding more of our kind for years. I believe that working together is the only way we'll succeed. Defeating Ambrose and restoring the Order has to be part of reaching our ultimate destinies. As guardian, yours is particularly special and I know it isn't easy, but I'll always be here for you.'

Ebony felt heat rise in her face and looked away.

A creak from upstairs made Aunt Ruby lower her voice. 'We should be careful what we tell Chiyoko from now on. Mr O'Hara may be part of the Order but he shoulders great responsibility and may not approve of our methods. Agreed?'

'I think we can trust her–' began Ebony but the look on her aunt's face silenced her. 'OK, agreed,' she said, her fingers crossed behind her back. Deep down, she knew that Chiyoko could be trusted, but convincing her aunt might be difficult. And so, until they had something concrete to show from their own investigations, she would let her aunt believe that Chiyoko wasn't involved.

'Oh, I almost forgot, I have something to give you,' said Aunt Ruby, pulling the memento mori photograph from her pocket. 'Quick, hide it!'

Taking it, Ebony's eyes widened. She was too shocked to speak.

'I thought you should have it. But I wouldn't go around showing it off.'

'You stole it? When?'

'Let's say I procured it a little while ago, but I wanted to make sure O'Hara hadn't noticed it was missing before passing it to you.'

'Th-thank you,' said Ebony, taking a peek.

Her eyes skimmed over the photograph, then rested on her mother's hands. They lay gently on top of each other, one slender finger jutting out. She checked her own hands for similarities; like her mother, she had long, slim fingers and a stubby thumb. This made her insides as warm as an open fire.

An easy quiet spread over the room: the hushed silence of plotting comrades. Inside, Ebony was buzzing with excitement; with her aunt's support, Icarus sharing his knowledge of the Shadowlands and her secret alliance with Chiyoko, she was sure she'd find her parents in no time and strengthen the Order's position against Ambrose and Zach. What could possibly go wrong?

Taking the stairs two at a time, Winston clinging onto her curls for safety, Ebony found Chiyoko at the top of the house, quietly closing her brother's bedroom door. Her hair was still wet and she looked small and frail in Ebony's blue-and-white-striped pyjamas.

'Have you seen this?' asked Chiyoko, holding out a newspaper. 'I found it next to his bed.'

Recognising the headline from earlier, Ebony read the whole story:

DUBLINERS HALLUCINATE: CROWD PSYCHOSIS OR FAULTY DRUG?

Over the last few weeks, sightings of ghoulish, shadow-like figures have been reported by multiple people in the Dublin City area. Several people have been so affected by these 'hallucinations' that they have had to be committed for their own safety. The first sighting was reported a few weeks ago, before the first body marked with a skull was recovered, but until reports reached excessive numbers, police didn't believe there was any need for concern.

'The person who reported the first sighting was intoxicated,' explained one of the officers on duty. 'We thought it was the alcohol causing hallucinations, so we kept him in custody overnight. He had stopped raving by morning and so we set him free.'

But since the initial sighting, several encounters with strange ghouls have been reported by people of all ages and from all walks of life. Puzzled investigators have yet to find a common link. Each report describes large, violent 'creatures' with bodies made of 'shadows'.

Police psychologists say this may be a form of mass psychosis, brought on by the recent spate of bodies – now four in total – pulled from the Liffey. A medical specialist says it could be a side effect of some type of medicine. As the backgrounds of those claiming sightings, as well as the dead bodies, are being investigated, police are appealing for reliable eyewitnesses to come forward and help with investigations.

'This is getting out of control – when do we start investigating?' asked Ebony.

As something clattered below, Chiyoko put a finger to her lips and looked down the stairs nervously. Only when they were in Ebony's room, door closed, did she reply.

'As soon as we can,' she said, reaching for her computer and settling herself on the bed.

Hearing footsteps in the street below, Ebony peeked out. The surveillance team was in place – one of the cars had been replaced by what looked like a mini olive-green tank, identical to the one that had driven straight at her when she was pulled into Mrs O'Hara's puppet show. The only other movement was a couple walking home, holding hands under a sky full of stars. Ebony's grandpa used to tell her that when the stars shone on you all your wishes would come true. After all the waiting, things were beginning to fall into place – she could almost feel starlight brushing against her skin. But she also knew that she had to play it smart and they had a long way to go.

'Actually, you'd better hide the computer for now,' said Ebony. 'Aunt Ruby will be in soon to say goodnight. We'll pretend to be asleep until everyone's in bed.'

'Got it.'

Ebony quickly showered and changed. As the pair settled under the duvet – Winston banished to his cage – Aunt Ruby, dressed in her purple silk dressing gown, quietly opened the door.

'Sleep tight, girls,' she whispered, pausing in the doorway. Ebony and Chiyoko snuggled down, squeezing their eyes closed. Eventually, the door clicked shut and Aunt Ruby's footsteps retreated. It took a while, but as soon as she heard the lights downstairs click off, Ebony lit a small candle. The girls sat up and huddled together.

'See what you can access,' said Ebony.

'Already on it,' replied Chiyoko, tapping at the keyboard. Eyebrows furrowed and head down, she entered a series of complex-looking commands that Ebony couldn't follow. Looking up, a grin plastered across her face, Chiyoko showed Ebony the screen. 'We're in – my father always uses variations of either my name or Seamus's for his passwords. What should we look at first?'

Ebony surveyed the seemingly endless list of files and folders – titles like Archives, Mineral Deposits, Tide Behaviour, Fish Counts and Activity. None seemed particularly alluring. Needing to start somewhere, Ebony suggested the Activity folder and Chiyoko clicked through. It led to multiple Excel documents, each workbook filled with row after row of figures – most of which, judging by the coloured key on the initial page, was a very complex way of saying that no suspicious shadow ships, submarines or even rubber dinghies had been spotted.

Chiyoko groaned and returned to the Activity folder. 'Wait!' she cried. 'There were so many options, I missed this folder! Seamus would have noticed it immediately – it's password-protected, again, so it might take me a minute or two.'

'Octopus?' said Ebony incredulously, as Chiyoko tried various password combinations. 'What's so interesting about a folder called Octopus?'

'When we were kids,' explained Chiyoko, trying to stifle a yawn, 'whenever there was something we had to keep secret, especially from Mum, Father used the code word octopus.' When Ebony pulled a face, Chiyoko continued. 'The giant octopus is the most loyal creature in the world. The female only ever lays eggs once. Do you know why?'

'No, why?' Ebony was genuinely interested. Her grandpa had always told her that the sea told stories, if you cared to watch and listen, and this sounded like something he would share.

'Because she dies for them. The mother finds a crevice to hide in – it has to be big because she's about nine metres tall – and lays thousands of eggs. Then she stays there, guarding them and gently blowing air on them to keep them alive. Slowly starving to death, she dies as they hatch. You don't get much more loyal than that.'

As Chiyoko spoke, it felt like something cold and heavy had settled in Ebony's stomach. How could her parents hide away from her like this for so many years and then refuse to come back? But then something else struck: what if, just like the giant octopus, her mum and dad were making sacrifices to keep her safe?

'OK,' said Ebony. 'I get it. So the code word means utmost loyalty is needed. But what's he hiding?'

Chiyoko finally figured out that the password was a variation of her name – Ch1Y0ko – but a small bleep quickly indicated it wasn't going to be that easy.

'Classified,' read Chiyoko, sounding irritated but undeterred at the message that flashed up on the screen. 'Don't worry, I should be able to crack this in a moment …'

But after a few minutes, Chiyoko shoved the computer away and rubbed her eyes. 'It's no use. I'm too tired, I can't concentrate.'

Ebony frowned. 'Please, Chiyoko, keep trying. We have to find out as much as we can as soon as possible.'

'I'm tired, Ebony, I can't think straight,' replied Chiyoko. However, she grudgingly picked up the computer again and entered one more command. Immediately an awful gushing noise sounded.

'Turn it off!' cried Ebony.

'I can't!' replied Chiyoko, frantically pushing buttons. Nothing worked. 'I think my computer is broken! Even Mute isn't working!'

Suddenly Ebony's palm began to hurt and a bright flash drew their attention to the mirror on the dressing table. They realised with a start that the sound was actually coming from there. It wasn't the first time this had happened: they both remembered Chiyoko being pulled onto Ambrose's pirate ship through the mirror. This time, they watched as a heavy mist swirled inside the glass. A pale light shone from one corner and Ebony recognised the gushing sound: it was wild and crashing waves, only magnified. A sea storm. The pain in her hand told her that the Shadow Walkers were coming.

There were voices now and, even in the dim light, Ebony could see Chiyoko's face turn deathly pale as their song rang out:

> ♪ Skull and bones flying on the main mast,
> Cutlasses and swords ready in hand ... ♫

Entranced, Chiyoko began to shake. The prow of a ship emerged from the mist, a giant spike at the helm where a red-gold dragon figurehead used to be. The ship changed course and turned towards them – there was an awful screeching as the spike began to push against the glass. The surface of the mirror curved outwards but somehow the ship failed to break through. Ebony leaped up, grabbed a towel and threw it over the mirror – this solution had worked before – and then raced back to the bed and slammed down the computer lid in case the two events were somehow linked. The sound of waves stopped but, under the towel, the ship's prow could be seen still trying to poke through the glass. In his cage, Winston quivered and shook, his teeth rattling. No one dared move.

Eventually, the point withdrew and the towel stopped moving.

'Shadow Walkers,' said Chiyoko.

'Their attacks are becoming more frequent,' replied Ebony. 'They'll come for me soon. I can feel it. We need a plan.' She reached into her bedside cabinet drawer for a pen and some paper. 'Let's break down what we need to do into achievable goals. That's how my grandpa used to plan our gardening and fishing schedules – and it always worked for him.'

Chiyoko called out her ideas while Ebony wrote them down alongside her own.

'OK,' said Ebony eventually, 'this is our to-do list.' She cleared her throat and read it aloud.

1. *Learn how to time travel the Shadowlands.*

2. *Help Seamus get better.*

3. *Rescue parents.*

4. *Get The Book of Learning back.*

5. *Defeat enemies.*

6. *Stay alive.*

Her enthusiasm for the list deflated with every word. None of it was going to be easy to achieve. As Chiyoko moved to close her computer down, Winston leaped onto the bed and proceeded to pat Ebony's leg and squeak. He twitched his nose and pointed at his chest.

'What is it, Winston?' asked Ebony. Winston drew a square with his paws, before miming being squashed flat, his tail snaking from side to side. 'I think he's talking about what happened at headquarters.'

Winston jumped up, holding his left paw in the air.

'Did you see what was in the file?' Chiyoko asked him.

Winston lifted his right paw and Ebony scooped him up onto her palm.

'He says no. But he definitely saw something.'

Winston lifted his left paw this time. Then, he scratched his head and pointed to Chiyoko's computer, his own eyes and back to the computer again. Ebony watched him carefully for a moment more. 'I've got it!' she cried. 'Why didn't I think of this before? Winston has cameras inside his eyes.'

Chiyoko recoiled. 'He has what?'

'Aunt Ruby inserted them. You noticed your dad hiding something at his office – well, Winston was on his desk all along. Your father accidentally knocked him onto the keyboard and I saw something moving on the screen. Whatever it was, if Winston saw it, it'll be recorded. We can go into the basement and check out the surveillance cameras.'

Chiyoko's eyes were drooping. 'Can it wait until tomorrow?'

Although raring to go, Ebony quelled her impatience; she could work the system downstairs, but she might need Chiyoko's computer knowledge to understand what she was looking at. 'OK. Get some sleep and we'll investigate after your mum's visit. How does that sound?'

'Like a good plan,' said Chiyoko, flopping back on the bed and cuddling her computer under the covers. 'Make sure the Shadow Walkers don't get me?'

'They're gone, you're quite safe,' said Ebony, hoping she was right.

In seconds, Chiyoko was snoring gently. Winston shuffled backwards so he was half-hidden under the pillow and closed his eyes. Soon, they were snoring together. Too alert for sleep, Ebony turned on her side and watched the candle flicker, but the snoring made it impossible for her to relax.

She shuffled out of bed, crept across the room and pulled the photograph from her trouser pocket. Holding it under the candlelight, she studied the image. Her eyes were drawn to her mother's hand once more, and this time Ebony realised that her mother was actually pointing. Tracing a line, Ebony's finger came to rest on the framed pictures. Puzzled, she wondered what this could mean, but there was only one way to find out. Picking up the lit candle, photo in hand, Ebony crept to the bedroom door. Leaving it slightly ajar, she tiptoed down the stairs.

Ebony crept into the living room, not a sound to be heard throughout the house, and began to compare the paintings on the wall to those in her photograph. Several of them were identical, so she reached for the closest painting and lifted it from the wall. The wallpaper behind it was much darker: the picture hadn't been moved for some time. Still, there was nothing interesting to be found. Leaning the painting carefully against the wall, Ebony removed a second and a third. Each time she found nothing, her disappointment grew; was she mistaken?

After removing the final picture without any luck, Ebony tried to hang the first painting back up. It wouldn't catch the nail so she put the candle down and turned it over to see if there was something wrong with the string. As she did so, something caught her eye: a piece of yellowing, folded paper was sticking out between the frame and the back of the painting. She removed the paper as gently as she could and unfolded it. Written at the top of the page was 'Week 1' – the writing was neat and careful – and at the bottom it was initialled 'R.S.' With a jolt, she realised that this must be a diary entry written by her father – Rufus Smart.

Quickly rechecking each painting, Ebony discovered more hidden papers and was left with a series of diary entries. After returning the paintings to their correct positions, she unfolded each find. She checked the entry numbers at the top and put them in order. Settling into a beanbag, the candle on a small table by her side, she began to read.

Week 1: Although we – myself, Ivy and Connie – are sad that Ruby has been removed from her position as weaponry specialist, our secret mission from Judge Ambrose makes it difficult to know what to feel. We are to build a weapon that will make the Order invincible should it ever come under attack from demonic or magical beings. Myself and Ivy are to design and build the machine and Connie has been put on other duties – what, exactly, we do not know. He doesn't seem overly thrilled but this is our biggest challenge yet, and although Ruby's help would be appreciated, we are under strict orders to mention our efforts to no one. This could be the making of our family within the Order and we're sure that Ruby will hold no grudge against us or her husband if our actions somehow secure our destinies. This diary will be our unofficial record of our new assignment. R.S.

Pausing, Ebony twiddled her amulet between her thumb and forefinger. So that was the secret project – her parents were working on a weapon! Had they been successful? Fingers crossed, she read on.

Week 5: After several frustrating weeks, at last we have had a breakthrough. Ivy has created a design – based on one of Ruby's past diagrams – that may just work. We have named it the D-STRUCTOR. It's a weapon that runs on regenerative power: to defeat the evil it is designed to fight, its power must be immensely strong and completely pure. Unfortunately, the D-STRUCTOR needs a lot of regenerative power and this kind of power only exists within the Reflectory, which none of us can enter. Despite this setback, Ambrose is pleased; he says he has a plan that will help us get the power that we need. He also promises that special honours will be bestowed upon us if this comes to fruition – but his mood is impatient. Ivy says we need to be careful but, since becoming a mother, she has grown extra cautious. Our baby daughter, Ebony, is restless. Ivy finds it difficult to leave her and concentrate on our work. She is such a beautiful child, and I can only console Ivy by reminding her that when this is all over we'll be able to spend all the time we wish with her. But this is our chance for

true recognition within the Order and we must not
mess it up. A peaceful future depends upon it.

Ebony had to stop. It was the first time she'd ever heard her
parents mention her. Granted, it was only a passing mention
in a diary, but it was clear that they loved her. Certain more
answers were to be found, she continued reading.

Week 11: Ambrose revealed his secret today: he has
somehow concocted a way to tap into the part of
Connie's soul that regenerates and reincarnates.
We are to harness this to create a power source
for our weapon. Despite the unethical nature of
the task, and Ivy's deep misgivings, Connie has
agreed – so what else can we do? Building of a
prototype is underway.

Week 21: The prototype is ready – all we need
now is to test it. Ambrose has captured a Shadow
Walker; even though it feels wrong, it's the
closest we can get to the kind of powerful threat
that might arise and so I must overcome my
misgivings. The initial test is scheduled for four
days' time. Connie is understandably restless, his
mood plummeting, but I can't help feeling excited.

Week 22: Finally, testing day arrived. Ambrose
hooked Connie up to some kind of machine to

draw the necessary power from him and transfer
it to the D-STRUCTOR. The procedure was
clearly painful. At first, Connie tried to bear it
in silence, but after a while, he began to writhe
and scream. Ivy pleaded for Ambrose to stop, but
he was completely unmoved. It took a long time
for enough power to be generated for each attempt
– four in total – and even then the weapon failed
to work as planned: the beam it created was not
strong enough to have the necessary effect. I'll
never forget Connie's cries of agony. Deep down, I
am thankful for the failure.

Ebony paused, taking deep breaths – the thought of her poor
uncle's soul being used to power a weapon made her sick to
her stomach. She recalled the excruciating pain she had felt
when Zach had used what must have been a similar machine
to try to transfer her soul to his mother's body and shuddered.
Desperate to know what happened next, she turned to the
next entry.

Week 24: Ambrose brought us a new power
source today: a special book that was created by
the ancients for the guardian. How he managed
to locate this book, and keep it secret, we do not
know, but by harnessing the power of The Book
of Learning, as it is called, the weapon should be

able to gather sufficient energy stores to discharge with force. We thought that with this new power source he would release Connie, but even with the book, Ambrose insists that Connie's energies will continue to be used, despite my wife's protests. Ambrose grows increasingly irritated by what he calls her 'emotional response' and has warned me to get her under control. His threat feels very real, but Ivy refuses to listen. Her trust in Ambrose is wavering. Connie has grown belligerent and difficult – and a strange dark pattern has appeared on the skin on his arm, which he tries to hide. It seems to writhe and twitch, like my wife's conscience. But if we succeed, there will be untold rewards and all will be forgotten. This is an investment in our family's future. The next testing is scheduled for two weeks' time.

Week 26: Another failure! We only managed to draw a small amount of the regenerative power from the pages of The Book of Learning and, even combined, the book and Connie do not create the energy that is needed for a strong and sustained blast capable of finishing off an enemy. It will only temporarily disable them. It also takes too long to charge: it would be useless against an enemy in an emergency situation. Maybe the book doesn't hold enough power after all. There is much testing still to do.

Week 33: We have managed to shorten the time taken for the D-STRUCTOR to charge but it still takes too long for Ambrose's liking. We have decided to bring the weapon home overnight, along with the blueprints, to see if we can find a way to increase the amount of power the weapon absorbs. That way, we can spend more time with Ebony and continue our work. Hopefully we will solve the power problem soon so that Connie's energy will no longer be needed. He is now weak and prone to violent fits; the mark on his arm has grown so big he can no longer hide it.

Sitting back and rubbing her chin, Ebony took a minute to let the facts sink in. How could her parents have been so gullible and blinded by the promise of power? Hearing a door bang somewhere upstairs, she folded the last few diary entries she hadn't read and slipped them into the waistband of her pyjamas. The others she ripped into pieces in case they were discovered and somehow fell into enemy hands – she didn't want Ambrose to find out that she knew what had happened to her parents, and she couldn't be too careful. She would tell her aunt about her findings once she'd had a chance to read and absorb everything. Sprinkling the pieces onto the glowing embers of the fire, Ebony watched flames spring up around the papers, the corners curling and turning brown. As the flames spread, Ebony felt her hatred for Ambrose grow.

She checked the hallway, then snuck back upstairs, memento mori in hand. Pausing outside her aunt's room, she heard gentle snores and quickly hurried by. But instead of going to her room, she slipped in to see Seamus. Placing the candle on the floor and lowering herself into the visitor's chair, Ebony took hold of his hand. Seamus's chest heaved up and down and the machine beside him emitted a slow beep, the only signs of life. The wires attached to his arms resembled octopus tentacles.

'I wish you'd wake up. Your sister misses you, you know. We all do. We're determined to help you. Don't worry – you have me and Chiyoko on the case now!'

Seeing his eyelids flutter, Ebony held her breath – was he going to wake up again? But it was only a spasm – a natural bodily reaction.

'Oh, what's wrong with you, Seamus? Can't you give me a clue?'

Hearing a creak, Ebony froze; she looked behind her, expecting Aunt Ruby to appear, but it was simply the house groaning, uncoiling from the heat of the day.

Letting go of Seamus's hand, Ebony rubbed at her face. Tiredness crept through her body, making it feel cold and shrivelled. She shuffled her chair as close to the bed as she could and settled the long edge of the bedcovers over her knees, careful not to pull them from Seamus. Holding up the memento mori and angling the photo in the candlelight, she studied the image. Her parents stared back, sallow and worn, as she tried to find something of herself in their faces. When she'd first arrived at Mercury Lane, Aunt Ruby had said her skin was like her mother's but, looking at the image, Ebony couldn't see it. Maybe it was the old-fashioned lighting, but she couldn't make the connection she was looking for. And the only emotion she could muster was disappointment – by refusing to return with Icarus, it felt like they had abandoned her a second time. Could she forgive them? Either way, she had to go to them. They might be the Order's only hope.

Laying the photo on the bed, Ebony took hold of Seamus's hand again. 'You're going to get better, I promise you.'

She hoped with all her heart that she was right, but the words felt fragile, like grains of sand that could be blown away. Leaning against the bed, Ebony placed her head on the covers and draped one arm across Seamus's body. Feeling her eyelids droop, but too worn out to move, she let sleep take her.

Faint sunlight dappled the window. Ebony sat up, stretched and rubbed her eyes. To her surprise, Seamus was sitting on the far edge of his bed, facing away from her.

'Seamus, you're awake! How are you feeling?'

The words tumbled out excitedly but Seamus didn't move or answer. He kept his face averted. The hairs lifted on Ebony's arms. She noticed that the air felt unnaturally cold. Icy cold. Ebony shivered.

'Seamus?'

Slowly, he turned to face her. Ebony held her breath, half-expecting his eyes to be black and empty, but thankfully they were normal. His lips pulled into a smile, but the corner of his eyes didn't wrinkle. His expression didn't look natural. It was like the skin on his face was too tight – but he had, after all, been sick for a while.

'Help me, Ebony,' said Seamus, his voice weak. 'He has me trapped.'

'I don't understand,' she said. 'What do you mean?'

To comfort him, Ebony reached out a hand. As her fingers connected with his cheek, his eyes rolled back and his skin stuck to her fingertips. She gasped and snatched back her hand, but to her horror his skin came with it, stretching and morphing.

Then she realised it wasn't skin but a mask: she recognised the way its left eye and the left side of its mouth sloped to one side. The mask was identical to the one that Seamus had worn to help her against the Deus-Umbra. And it was glued to her fingertips.

Ebony tried pulling and yanking and biting, but nothing would remove it. The mask was stuck fast. A hacking cough made her look up. Seamus was now black-eyed, his skin pallid and his body shivering. The Deus-Umbra had returned. *If only I had* The Book of Learning, thought Ebony. *It might have given me some clues about how to help him.* The demon inside Seamus made his body lurch forward violently, and his mouth twisted in pain.

'No!' cried Ebony. 'Stop it!'

As she yelled, there was a terrible ripping noise as something pushed its way out of the back of Seamus's shoulder. It was black and pointed, like a shark's fin. Was Seamus's skin splitting?

'Leave him alone!'

Despite her show of bravado, Ebony couldn't move; trembling legs froze her to the seat. As the pointed fin grew, getting sharper and longer, it flapped menacingly. Another appeared behind his other shoulder, surrounded by slime and mucus, and Ebony felt the blood drain from her face.

They weren't fins, they were wings.

Big, black, leathery wings belonging to the Deus-Umbra.

Seamus's head shuddered and shook, moving from side to side at incredible speed, his eyes rolling in their sockets. His head turned transparent, the details on his face fading away. Inside the vague outline of his skull, Ebony could see the face of the Deus-Umbra, its fanged jaws and searing eyes, morphing with Seamus's features.

Ebony remained frozen for a moment longer, but then her instincts kicked in. 'No! Leave him alone!' she cried, reaching out with her free hand and grabbing one of Seamus's arms. 'Seamus, if you can hear me, you have to fight it. Don't let it do this to you. *Please.*'

Seamus's body jerked and staggered; she watched as a tremor rumbled through him. Then, suddenly, he lifted his hands and reached behind, grabbing hold of one of the demon's wings. Yanking and tugging, Seamus began to fight back, as if trying to wrench the demon out of his body.

'Put the mask on, Ebony,' he said in a weak voice.

Leaving Seamus and the Deus-Umbra locked in battle, Ebony lifted the mask to her face. As she did, it came away from her fingers, so she slipped it on. Once the mask was in place, a bright light blinded her, making her close her eyes. When she opened them again, she saw dust motes dancing in front of her eyes where coloured lights beamed from the sockets: the mask was projecting an image. Turning to the wall to make the image clear, she saw a ridge of dark rocks, a splash of white shaped like lightning running through them.

The image was rippling. Realising she was under water, Ebony gasped and looked around her. Behind there was a seaweed forest and, in front, a sheer rock face. Looking up, way above, she could see sunlight dappling the water's surface. *What do you want to show me?* thought Ebony.

As though responding to her will, the image began to move upwards, scaling the rock until it levelled into a spiky plateau with towering rocks on either side. Eventually, the plateau dropped away, revealing a much shallower ocean floor, littered with splintered wood and, just beyond, there was a mask, half-submerged in the sandy bottom. *Where is this?* thought Ebony. *There's something about those rocks ... it's linked to my grandpa ...* Drawn to the image, her hand reaching out, Ebony took a step towards it.

Then, hearing a scream from Seamus, Ebony yanked the mask from her face. Looking back, she shuddered, hardly able to believe her eyes. A trickle of blood dripped down the centre of Seamus's forehead. Then there was a terrible tearing sound as a crack appeared near his hairline. The crack grew, travelling down his face as though chasing the drop of blood. The skin on Seamus's face was beginning to split. When the crack reached Seamus's chin, the demon screeched triumphantly. As Seamus cracked in two and the demon turned to face her, Ebony screamed and the world turned black before slipping away.

'Are you OK, Ebony?' Aunt Ruby gave her niece a firm shake.

Ebony woke with a start. The candle had burned out long ago, leaving the room chilly and dark, but morning had arrived, the greyish-green sky signalling a cloudy dawn.

'I heard you screaming. I didn't want to disturb you but you were shuddering and murmuring. You looked terrified.'

Gathering her senses, Ebony leapt to her feet, expecting to see Seamus's body torn to shreds. Instead, he was curled on his side, unharmed, a peaceful expression on his face.

'I couldn't sleep, so I came to talk to Seamus. I must have had a bad dream.' The words felt like a lie – it had seemed so real. Checking around for the photo of her parents, she found it on the bed, where she'd dropped it. Relieved, Ebony tucked it into her pyjamas waistband. 'What time is it?'

'Early. You should go back to bed, get some proper rest.'

Ebony cracked her neck and twisted it from side to side. 'I will.'

But her brain throbbed – what was the dream trying to tell her? *What if I'd kept the mask on – what else would I have seen?* One thing was clear to her: Seamus's condition and the mask were linked.

Aunt Ruby rested a hand on Ebony's shoulder, pulling her from her thoughts. In the half-light they watched Seamus for a moment, his chest rising and falling.

'Do you think he can hear us?' asked Ebony.

'I don't know, but there's nothing to lose by talking to him.'

A small, painful wheeze sounded from Seamus's throat as he sucked in air and the image of the Deus-Umbra ripping his body apart appeared fresh in Ebony's mind again. When he exhaled, his breath returning to normal, Ebony and her aunt relaxed.

'You know this isn't your fault, don't you?' said Aunt Ruby. 'Seamus chose to help you. As for your parents, we will reach them. I'll persuade Icarus – it might just take a little time.'

'What if we don't have time? You saw that Shadow Walker today, assaulting a civilian in broad daylight. It seems as if Ambrose has no regard for the Order's secrecy any more.'

'That may be so, but we may have no choice but to wait.'

'Well, as soon as I bring my parents back, I'm going to make war against Ambrose and Zach. I'll end this once and for all when I kill our enemies.'

'Winning is not about killing, Ebony, it's about staying alive and bringing our enemies to justice.'

Getting to her feet and taking hold of the candle, Ebony looked her aunt in the eye. 'Destroying Zach and Ambrose is my destiny,' she said. 'That's what everything has been leading up to. How else will I achieve Ultimation and get to spend ·eternity with the ones I love?'

'You've got a special connection to the Reflectory, Ebony. A place that doesn't allow death. A place that welcomes regeneration. Think about it – what if you're wrong?'

'I'm not wrong,' said Ebony, turning to leave. 'You'll see.'

Back in her room, Ebony found Chiyoko still sound

asleep, her hair spilling across the pillow. Climbing into bed beside her friend, Ebony waited to make sure her aunt wasn't going to follow and that she hadn't disturbed the sleeping girl. Chiyoko mumbled something and turned over, but didn't wake. Lying still, Ebony waited a moment more, the lack of sleep making her limbs and neck ache. Hearing her aunt go back down to her own room, she pulled out the last few diary entries.

Week 34: Ambrose grows increasingly agitated. Every day he swears us to secrecy, as though afraid of the weapon's detection. When Ivy asked him when we were to present it to the rest of the Order, Ambrose gave her a cold stare and said, 'That's supposing you ever manage to make it work properly.' Ivy has outrageous suspicions I dare not voice. At night, she does not sleep. Sneaking out of bed, she pores over the blueprints. Last night, I heard her sobbing. I peered through the crack in the door and saw her hugging our daughter close, apologising. I understand her feelings, but we're in too deep to stop now.

Week 34 (continued): Things have taken a sinister turn. Someone broke into our lab last night and tried to steal the weapon: the place was destroyed. Thankfully, the weapon was safe with us at home, as were the blueprints. We had no choice but to report it to Ambrose. We expected to be reprimanded, but Ambrose flew into a rage. He said he knew we had betrayed him and he threatened us and Ebony. I managed to talk him round, pretended to understand his concern, but I must find a way for us to remove ourselves from this project. Ambrose's moods are erratic and Connie is increasingly violent – it must be the effect of the machine draining his regenerative power – but there's no way for us to help him. We fear for his life. I don't believe Ambrose intends to tell the Order about the weapon and, if I'm right, then his intentions can only be for ill. We are meeting Connie in secret tonight to make a plan of action.

Week 34 (continued): Connie came to us earlier, shaken. He believes our lives are in imminent danger and begged us to put our plan to disappear into action immediately; he overheard Ambrose making arrangements to remove our child from us. We will take the weapon with us. If we leave it behind, who knows what will happen to Connie? If something bad should happen, we'd never forgive ourselves. We'll hide The Book of Learning in the High Court library and leave instructions to Ruby about its whereabouts. We have no idea if our escape plan will work or if we will survive, so rather than risk our baby daughter's life, she will be left in my father's care. If we are to create a safe future for her, this is our only option. If Ambrose believes we are dead, hopefully he will leave her alone. Regardless, I know my father will protect her to his last breath.

So, her parents hadn't been successful, but they were close enough to feel that the weapon needed protecting. Her aunt knew that her husband's alteration had something to do with Ambrose and the mark on his arm, but she clearly didn't know what had been happening – should Ebony tell her? Or, with Connie long dead, would it just reopen old wounds? The question weighed heavily on her as she tucked the final diary entries into her pillowcase, closed her eyes and tried to relax, but thoughts continued to tumble through her head. Without Connie, would her parents be able to make the weapon work? Her parents' instincts had been right – what they hadn't anticipated was that Ambrose would raise the Deus-Umbra and use its power to help him achieve his plans, which meant he needed a way to control it. And although Ambrose had found another way to control the demon – the magical silver restraint – the weapon was the Order's only hope against its power. It was up to her to get it back.

As fatigue took hold, Ebony snuggled down and tried to let her worries drop away – at least her instruction on how to reach her parents would begin soon. Aunt Ruby would make sure of it. And then she would get the answers she needed.

Later that morning, Ebony woke to the sound of singing in the next room. The light was strong, streaming in through the window, and Chiyoko and Winston were already gone. Dressing quickly, Ebony followed the melody.

As she pushed the door to Seamus's room open, a cloud of sparkling dragonflies, seahorses and butterflies gushed out, fluttering delicately. Ebony watched their glistening wings pass overhead as they floated towards the stairs; halfway down the first flight, they popped, one by one, like bubbles. Inside, Mrs O'Hara was in front of Seamus's bed wearing her mask, her hair coiled on top of her head, secured with a single gold leaf-shaped pin. She had a small screen placed in front of her knees, between her and the bed, and held a single black puppet. It was shaped like a boy with spiked hair – Ebony knew right away it was meant to be Seamus, but she couldn't see the effect it was having, if any, as Uncle Cornelius's bulk obscured her view.

Mrs O'Hara moved the sticks attached to the puppets this way and that, swaying from side to side, while Chiyoko and Uncle Cornelius stood by her and sang, the sparkling creatures springing from their lips. The creatures shimmered and fluttered in circles, reminding Ebony of a bait ball – when gannets, dolphins and seals came together in a feeding frenzy, the fish they hunted gathered in a giant moving ball, trying to confuse their predators. Only instead of in the sea, this writhing ball of creatures was in the air. The more the pair sang, the more creatures appeared, and the bait ball grew, spinning in circles above everyone's heads. Impressed – she had suspected that Chiyoko possessed secret skills, but she hadn't previously seen the evidence – Ebony peered round and saw that both singers had their eyes closed as if in a deep trance. Peeping over Chiyoko's shoulder, Ebony finally saw Seamus.

No longer lying down or attached to wires, he was on his knees, smiling and swaying like the puppet Mrs O'Hara was manipulating. With every twist and turn, Seamus mimicked the move. His face looked rosier than earlier and he moved steadily. He looked like he had fully recovered. Not daring to break the spell, Ebony watched quietly. Speeding up the rhythm, Mrs O'Hara began to sweep her arms wider and wider. Seamus began to giggle, his body responding like a dancer. Moving closer to the screen, Ebony saw that Mrs O'Hara was recording the whole thing; her trance was so deep, she probably wouldn't be able to recall what had happened and needed it for reference. Giving the camera a small, awkward wave, Ebony stepped out of the way.

On the next upwards swoosh of Mrs O'Hara's arm, a ghostly version of herself separated from her body, and stepped to the side. Ebony rubbed her eyes, thinking she was seeing double. But as Mrs O'Hara dropped her hands, the ghostly twin stood right in front of Ebony, nose to nose, the tip cool. Her big eyes stared deep into Ebony's soul. Strangely, Ebony didn't feel scared.

'Are you ready for the battle, guardian?' the phantom asked. 'We're all counting on you.'

Not daring to reply in case it broke the spell, Ebony nodded. The phantom Mrs O'Hara leaned in so their foreheads touched: she felt like chilled porcelain. Smiling, the phantom pulled back, shattering into a thousand pieces. Each piece swirled like dust, then grew into a seahorse, dragonfly or butterfly and joined the whirlwind of creatures that was now spinning furiously. Lifting her arms high, Mrs O'Hara shoved the puppet towards her son, and as she did so, Seamus laughed and lifted onto his feet. At the same time, the whirlwind of creatures spun forward, flapping around Seamus as the voices of Chiyoko and Uncle Cornelius lifted higher and higher. Unable to look away, Ebony watched as the creatures hid Seamus's head, then his shoulders, moving down his body until he was completely covered. Dark shadows shot out in all directions, disintegrating mid-air, reminding Ebony of the souls expelling their bad memories in the Reflectory. Did Mrs O'Hara have a similar power as a Shadow Custodian?

Their voices reaching fever pitch, Uncle Cornelius and Chiyoko began to sway. Lowering the puppet of Seamus, Mrs O'Hara copied their rhythm and, together, they moved in perfect time. Meanwhile, the exploding shadows lessened, eventually stopping, and the creatures began to land on Seamus's bed. As they touched his sheets, they popped, disappearing one by one. Their frenzied spinning slowed as their numbers dwindled. Moments later, every remaining creature popped, the air filling with the tinkling of a thousand crystal bells. The singing stopped and Ebony held her breath as an explosion of glitter shimmied towards the floor, blocking everything from view. When it settled, Seamus lay down and closed his eyes, still smiling. The colour in his cheeks remained, making Ebony's heart skip with joy.

Mrs O'Hara removed her mask, felt his forehead and nodded at Ebony. 'I think it helped.'

Beside the bed, Chiyoko and Uncle Cornelius leaned forward, hands on their knees as they panted as if they had just completed a sprint. Sweat glistened on their foreheads.

'What did you see, Ebony?' asked Chiyoko. 'Did I go into a trance?'

'I've never seen or heard anything like it,' replied Ebony. 'Singing like that, like Uncle Cornelius, I didn't know you could do that. It was magical.'

'When we released the music note from the silver box for the Silent Peregrine, the urge to sing was all-consuming. It was like I would no longer be in control of my own body until I gave it a try. I've been practising, but I have a long way to go – even with a great teacher.'

Looking to the floor, Uncle Cornelius hopped from one foot to the other.

'You looked and sounded like a master to me,' said Ebony. 'We need special skills like yours.' Seeing Chiyoko's face glow, she added, 'Seamus was on his feet, dancing and laughing. I think he's better. Look at the colour in his cheeks!'

Gathering round, Chiyoko and Uncle Cornelius looked decidedly pleased with themselves – only Ebony noticed the crease in Mrs O'Hara's forehead. 'Let's report this to Ruby,' she said. There was a red dent around her face where the mask had been resting. 'She will be happy to hear our progress. Afterwards, I will study the recording to see what I can learn.'

Letting Uncle Cornelius and Chiyoko file out of the room first, Ebony hovered as Mrs O'Hara began packing her puppet equipment away.

'Can I ask you a question?' asked Ebony. 'What happened to Seamus's mask when he fought in Oddley Cove?'

Mrs O'Hara's eyelashes fluttered gently. 'It disappeared.'

'Do you think the disappearance of the mask could be linked to his condition?'

'I know it is,' said Mrs O'Hara. 'I had my husband search the cottage multiple times, but there was no sign of it. Why do you ask?'

'Last night I had a dream, or a vision – I'm not sure which. In it Seamus showed me a scene of a mask stuck in the sea bed. But how could that be? Seamus was in the cottage the whole time we were fighting and Mr O'Hara was there with him – if someone had entered and taken the mask, then surely he would have seen them.'

'As you know, the Shadowlands lie between worlds – and as Shadow Custodians, when Seamus and I wear our masks we occupy yet another space between this world and the Shadowlands. Although Seamus's body was in the cottage, his soul was not. The masks we use have magical properties of their own. Where our soul goes, a part of them goes too, acting as a tether to the soul's body. So if the mask was taken from his soul, then its physical manifestation would disappear too. Whatever he was fighting could have stolen the mask and, travelling through this in-between space, discarded it elsewhere in either world, leaving Seamus trapped in the in-between world, drifting. If we can return the physical mask to his body, then that might recall his soul. As the only enemy we were fighting that was strong enough to do this was the Deus-Umbra, I shall concentrate our search on the sea bed around Oddley Cove – although the shifting tides and sands will make it tricky, I trust your vision. Thank you.'

Mrs O'Hara laid a hand on Ebony's arm, and as she did so, the image of her shifting out of her skin assaulted Ebony's mind. When Mrs O'Hara secured the lid on her storage box and headed towards the door, Ebony blocked her way.

'One more question – how did you split from yourself like that?'

'Split?' asked Mrs O'Hara.

'Yes. You left your body during the trance and a second version of you, a phantom-like version, spoke to me.'

'Are you sure? What did it say?' Her face was solemn.

'I'm positive,' said Ebony. 'It asked me if I was ready for the battle.'

'Then the end draws near. This other self you saw is the part that sees the future. When it splits from me, its visions are more reliable – and Ebony, I sensed the demon near.' Looking at Seamus, she laid the back of her hand against his cheek. 'I fear for my son.'

21

Waiting until Mrs O'Hara, Uncle Cornelius and Aunt Ruby departed to view the shadow-work recording, Ebony collected Winston and her rucksack.

'Come on,' she said to Chiyoko, 'it's time to visit the basement.'

'The basement? Is that thing down there?' asked Chiyoko, looking a little sick.

'Mulligan? Probably,' replied Ebony, 'but we need to know what Winston discovered – he wouldn't bring this to our attention if it wasn't important. And now's the perfect time. Don't worry, we'll take the whistle with us. Mulligan is used to me, but he might be wary of you.'

'A whistle? That's our only protection?'

'Don't worry. It works.'

But Chiyoko's eyes fell on Ebony's bulging sleeve where Winston fidgeted in protest. 'Is there any way I can convince you to look for another way to find out what Winston saw?' asked Chiyoko, her face pale.

'None,' replied Ebony, firmly. 'Let's go.'

Collecting Mulligan's whistle from the kitchen drawer,

Ebony pushed her way under the sink with Chiyoko in tow. The air was damp and a cold draft gusted. Dripping water could be heard somewhere up ahead in the darkness. Moving slowly so Chiyoko could keep up, her rucksack snagging on the low ceiling, Ebony crawled along the cold flagstones to the back and positioned herself on the dumbwaiter, ready to sink to the basement.

'Will this hold our weight?' asked Chiyoko as she found the dangling rope and tugged, helping Ebony lower the dumbwaiter into the basement's depths.

'It's fine, I've used it lots of times. Mulligan uses it and he's heavier than both of us put together.'

Ebony heard Chiyoko's breath quicken as she struggled with the rope – she was much smaller than Ebony and not as strong. But together, they made their way down. When they reached the bottom, the two girls covered their eyes for a moment, squinting while they adjusted to the bright glare of the television screens. Hearing a slight whimper from Chiyoko moments later, Ebony tried to open her eyes but the glare was still too bright. Her other senses heightened, she felt warm, foul-smelling wind on her face.

No, not wind, breath.

The breath of a creature that regularly digested a mountain of raw flesh.

Finally adjusting to the light and opening her eyes, Ebony found herself nose to nose with Mulligan.

'Hello, boy,' she said. 'Go back. We need to pass.'

But Mulligan refused and, peering at Chiyoko, stayed put. Ebony stared into his eyes, her breath ruffling Mulligan's fur.

'Chiyoko's a friend,' said Ebony impatiently. 'Come on, let us pass!'

Scrunching up his nose, Mulligan eyed Chiyoko, bared his teeth and growled. Feeling a wisp of fur brushing the tip of her nose, Ebony reached for the whistle in her pocket. Bringing it to her lips, she paused.

Mulligan's eyes dropped to the whistle. He butted her once against her cheekbone, then backed away, shaking his head and bellowing. Winston trembled, his tail sticking out straight and catching her sleeve. Giving a slow blink, Mulligan bowed his head and turned away, his tail swishing like an angry python as he slunk off down the passageway on the far side of the room.

'Don't worry, he's just being territorial,' said Ebony.

However, just in case, she grabbed the whip that her aunt used to control Mulligan from its hook on the wall. Although Mulligan was her aunt's pet, he was still a wild animal at heart and, therefore, unpredictable. She knew better than to believe that a wild animal could be completely tamed.

Together, the two girls dived for the armchair in the centre of the room. Above their heads, a vast number of cages hung, rusted and empty. A few containing small animals began to swing as their inhabitants came to life, twittering and croaking, but most of Aunt Ruby's animal spies were out on duty. Ebony reached for the TV remote control while

Chiyoko surveyed her surroundings, taking it all in. The screens were muted but several images were showing, each displaying a different communal room in the house, as well as a few scenes from outdoors.

'This place is so cool,' she said.

'The images recorded by the cameras implanted in the animals' eyes are stored for forty-eight hours,' explained Ebony, coiling the whip on her lap.

One of the screen recordings was bobbing up and down into a heap of rubbish. Ebony guessed from the beak that it was herring gull, probably scavenging someone's leftovers from a bin.

'What do we do with Winston? Plug him in?'

Winston squealed and hid behind Ebony, making her choke with laughter. It took a moment for her to control herself, and when she finally stopped laughing, she was so breathless that she could hardly speak.

'The r-recordings are auto-m-matically transmitted and saved.' Changing the screens so that they showed one collective image, like a mosaic, Ebony began clicking through the channels until she found one showing what Winston was looking at now – the screens in front of them – and set it into fast rewind. 'We need to go back to yesterday and … ah yes, here we go.'

Winston puffed out his fur as images from the Botanic Gardens began to show on-screen: giant glossy leaves, glinting panes of glass and large dusty flagstones. The world looked huge through Winston's eyes – expanded and distorted – and everything seemed to move more quickly. Ebony hugged Winston close and began to rewind further. When it was time to check again, she slowed it down so they could watch without feeling dizzy.

'Here, you have a turn,' said Ebony, handing the remote over.

Chiyoko's face brightened and a smile stretched across her face as she mastered the controls right away. On the screen, the image turned dark. All glimpses of headquarters disappeared and Ebony guessed that her friend must have rewound too far.

'Stop!' she cried. 'Go forward a little.'

Chiyoko fumbled with the remote. Forwarding, she kept a close eye. Suddenly, Winston pounced, hitting the pause button to freeze the frame. His quick movement made Chiyoko jump, and the remote flew through the air, spinning like a wheel before landing at Mulligan's feet. Ebony hadn't heard him return. Carefully, whip and whistle in hand, she stood up and edged towards the remote. Mulligan gave it a swipe in her direction, then sniffed around, before heading to the chair. Chiyoko froze, her legs curled under her – if Mulligan attacked, there was no way she would escape.

Ebony held her breath, whistle between her teeth and whip poised, as Mulligan placed his front paws up on the chair cushion. Bringing his face right up to Winston, the wildcat's nose twitched and his jowls filled with saliva as a rumble escaped from his throat. Winston shuddered and shook, but stood his ground; Ebony could see his back legs tensed, ready to leap from harm's way if the wildcat pounced. Instead, Mulligan shoved past and sank his nose deep behind the cushion and tugged. Pulling out an old, stinky bone, covered in fluff and hairs, he dropped back onto the floor, his growl still rumbling like thunder, and padded away into the darkness.

'Th-that was a close one,' said Chiyoko.

'Honestly, we're safe,' replied Ebony.

Returning her attention to the screens, Ebony tried to figure out what she was seeing. The image was too close – a fuzzy mix of grey and greenish tones. Beside her, Chiyoko's brow was furrowed. Soon, the image cleared and the world arced as they watched the recording of Winston's leap onto O'Hara's computer desk.

'That's it! Let's watch from here,' said Ebony.

At first there was nothing exciting to see, only Winston glancing at everyone in the room in turn. The speed with which he turned his head made the girls feel dizzy and Chiyoko had to look away. But Ebony slowed the image and persevered. Soon they were staring at Mr O'Hara's computer monitor: it showed a list of emails, the top one from Ambrose. Its subject line read: **IS ICARUS A TRAITOR?**

The image on screen jiggled and rushed closer – Ebony realised it must have been when Winston was knocked forward. When the image righted, a video was playing, showing Ambrose waiting on an empty canal path, lit by a single orange streetlight. It was dated several weeks earlier.

Chiyoko leaned closer as Winston began to tremble.

When Icarus also appeared on-screen, the basement air seemed to chill.

'This must be when he went to find out the truth from Ambrose,' said Ebony. 'I'm almost afraid to watch.'

Ebony looked at her friend; Chiyoko's face had turned deathly white. Neither of them dared speak as the scene played out.

Icarus looked wary as he approached. Checking behind him every few seconds, his cheekbones and jaw twitched as he marched towards Ambrose.

'Why did he even meet Ambrose?' asked Chiyoko.

'Wouldn't you, if you'd been told you were adopted and you thought Ambrose had some proof? He looks nervous,' replied Ebony.

Her brain thumped as she tried to make sense of what she was seeing. Reaching Ambrose, Icarus watched him carefully, his eyes narrowed. As the two men faced each other, Icarus's mouth began to move, but he remained silent on screen.

'There's no sound!' cried Chiyoko.

'We'll have to watch carefully,' replied Ebony, 'and figure it out the best we can.'

Eyes glued to the screen, Ebony tried to lip-read as Ambrose and Icarus exchanged words, their faces full of hatred. With each sentence, they both looked angrier and angrier. Ambrose pulled a document from his pocket and held it out. As he read it, Icarus's face dropped, his eyes widening. Ambrose laughed, while Icarus's face crumpled and he covered his face with his hands.

'I wonder what they're saying,' said Ebony. 'And I can't read the document either. This is so frustrating – it's not going to help us at all.'

With Icarus distracted, two Shadow Walkers appeared suddenly from the darkness behind him. They grasped an arm each, forcing him to his knees. Despite his struggles, the Shadow Walkers held him tight.

A moment later Zach appeared, wearing a wry grin, and Icarus shook his head sadly, his eyes darting left and right. One of the Shadow Walkers forced his arm out in front of him, palm up, and Ambrose grabbed it. As their hands connected, Icarus tilted his head back, mouth wide open as though roaring. When Ambrose pulled away, Ebony saw that he held a small, sharp spike in his palm. As Icarus jerked his hand up to see what had been done to it, a streak of blood ran down his forearm. The cut was clearly painful: Icarus was shaking and juddering, his teeth clenched and eyes squeezed shut. The Shadow Walkers released him, their job complete.

'What did Ambrose do?' asked Chiyoko.

Beside her, Winston cowered and shook, his teeth bared and tail out straight. Then, he nudged Ebony's hand until she pulled it away. 'I'm trying to watch, Winston.'

But Winston was persistent and nudged her hand again. Realising what he meant, she looked at her palm, where the mark of the Shadow Walkers sat. Ambrose had triggered that mark by creating a trap for her in a door handle where she spiked her hand. It seemed that he had used something similar on Icarus. Sure enough, as Icarus gripped his wrist, she could see the beginnings of the inky black mark on his hand. But it was different to hers. Icarus's mark was a snaking black coil, centimetres long.

When Icarus raised his head to look at Ambrose, instead of his own eyes all they could see were two black pits.

Ebony, Chiyoko and Winston leaned back.

'He's possessed!' cried Chiyoko.

Laughing, Ambrose said something to Zach and then raised his arms slowly. Icarus responded, rising slowly. Once upright he stared at Ambrose, his expression lifeless. Zach stepped forward and waved a hand in front of his father's eyes, a sneer on his lips. Without warning he slapped him across the face, making him sway to one side. The hit looked powerful, but Icarus simply righted himself and stared on, as though completely unaware. Zach lashed out a second time, returning to his original spot when Ambrose shouted a command.

When the shot panned out to a wider angle, Ebony and Chiyoko gasped. The two Shadow Walkers were now dragging a man from the Order into the light, his hands and feet tightly bound, the mark of the Shadow Walkers visible on his forehead. They propped him against the lamp post, wriggling and crying out, but no one took any notice. Icarus was still staring dead ahead and Zach was enjoying the show. Then Ambrose's arm flew out, a finger pointing towards their captive, and Icarus turned. The man's struggle grew more frantic as Icarus crept towards him. His eyes were still as black as tar. Kneeling down, Icarus leaned in towards the man, his hands outstretched, heading for the throat. His body covered the scene, but the captive's legs could be seen kicking wildly.

'He's strangling him,' cried Chiyoko.

'Ambrose is controlling him,' said Ebony, steadying her shaky voice. 'Whatever happens, Icarus is not to blame.'

They watched Icarus jerk suddenly, as if he had just woken from a bad dream. His shoulders slumped, then he dropped the man and stepped back, covering his mouth with his hand. The man choked and spluttered on the ground. Icarus turned away; as he faced the camera, Ebony could see his eyes were back to normal and his lips moved, saying 'sorry' over and over.

'He fought back,' said Ebony. But she fell silent as Zach Stone threw back his head and laughed, clutching his chest. Then he pointed and, as one Shadow Walker restrained Icarus, the other creature moved in, finishing off the Order's man. When it backed away, the man was dead. Chiyoko covered her eyes. Ebony continued watching as, slowly, Zach, Ambrose and the Shadow Walkers walked away, fading into the shadows. At the last second Zach turned and, Ebony thought, looked straight towards whatever was recording the scene and winked – but it happened too fast for her to be sure.

When they disappeared, Icarus looked around in panic, his face ashen. He turned to the dead man at his feet, dropped to the ground and tried to revive him. Realising it was too late, he covered his face and started to sob. His shoulders shook and tears streamed from under his fingers. When the sobbing subsided, Icarus wiped his eyes and crouched next to the body, inspecting the sign of the Shadow Walkers imprinted on the man's forehead. Then he started, as though hearing a noise, and ran off into the darkness.

'No wonder Father wants to arrest Icarus!' cried Chiyoko. 'He's out of control.'

'That's not fair,' replied Ebony. 'This email arrived after your father made his decision. And although Icarus was under Ambrose's control, he fought him off. There's still hope, despite the vision your mother saw.'

'It doesn't excuse the fact that he tried to kill someone.'

But Ebony shook her head. 'Ambrose set this whole thing up. I'm sure Zach winked at the camera before they disappeared – Ambrose knew that if your father saw this he'd take Icarus out of the game. I trust my uncle. Your father is wrong to arrest him. It's exactly what Ambrose wants. It weakens us.'

'Now that my father believes in you as guardian, he's determined to protect you. Can't you see that? You've seen what control Ambrose has – aren't you scared?'

'No more so than before,' answered Ebony. 'But this is proof that we have to act now – we have to find them and stop them. Ambrose's power over Icarus is clearly strong, but there's still time to get to them before they destroy him completely. We have to find a way to convince your father to be more proactive – otherwise we'll be wiped out. Ambrose means business.'

Unable to look in Chiyoko's eyes – afraid that her fear would show – Ebony looked down at her hands. As she did, something caught her eye on the handle of the whip that was sitting in her lap. Ebony held the whip up and took a closer look. Scratched into its handle were the words 'Property of Ebony Smart'. Ebony gasped – it must be a family heirloom that belonged to her! Remembering her past cowboy self, who always carried a whip, she wondered whether this was the same one. Coiling the whip as small as she could, she shoved it into her rucksack, intending to bring it back once she'd done some investigating.

'Why don't we go and check out that Octopus file of my father's – see if it gives us any more info on top of Winston's recording?' suggested Chiyoko.

'You're not worried that the pirate ship might come back?'

'I'm willing to take the risk – somewhere away from the mirror.'

Smiling, Ebony led the way to the dumbwaiter and together they hauled themselves up. As they crawled out of the swing door under the sink, Ebony bumped her head against Uncle Cornelius's leg. He yowled and jumped out of the way.

'Good timing,' said Aunt Ruby, loading a mini helicopter with raw sausages. 'I was about to cook lunch.' Noticing

Ebony looked a bit peaky, she added, 'What were you up to down there?'

'I wanted to show Chiyoko our surveillance so she knew Seamus would be safe. Chiyoko wants to see the Hideout but the park will be full.' As her stomach grumbled loudly, she realised she'd skipped breakfast. 'Can we have lunch to go? And can you send a swarm of bees?'

'Bees?' asked Chiyoko.

Aunt Ruby surveyed her niece for a minute. Ebony tried not to squirm under her aunt's piercing gaze.

'I was telling her how you put cameras in the bugs and animals and made them smart.'

'Cameras, yes. I didn't make them smart, though – I'm not a magician!'

'But Winston's practically a genius,' said Ebony.

'Winston – he has abilities of his own,' said Aunt Ruby hesitantly. Before Ebony could ask anything else, she continued, 'I'll send the bees. So long as you stay together and one of the surveillance teams goes with you. I'll have everything ready in a jiffy.'

Ebony and Chiyoko hurried to the Hideout, two security men close behind and the swarm of bees buzzing violently up ahead. Winston was secured in Ebony's trouser pocket and in her rucksack she had some sausage sandwiches wrapped in tinfoil; although, after what they had witnessed in the basement, she had little appetite. They soon lost sight of the swarm, but reaching the gates at the nearest entrance, they met crowds of people running as though their lives depended on it. Stray bees darted this way and that, and Ebony could see the swarm had separated into three to chase the stragglers. Checking around to make sure no one was watching, Ebony grabbed Chiyoko's hand and pulled her into the park before the warden could appear and lock the gates.

They sped across the grass. At the marble seat, Ebony quickly positioned her eye over the security system. There was a click as it registered her iris, and the doorway began to open. Lights on either side of the steps leading down underneath the pond flickered on. After convincing the security men to wait outside, hidden out of view but where they could clearly see the Hideout entrance, Ebony and Chiyoko raced to the bottom and sealed up the entrance. Turning her computer on, Ebony entered her password – GPA_TOB1A5 – and let Chiyoko take the chair. Winston positioned himself next to the keyboard, his eyes glued to the screen. Chiyoko was instantly engrossed. Her jaw tensed as she tried to break the security code her father had put in place. Feeling helpless, Ebony paced the room, trying to think of some way to help. She marched up and down in time to Chiyoko's rhythmic tapping on the keys.

'Are you hungry?' asked Ebony, but there was no reply.

Chiyoko was busy concentrating on the task in hand. 'I'm in!' she cried after a while, breaking the silence and making

Winston leap an inch off the desk. But then she made a strange harrumphing noise. 'There's only one file. All that effort to get to one file? This had better be good!'

'It must be important,' said Ebony. 'Open it!'

As Chiyoko clicked on the icon, the two girls expected Ambrose and Zach to fill the screen. Instead, there was a giant shark. Ebony thumped the desk with excitement.

'I'd know that creature anywhere,' she said. 'That's Cedric, the Order's shark submarine!'

As they clicked Play, the scene before them changed: the recording was from inside the shark's body, looking out through his eyes. Chiyoko's face crumpled in concentration. 'What's so special about Cedric that father has to keep him hidden?'

'Be quiet and watch,' said Ebony.

'It's only three minutes long,' said Chiyoko, pointing to the timer in the corner. 'It shouldn't take us long to find out!'

Everyone leaned in, including Winston, as Cedric wiggled his way through the water. The sea was blue and clear, islands of green-brown seaweed floating past, schools of darting sprats and mackerel in hot pursuit, their down-turned mouths looking grumpy as they sped after their prey. In some parts, the water turned milky, where crowds of tiny shrimp propelled their legs through the water. Before they knew it, the video had finished.

'Let's try it again,' said Ebony, her breath quickening. 'We must have missed something.'

Chiyoko set the recording in motion again, but no matter how much they stared, there was nothing obvious that could make the recording worth hiding behind such strong security protocols.

'I must admit, this is pretty cool!' said Chiyoko. 'But if it's a submarine, who's controlling it?'

'When I was inside, Uncle Cornelius was piloting it.'

'Two of you were in there – it's that big?'

'It could hold four people easily,' replied Ebony. 'And that's just in its belly. I didn't get to see much else.'

Thinking back to the fishing boat disaster that had brought her to Cedric, the sound of her grandpa's beloved vessel – the boat she had spent most of her youth on – being ripped to shreds by rocks and tide, Ebony fell quiet. It was a memory she didn't want to share; not all problems shared were problems halved. Some nights, Ebony would dream of loading the deck with pots and lines, waking suddenly, expecting her grandpa and the boat to be right there. The sadness that flooded her heart when she remembered the truth was too much to bear.

As the recording finished, Chiyoko murmured, 'Let me just try something …'

Ebony watched as she opened the recording using a different programme and altered the settings, her fingers moving quickly and her eyes fixed on the screen.

'Here goes,' said Chiyoko as the recording played once more.

'Wait!' said Ebony, as an embedded anchor appeared on

the screen. 'That's not the same recording. We didn't see that before.'

'That's impossible,' said Chiyoko, moving closer to the screen.

Without warning, Winston had a fit of excitement and began twirling in circles. When he had both girls' attention, he headed for the screen and pointed at the bottom corner.

'Look!' said Chiyoko. 'The timer has gone.'

Noticing a spot of dirt on the screen, Chiyoko brushed it away with her finger. As she did, the words Autopilot in green and Manual in red showed up at the bottom of the screen. Touching her finger to Manual, making it turn green, she then swiped the screen to the right. Cedric juddered and changed direction slightly. Chiyoko tried again, this time rubbing her finger the other way, and Cedric followed her.

'Hey! I didn't realise this was a touch screen – I think we can control the shark. Look!'

Ebony and Winston watched as Chiyoko moved her finger on the screen, guiding the shark left and right, up and down, as he powered through the water.

'Are you serious?' asked Ebony.

'Haven't you noticed that the video isn't running out?' said Chiyoko. 'There's no timer any more. The video is live.'

'Live? Right now?' Ebony turned back to the screen. 'Great! Then let's see where we can go. Can you make the shark breach? I want to see where we are.'

'I can try.'

Chiyoko tried swiping up, then tapping on the screen, but nothing worked. She then tried the mouse and, after clicking a few times, the trio leaned back from the screen as Cedric suddenly shot upwards, the waterline rushing towards them at dizzying speed as he headed for the surface. Seconds later, he was on the surface, the sky blue and cloud-filled. Chiyoko steered him in a circle so they could get a look at the surroundings, before plunging him back down into the depths. As Ebony squealed, bubbles filled the screen and, when they cleared, Cedric was back in the ocean.

'We're near Oddley Cove,' said Ebony. 'I recognised the land in the distance. That was Roaring Water Bay.' Thinking of her earlier vision and conversation with Mrs O'Hara, she added, 'Watch out for Seamus's mask.'

Confused, Chiyoko frowned. 'My brother's mask?'

'Your mum told me about Seamus's mask getting lost during the battle and I had a vision of it lying on the ocean bed. I think that's what's wrong with Seamus. By losing his mask part of him has somehow become trapped in the shadows.'

'Trapped how? He's at your house!'

'Your mum told me that when a Shadow Custodian is working they somehow split and their soul enters an in-between world somewhere between our world and the Shadowlands. The mask is their link back to reality. We think the Deus-Umbra took Seamus's mask from him in the in-between world and now that part of him is trapped there, unable to get back to his body. The vision I had suggests that, after it took the mask, the demon threw it into the sea. I'm not sure how it works, but if we can find the mask we might be able to get him back.'

'I didn't know that.' Returning her attention to controlling Cedric, Chiyoko's frown deepened. 'OK. Let's keep our eyes peeled. I saw a rock sticking out of the sea and seeing as I'm not quite confident in piloting this thing yet, we'd better avoid that.'

'No, head for it!' said Ebony, a memory triggering. 'In my vision, Seamus's mask was near an underwater rock face. It's a long shot but it's worth a try.'

Ebony and Winston watched as Chiyoko guided Cedric forward.

Winston moved closer, whiskers twitching, as Chiyoko guided the shark right, towards a dark area of water that turned out to be a forest of kelp and seaweed. The display was spectacular: some of it was blistered, some was oily and flat with frilled edges and some was long and wispy like spaghetti. Around the fronds climbed crabs of all shapes and sizes, sea spiders and small, fast-moving creatures that resembled woodlice.

Chiyoko shuddered. 'I prefer the cicadas back in Japan.'

'Careful, it looks like we're going to lose visibility,' said Ebony as Cedric pushed his way into the kelp, but a moment later, the underwater forest parted revealing a wall of jagged granite rock up ahead, several metres wide. There was a shock of glistening white quartz running through it, shaped like a lightning bolt.

'This is the place!' cried Ebony. 'You need to go up.'

Concentrating hard, Chiyoko made the shark circle in the water. Unable to move forward because of the wall of rock, she used each circle to spiral higher. Eventually, the rock levelled into a plateau of dangerous spikes. At this level, above the main ridge, pollack and conners swam, their muscular bodies flicking their tails from side to side, creating rainbow colours with every twitch and twist. But as Chiyoko tried to turn Cedric, she suddenly had to swerve. To the right, a tower of granite soared upwards towards the surface like a mountain peak. As Chiyoko guided the shark in a circle in an attempt to double back, she had to swerve again as another towering rock filled the screen.

'I know those rocks!' cried Ebony. She could almost smell the tang of salt lifting from the screen. 'Those two peaks are the Razor Rocks. They're in Man O'War sound, not far from Gun Point. When the tide is out, you can see them poking out of the sea. At high tide a punt can easily pass through the crevice – a small fishing boat even – but there are lots of jagged rocks below. The seabed falls away very quickly; one side is deep water, while the other is much shallower. It's really dangerous unless you know the area well and even then it's risky to get too close. There are cross currents and a strong draw so boats risk getting dashed on the rocks or having their keels ripped off. Grandpa used to steer clear of that area. He said that it had a mind of its own and any vessel stupid enough to get too close would be sucked in and lost forever.'

'Like the Bermuda Triangle?' laughed Chiyoko, shaking her head.

'I trust my grandpa's judgement. There are tales of lost fishermen's souls rising out of those waters at night.' She waited until Chiyoko stopped shuddering before continuing. 'I only ever saw the rocks up close once, but I'll never forget them. We were fishing for pollack. My grandpa had thrown his net out the day before and we were returning to haul it in. The wind was gentle and the weather fine so we were expecting a good catch. But as we hauled in the last buoy, the weather turned and our engine cut out. The waves were growing and the pull was strong – we drifted pretty fast.'

'Were you frightened?'

'Not really – not with Grandpa. At least, not until we drifted into Man O'War sound. At first, I could only see the breakers over the Razor Rocks, but they were huge so I knew there was something dangerous underneath. The tide turned and soon the rocks emerged. Two great big spikes of granite, covered in jagged points and sharp edges – and we only saw the tips. When Grandpa spotted them, he panicked; it's the only time I saw him lose his cool. And I knew right away why: those sharp points would destroy the boat in no time.'

'What did you do?' asked Chiyoko, eyes wide.

'Grandpa guessed that we had some dirty diesel and when he checked inside the diesel barrel we'd used, he found clumps of rust. So he disconnected the fuel pipe and bled the engine to get rid of the dirt.' Ebony took a breath, picturing the scene in her mind. 'I kept watch because we were drifting really fast. Thankfully, Grandpa was quick. Some rust came out and he got everything connected again as fast as he could. After a few splutters, the engine kicked into action and we were out of there.'

'How close did you get to the rocks?'

'Close enough to get a good view of the razor-sharp edges that give them their name. Close enough to have them imprinted on my mind. I've never forgotten that moment … But right now, we need to keep our eyes peeled. Go through the rocks to the shallow side.'

Chiyoko did as requested. Although the water was still deep, it was brighter and visibility improved.

'Wait! What's that?' said Ebony, pointing at the screen as Cedric dived.

Something lay up ahead in a tangle of kelp. It looked like a rabble of giant bones. Cedric pushed through, with Chiyoko steering, eventually reaching their goal. The bones turned out to be planks of wood in a crumpled heap, thick and rotting; they looked old but not ancient.

'It's a boat,' said Ebony. 'There's not much left, but look: there's the rudder and a name written on one of the planks. Can you get closer?'

After fiddling with the screen and then pressing a number of buttons on the keyboard, Chiyoko managed to zoom in. Ebony twisted her head to one side to read the letters. They were chunky and decorative, the same style as the lettering many boats used in the Oddley Cove area: **P-H-I-R-E**

Next to the letters was an anchor, with a feather behind it.

'Some letters are missing,' said Ebony. 'But that anchor symbol shows where it's from. Every boat has one if it's built within twenty-five miles of Oddley Cove. It was an old tradition among the sailors so they could recognise people from home when they passed on the sea.'

Cedric swam over the wreckage too quickly to see much else, so Chiyoko turned the shark around. Seconds later, he was cruising back towards the debris. This time they stumbled upon a rusted engine and they could make out the outline of the name, Yamaha 15, on the side. And nearby were an anchor and a lobster pot like those Ebony's grandpa would have used.

'The boat can't be that old,' said Ebony. 'It must have gone down within the last twenty years. Old Joe or one of his friends must know about it. See if you can make Cedric shift some of that sand so we can get the full name.'

After a few attempts, Chiyoko managed to position Cedric near the plank with the name on it and then, moving her finger back and forth quickly, she made the shark's head flail about enough to disturb the sediment on the bottom. The water turned murky and milky as mounds of sand grains shifted. Eventually, the grains scattered and settled, leaving the name visible. It read: **S-A-M-P-H-I-R-E**.

'*Samphire*? I've never heard that boat mentioned back home,' said Ebony. 'But at least we have the start of something interesting.' A glint on the newly settled seabed caught her eye and Ebony pointed at it. 'Let's go check that out.'

As Cedric neared, Ebony's stomach flipped. Something white and curved was half-buried in the sand – with holes for eyes and a crooked mouth clearly visible.

'Seamus's mask! It must have been buried among the wreckage,' said Chiyoko. 'I disturbed it when I made Cedric flip about.'

'We found it!' said Ebony, hardly believing her eyes. 'Now we know where it is, it's just a case of retrieving it.'

'And what's that?' asked Chiyoko, steering Cedric towards her find.

Sticking up out of the ocean floor was a copper photo frame, now covered in a lime-green patina, decorated with frilled roses – blooms that Ebony knew only too well: the *Ebonius Tobinius* rose. Holding her breath, Ebony barely dared to look, but she had to see whether the boat was linked in any way to her parents.

Chiyoko made Cedric dislodge some more of the sand. As soon as the photo came into view, Ebony could see that most of it had eroded away. But a tiny piece remained intact and she recognised the face staring back immediately.

'That's a picture of me as a baby. The *Samphire* must have been my parents' boat,' said Ebony in a quiet voice. 'No wonder no one ever found it: it's a wreck – look at it. How did they survive? And as for the mask – how did it get there?'

'Are you sure that's you?'

'Yes,' said Ebony. 'My grandpa had a copy of the same photo. But what's it doing there?'

'My guess is they were taking it with them to remember you by,' said Chiyoko. 'They must have lost it in the wreckage.'

Pulling the Victorian photo out of her rucksack, she handed it to Chiyoko. 'I can't believe they had a photo of me! This is the only photo I've ever had of them. Grandpa didn't like sentimental reminders of those he'd lost.'

'That's the one my dad had. Where did you get it?'

'My aunt gave it to me last night – I think she stole it. I was going to tell you, but I forgot all about it.'

'Forgot all about it?' said Chiyoko. 'I'd have thought you'd have been too worried to do that.'

'Worried – why?'

'Look. The rest of the photograph is fine but your mother – her image is fading.'

Snatching the photo back, Ebony examined it. Chiyoko was right. The image had looked slightly shaky before, but she had thought that was because of the long exposure needed for old photographs. However, now her mother was almost transparent, while the surroundings and everyone else – her past self and her father – were unchanged. The two girls stared at the photo for a minute, their brains in overdrive.

Chiyoko was the first to break the silence. 'Maybe it's the old-fashioned printing methods?'

'I've seen Victorian photos in antique shops – they were designed to last. This is nothing to do with technique. The photo was perfectly fine last night – and why would it be just my mother fading?'

'What does it mean?'

'I don't know, but something must be wrong. And there's only one way to find out.' Winston hid behind Ebony's rucksack, his quivering tail sticking out. 'Things are moving too slowly. I'm going to sneak into the Shadowlands to see if I can reach them. When I get back, we'll figure out a way to get Seamus's mask.'

'No,' cried Chiyoko, 'it's too dangerous! You don't even know how to travel in time.'

'Waiting is more dangerous. It's been a while, but I've travelled from one spot to another. I'll apply the same techniques and try transporting myself back to 1871. How difficult can it be?'

'Without Icarus's help, it's suicide!'

'It has to be done.' Ebony took a deep breath. 'Look, I haven't had a chance to tell anyone yet, but I found out about the project my parents were working on – it was a gun. A gun that might be powerful enough to defeat a demon.'

'You think it might be able to kill the Deus-Umbra?'

'That's what I'm hoping. So I need to find my parents – even if it means risking my life.'

Striding to the middle of the room and positioning herself under the glass roof, where the rippling pond cast waves of shadow on the floor around her, Ebony took a deep breath. Her rucksack was firmly in place but Winston was on the ground, glaring at her.

'You stay with Chiyoko, Winston. I don't know what the effects are on rats and I don't want to hurt you.'

Winston shook his head and tried to scurry up Ebony's leg. She gently prised his claws off her trousers one by one, then handed him to Chiyoko.

'Wait here together. It might seem like I've been gone for seconds – or it might seem like hours. Time works differently in the Shadowlands but, trust me, I'll be back.'

Squirming to break free from Chiyoko's grasp, Winston gave a series of angry squeaks. Putting her lips to his ear, Chiyoko whispered, 'Don't worry, little friend. Looking out for you will only distract her and what she's doing is dangerous enough already.'

As Winston's body relaxed, Chiyoko loosened her hold and placed him on her shoulder. Winston gripped on with all four paws and continued squeaking, his eyes locked on Ebony as she fixed her stare on the shadow of the computer and desk, breathing slowly and deeply. Taking hold of the amulet around her neck, she concentrated until the shadow blurred and moved.

'Please be careful, Ebony,' said Chiyoko, 'and come back in one piece!'

Sweat beaded on Ebony's upper lip as she fought to clear her brain of worries. A weird mix of fear and excitement rippled through her, but she stayed focused, her gaze on the shadow until it blurred and shimmered. Claustrophobia crept over her, begging her to break concentration, but Ebony was determined. When the shadow began to wrap itself around her, she knew she was nearly there. Her head turned light and dizzy.

Soon the world around her seemed to drop away. Ebony could hear Chiyoko's voice gently soothing Winston, but she could no longer see her. Everything turned fuzzy, made up of faint lines and grey smudges, like a charcoal drawing that had been brought to life. Chiyoko's voice turned slurred and distant so Ebony could no longer make out her words.

When Chiyoko's voice dropped away completely, Ebony knew she had passed through to the Shadowlands. In the distance there was a rumble of heavy footsteps marching in time. She knew the sound: an army of Shadow Walkers on the move. As the drumming feet grew louder, Ebony spotted a far-off line of marching Shadow Walkers, their red eyes gleaming like laser beams. Lightning crackled and Ebony's eyes followed the sound, coming to rest on a whip that fizzed and sparked. It belonged to Zachariah Stone.

Zach was marching alongside the Shadow Walkers, huge electric whip in hand, his face contorted with hatred. In the Shadowlands, with its grey tones and smudges, his face looked completely transformed, almost skeletal, with deep sunken eyes. He looked more like a Shadow Walker each time she saw him. Automatically taking a step back from view, Ebony tried to merge with the darkest shadows so she couldn't be seen, in case they marched by.

I need to get out of here, and quick! she thought, trying to picture her destination. The Shadow Walkers were still reasonably far away, so she had a little time. Without a second to lose, Ebony set to work. Bending down, she scored a line wider than her into the ground with her pocket knife. Then at either end she added arrows pointing from the Hideout in the direction of 23 Mercury Lane, as that was where her parents had taken the photograph. She knew this would take her to the right place. But what about the right time? She thought about it for a moment – if an arrow would take her to a certain destination, maybe to get to another time she needed to score the year into the ground?

It was the only thing she could think of, and Zach and his Shadow Walkers were getting closer, so she wrote 1871 under each of the arrows pointing to Mercury Lane. Even if it didn't work, it would take her safely back to Mercury

Lane and out of Zach's reach. Finally, she reached down and worked her hands under the edges of the scored earth until she had a firm enough grip that she could pull up part of the ground, like lifting the edge of a rolled-up carpet. She counted to three and yanked as hard as she could. As before, the ground began to move. Watching the spreading ripples carefully, Ebony waited until she saw the third one form and then leapt on. Landing on her belly, she skidded and slid, twisting her body so that she didn't fall off the edge. She had no idea what would happen if she fell off and she didn't want to find out!

Racing along at top speed, Ebony steadied herself and pushed up into a seated position. It was like riding a toboggan. It was more difficult than she remembered, but seeing the ripples stretching out in front of her, Ebony focused her mind on the photograph her parents had sent. Their faces, the shutters, the mirror, everything except her own dead face. Her head throbbed with the effort, but if she was to succeed, she had to concentrate.

The ride was bumpy and much longer than when she had ridden the shadows with Icarus by her side. Back then, it had seemed to be over in moments. Ebony knew that time in the Shadowlands worked very differently to time in the outside world – was the delay because she'd succeeded? Was she travelling back in time? Heartened by the idea, Ebony hurtled along, hands on knees and her eyes fixed on the horizon. Seeing the end of the ribbon of earth up ahead –

a sign that her journey was coming to an end – she took a deep breath and tried to focus as hard as she could on the memento mori, her parents' faces and the room reflected in the mirror. *They will be so proud of me!* she thought.

But as she relaxed her brain for an instant, an image of Seamus's mask lying at the bottom of the sea beside the Razor Rocks took over her mind. She tried to shake it away, but the rushing waves, the threatening rocks, the image of the rusted engine and anchor symbol were too vivid for her to ignore. The end of the ribbon of earth drew closer and Ebony felt her heart rate rise with panic, her thoughts turning fuzzy.

'Think of Victorian times, think of Victorian times,' she chanted, but her brain wouldn't listen.

As she reached the end of the line and was flung up into the air, Ebony crossed her fingers, but the image of the mask at the bottom of the ocean returned to her thoughts. In the next instant her mouth was filled with salt water and she was choking.

Ebony kicked and fought to reach the surface, her brain trying to comprehend what was happening. A school of sprats flashed by, like a murmuration of underwater starlings. She surfaced momentarily, enough to gulp in a mouthful of air, before being sucked down by the cross currents. Around her, the sea curled and raged like an underwater twister, pulling her down and spinning her around until she could hardly tell which way was up. She had to locate the sun to find her way to the surface! Searching out the brightest shade of blue, Ebony tried swimming towards it, against the pulling tides.

As her surroundings twinkled and glistened, the water shoving her this way and that, Ebony's brain kicked into gear. She realised she was where she'd been thinking of, back in Oddley Cove, where the baby photograph and Seamus's mask lay on the seabed. Spotting a wall of granite below her, and a towering slab to either side, a shock of glistening white running through, Ebony realised she had landed in the crevice between the Razor Rocks in Man O'War Sound. She would have to be careful: if she bashed against them, she could be killed.

As panic set in, Ebony kicked with all her might and managed to propel her body upwards. Breaking the surface, she searched around her for something to grab onto, but the sea pulled her down again. Ready for it this time, Ebony took a gulp of air, letting only tiny bubbles of breath out as she sank down and down, trying to figure out her position. Was there a way she could swim free of the currents? It was difficult to tell in the swell and swirl of sea, and travelling in the Shadowlands had sapped her of most of her energy.

Deciding that going with, rather than against, the current was her best bet, Ebony let her body relax and be carried, keeping her eyes peeled for Seamus's mask. As she began to understand the water's rhythm, she figured out how to move with it to conserve energy. Kicking her way up and surfacing for breath, Ebony spied an area up ahead that seemed calmer. As she was dragged back down, she aimed herself straight for the calm spot. Every few seconds, in time with the sea, she pushed forward.

Just as she felt the current drop away and she was about to propel herself to the surface, Ebony caught a glimpse of what looked like a large, white scallop shell, stuck in the sand. It was Seamus's mask, she was sure of it – the scene looked exactly like the one they had seen through Cedric's eyes. But the mask was too far down for her to reach. She knew there was no way she had enough strength left to dive for the mask and make it back to the surface safely. Her lungs were already screaming and her limbs aching, and Ebony knew she needed to conserve what little energy she had left to survive. Heading for the surface again, she tried to make each stroke count. Her head pulsating with the pressure of holding her breath for so long, she pushed and kicked her way up to where sunshine dappled the water. Moments later, she broke the surface and this time, although gasping for air, she wasn't dragged back down – she'd escaped the cross currents.

Treading water, Ebony looked around, planning her next move. As she spun in a slow circle, the biggest Razor Rock loomed up in front of her. Rising out of the water about three feet high and several feet wide, it obscured part of her view out to deeper waters. As she continued to turn she realised that the land in the distance was too far away for her to swim to and, with no boats visible, she was on her own. The cold was already making her toes and fingers numb. Soon, she would lose all feeling in her extremities. Despite its jagged edges, she decided to cling to the closest of the Razor Rocks to conserve her energy. Treading water would keep her blood circulating and her limbs from seizing up, and maybe there was something on the other side that could help her – some stray driftwood she could use as a float to help her get to shore? The dangerous rock was her only chance.

Hoping the tide was on its way out – an incoming tide would begin to cover the rocks and she'd have no way to hold on – Ebony tried to swim towards the jagged granite. But even with her arms whirling, she progressed very little, despite her life depending on it. Waves and sea debris smashed into her face – thick, slippery seaweed, a floating plastic bottle and some stray nylon fishing net. Switching to breaststroke, thinking it might require less energy, Ebony found that she moved even less. Despite her best efforts, she was staying in practically the same spot. Feeling numbness beginning to climb up her legs, panic set in, giving her a surge of adrenaline. Ebony kicked with all her might and finally inched her way to the rock.

Reaching out, her body freezing despite the exertion, Ebony found it difficult to get a grip. The rock was cold and wet, but also painfully sharp, and the in-between bits were slippery where seaweed had left its oily residue. Trying not to lose hope, she finally managed to grab hold, slicing the skin on her fingers as she did so. Grappling her way round the rock, she pulled herself along, traces of blood colouring the water. Her lungs screamed with cold.

Don't give up, she told herself. *Don't give up*. But the thought was easier than the action. If she gave up and sank to the sea's depths, she could forget all about everyone and everything for once. Let the others deal with Zach and Ambrose …

The thought of her enemies spurred her on; she knew she still had to fulfil her destiny and she couldn't let herself, her family or the Order down. Looking back to where the sea was boiling and bubbling, she realised how far she had come already. *I can do this*, she willed. Finding a grip on a less jagged part of the rock, Ebony pulled herself close and clung on. Taking a few moments to breathe deeply and regain her composure, as well as a little energy, she pulled herself around.

Her nails digging into the rock for leverage, Ebony moved, inch by inch, until finally she could see beyond it. There, lifting and lilting with the waves, was a green and red fishing boat. Ebony lost her grip and nearly slipped under the water. She was lucky the boat was there, but how would she attract the occupant's attention?

A short and stocky old man appeared on deck. He wore a navy captain's cap with a gold crest on the front and a thick black polo neck underneath bright yellow waterproofs. Ebony gripped on as best she could with one hand and waved with the other, yelling, 'Over here!' But her grip was not strong enough and she fell back into the sea. Gulping down sea water, Ebony spluttered and choked, trying to keep her head above water. Kicking her legs, she realised she could no longer feel her calves; her lungs hurt and her mind felt hazy. Controlling her limbs was becoming increasingly difficult; she was losing coordination. Having lived by the sea most of her life, she knew what was happening. It wouldn't be long until hypothermia kicked in. The water was too cold – she had to get the fisherman's attention, and quick!

Oblivious, the fisherman began hauling in a string of lobster pots. It reminded Ebony of her grandpa and she gave one last push. The tide would take her towards the boat but the clanking pots would drown out her cries. She would have to swim for it. If she didn't, the cold would get her and she would drown.

With very little energy left in her freezing limbs, Ebony pushed herself away from the rock. The swells in the water crashed and broke against her. Swimming was difficult, but she fought to stay afloat, inching towards the boat. Desperate now, Ebony cried out and waved her arms once more, then spluttered and choked as she sank under the surface.

As Ebony resurfaced, the fisherman finally spotted her struggling in the water. He cursed and dropped his pots, then quickly turned the boat towards her and powered his vessel through the water. He pulled up as close as he could get without risking his boat.

'Catch!' he yelled, as she broke the surface once more.

She watched as he grabbed a lifebuoy and threw it with perfect precision over the side so that it landed a few metres from her reach. Using her last bit of energy, she swam towards it, caught hold and clung on for dear life. The fisherman pulled her in. Seconds seemed like hours before she was hauled up over the side and into the boat. Ebony felt warm tears sliding down her frozen cheeks as the fisherman wrapped a thick, scratchy woollen blanket around her shoulders. After almost drowning, it felt like silk to Ebony. She hugged the blanket tightly, taking deep breaths as she considered how lucky she was, how silly she'd been – and how much trouble she was going to be in.

'Aren't you Tobias's granddaughter?' asked the fisherman, looking around him. He had a thick black beard and silver-grey hair, both long and shaggy. Ebony nodded, recognising him as one of her grandpa's old friends. She had seen them together a few times. 'How did you end up out here? Are there others? Do I need to raise the alarm?'

Ebony shook her head, too exhausted and shaken to speak.

'You were alone? Out here?'

Nodding, more tears streamed down her face. Seamus's mask had been so close.

'I'll throw back these pots – they can wait another day – and then I'd better get you home.'

His eyes were warm and kindly, concern seeping out of every crevice on his weatherworn face.

Feeling more hot tears streaking her cheeks – how she wished Oddley Cove was still home, that her grandpa hadn't died and none of this had happened – Ebony covered her face with her hands and sobbed. As the fisherman tucked the blanket more tightly around her, she looked up through tear-stained eyes and thanked him. Her hands shook as she accepted a tin mug of lukewarm tea. Having done all he could, the fisherman set to work, turning the nose of the boat back on course and throwing the pots over the side at calculated intervals.

Listening to the heave and splash of the pots, Ebony realised that she was far too exhausted to travel back to the Hideout through the Shadowlands. The initial journey and the struggle in the sea had sapped all her energy. She could stay with Old Joe – it would delay the grilling from Aunt Ruby – but she had to let her aunt know her whereabouts. Especially since Chiyoko and Winston would be at the Hideout worried sick. Chiyoko wouldn't be able to trigger the Hideout's security: it used iris recognition and she wasn't in the system. The surveillance team that had followed wouldn't be able to help either; Aunt Ruby would have to fetch Chiyoko and secure the place.

But at least she was alive.

'Thanks for saving my life,' said Ebony through chattering teeth before slurping a mouthful of tea. 'I'm so lucky you were here.'

'You're lucky all right. This is my fishing ground so I'd have strayed across you at some point – but I've found bodies around here before and it's not pretty.'

Despite her elation at being rescued, Ebony felt a sinking feeling in her stomach. 'I thought no one fished here – it's such a dangerous spot.'

'Don't worry, we're safe. The sea's dangerous, all right, but this spot's no more worrisome than anywhere else round here. I've been fishing here for over forty years.'

He laughed a deep, hearty chuckle that reminded her of Old Joe. Huddling into the blanket to get warm, Ebony tried to accept his words and to not feel afraid. As the boat chugged towards shore and her teeth chattered, she used the little energy she had left to plot ways of finding Ambrose and Zach and getting rid of them once and for all. They had to be in the city, but where?

In the corner of Old Joe's kitchen, Ebony sat on a tattered armchair with Mitzi – the one-eyed Shih Tzu that Grandpa Tobias had rescued and Joe had acquired after Ebony moved to Dublin – on her knee. She was wrapped in a dressing-gown and surrounded by cushions, a mug of hot chocolate in her hand and a hot-water bottle tucked under the several layers of blankets. The stove in the living room was lit and the oven was on high, potatoes roasting inside. The thought of their crunchy skins made Ebony's mouth water.

Although Ebony had warmed up, the shivers still attacked now and again, making her teeth chatter. For an instant out there she had almost lost her nerve and it played on her mind. As did the mask – Old Joe admitted he wasn't skilled enough to pilot Cedric to that spot, so she still had no idea how to retrieve it. Old Joe was keeping watch while gutting some pollack the fisherman had given him. Ebony watched silently as he sliced and deboned the fish, the scales dotting his hands like pearlescent eyes. It made her think of Aunt Ruby's animal spies. A shiver ran through Ebony's bones and she began to cough. Old Joe paused, waiting until the coughing fit had passed.

'Are you all right, girleen?'

Ebony nodded, despite the sense of dread lingering in her mind – she would have to face the wrath of Aunt Ruby soon. Old Joe had phoned to let her know that Ebony was there, to ask her to collect Chiyoko and seal up the Hideout. He had buffered her requests to speak to Ebony, even when she called back, saying the girl was too fragile and exhausted to speak. It was true, but Ebony knew her aunt wouldn't be appeased for long. She kept expecting the shrill wail of the telephone to start up.

Old Joe checked in the oven, then lit the gas hob and heated some oil, glancing at Ebony now and again as though expecting something terrible to suddenly happen. He started frying, the fat spitting and sizzling as he squashed the fish down into the pan with a wooden spatula.

'Think you could manage some?' asked Old Joe.

Ebony sucked a deep breath in through her nose and her nostrils filled with the whiff of warm potatoes and salted fish. Her stomach rumbled hungrily in reply. But before she could answer, the room turned dark and cold as something blocked the sunlight from the window. Just as suddenly, whatever it was disappeared.

'What the …?' shouted Old Joe.

Ebony struggled to her feet and hobbled to the window, trying to ignore the pins and needles in her legs. Outside, a huge bird was circling. Ebony recognised the creature, its bald head and neck, purple and scarlet in colour, a neon-orange wattle on its beak. Aunt Ruby had sent a King Vulture.

'Do you have any rashers?' asked Ebony.

A quizzical look on his face, Old Joe pointed to the fridge.

Moving as fast as her tingling limbs would allow, Ebony took two rashers from the fridge, cold and sticky in her fingers. As she headed for the back door, she looked out the window:

the King Vulture was circling the garden. Tugging the door open – it took more effort than she expected – Ebony rushed out, rashers in hand. With two muscular flaps of its wings, the vulture powered her way.

As it neared, Ebony saw an envelope in its slate-grey claws and her heart began to race. Was her aunt angry? Was she coming to get her or would she make her travel on the bus? She didn't fancy travelling alone right now.

The day was reasonably bright, a mild yellow sun high in the sky, but as the bird swooped, Ebony was covered in shadow. Flashes of Zach and Ambrose at the altar, of Zach and Seamus's eyes turning black, zipped through her mind and chilled her bones. Bunching the dressing-gown tighter around her, Ebony looked into the vulture's piercing pale-yellow eyes and reached for the envelope, snatching it from its claws. The bird turned again and swooped, more slowly this time, to hook the rashers – its payment for delivery. The vulture snatched up the rashers and shrieked twice. Then, flapping its wings, the huge bird soared towards the horizon. In no time at all it was a distant speck. Taking a deep breath, Ebony turned the envelope over in her hands. It had a delicate curlicue 'C' in the corner – Uncle Cornelius's personalised paper.

'It's a letter from home.'

'Open it,' said Old Joe. 'What does it say?'

Slowly unpicking the envelope, Ebony pulled out the note. It was in her aunt's hand.

Dear Ebony,

As you won't speak on the phone, I decided to send a King Vulture. The Hideout is secured and Chiyoko is fine, if a little shaken. And she told me about your parents' gun. What were you thinking, keeping that information from me and going into the Shadowlands alone?

I'm needed at Headquarters and I don't want to raise any alarm – the less O'Hara knows about this, the better. He has already banned you from Shadowlands activity and the penalty would be severe. Chiyoko has promised to stay quiet this time, but any more scares and I believe she'll squeal. The last thing we need is for you to end up in the Order's bad books and out of action.

The city is suddenly under attack – Shadow Walkers openly march in the streets, injuring anyone they come across. Civilian forces have no idea how to fight them, so O'Hara has declared a state of emergency in the Order and it's all hands on deck. We need a full team. Caught up in official business, he hasn't realised you're gone yet, so we've covered your tracks so far – but we need you home as soon as possible.

We've snuck Icarus out – it was the only way to set him free and O'Hara is so preoccupied he hasn't yet noticed. Icarus will come to you and bring you home.

Until he arrives, keep out of trouble and away from the Shadowlands.

For once, please listen. It's for your own safety.

Aunt Ruby

After reading the letter aloud to Old Joe, Ebony scrunched it into a ball.

'That sounds bad,' said Old Joe, his eyebrows pushed up high under the rim of his flat cap.

'It does,' said Ebony, her stomach in bits.

When Icarus had returned from the Shadowlands, he had made it clear that he didn't want to be involved with Ebony's parents any further. And after seeing what Winston had recorded, she knew why he didn't trust himself. So even though he was coming to help, she didn't expect a friendly reunion. But maybe he would see that she was determined, with or without his help, to get back to her parents and would realise that it was best to share his knowledge and avoid unnecessary problems. And maybe he would help her with Seamus's mask? It was the only way Seamus would get better, and it might help Mr O'Hara to see that Icarus was on the Order's side. Surely Icarus would understand. After all, she had risked her life – and she would do so over and over until her enemies were defeated.

That night, after a long, hot bath, Ebony wrapped herself in one of Old Joe's shirts and the fleecy dressing-gown. 'I'm going to the sea to say a blessing.'

'Take this to find your way,' said Old Joe, offering her a big farmer's torch.

Taking it, so as not to offend, Ebony laughed. 'It's not that long since I lived here, Joe! I could find my way around the place blindfolded.'

A spot of red tinged Old Joe's cheeks. 'But you're a city girl now.'

The comment stung. Despite the day's events, Ebony felt the sea calling her, whispering to her bones and sinews, her blood. She was made of sea air and bird song, salt water and earth, and no matter how long she stayed in Dublin that was never going to change. Ebony jumped to her feet, tugged the dressing-gown around her neck and rushed outside without switching the torch on or saying another word.

The freezing night air assaulted her face as she wandered down to the rocks at the bottom of the garden. A herd of early wintering curlews began to call; something must have disturbed their sleep. She followed the sound by the light of the moon. Just like her old cottage, Joe's land backed straight onto the wild Atlantic, the garden edged with black rocks and grassy ledges skimmed by waves. When the tide was really high, the sea left a scattering of seaweed. Wagtails and crows would flock to peck at the stranded fronds, looking for minuscule shrimp and crabs that had dried in the sun.

That night, the tide was low and the sea was calm. Somewhere nearby, Ebony heard another curlew call. Staring out across the ocean, there was nothing to see except an endless black blanket under the dark night sky. On the surface, the moon reflected so perfectly that Ebony could almost believe she was looking into a parallel world.

'Perhaps in that world, Grandpa's still alive and my parents didn't disappear,' said Ebony aloud. As silly as it sounded, she wished it were true. As she spoke, the water rippled and the moon fractured into several pieces, before re-forming again. Above her head there was a wash of blinking stars. Ebony stared at the sky's vastness, imagining the world of ocean below it. She had grown up knowing the power of the sea – its whims and duplicity only made her respect it more.

Facing the water Ebony gave a salute. A star flared brightly before dying out and Ebony made a wish. Her grandpa had said that when you lost someone you only had to look to the treetops or wind or waves to feel them. Ebony could sense him watching. Ever since she had released his soul she had hoped that he had passed through to Ultimation, mingling with the universe for eternity. In the moonlight next to the whispering sea he felt near and, although she knew he would no longer have need for an earthly body, she could clearly picture his warm eyes and broad shoulders, his calloused hands and hearty laugh. Spotting another shooting star and another, Ebony clapped her hands and made two more wishes. By the time the seventh star arced across the sky, her heart was racing.

'It's a good omen,' she whispered. 'It has to be.'

At that moment something floating in the water caught her eye. At first she thought it was an island of kelp but as it neared she realised it was human-shaped.

A sea corpse.

The figure was large and bald, so she guessed it was a man. He wasn't wearing a life jacket, but he was floating. Ebony leapt to her feet and, after shouting to Old Joe for help, she switched on the torch and searched the nearby ground for something to haul the body in. There was no point throwing Old Joe's life ring – as the torch beam settled on the corpse, covered in markings and barnacles, it was clear that the man was long dead. Bodies had washed ashore in Oddley Cove before, so she knew what to do.

Checking back, there was no sign of Old Joe, so she called again as loudly as she could. Then, finding a branch that was drying for firewood, Ebony reached out from the rocks, trying to hook the body, but it was just out of reach. In the light of the torch she saw that the markings on his head were like a tattoo. A long, continuous tattoo that wound around the top of the skull and down to the neck, below the shirt collar – it was almost identical to the one Icarus had revealed on his arm. There was only one other person she had heard of that bore the same type of mark. *But it can't be my aunt's husband,* thought Ebony, *he died years ago.* The corpse inched closer, still too far to reach, but the tide was coming in.

Hoping Old Joe would arrive soon – she just had to be patient – she waited and watched as the body drew nearer, bobbing on the gently undulating surface. As soon as it was close enough, she reached out again with her branch and was close to hooking the wet shirt when the corpse's face suddenly lifted up, a moan escaping from between its barnacled lips. As Ebony sprang backwards with a startled cry, a cacophony of nearby curlews cried out, their wing beats filling the night sky as they flew away. The man's face had a tuft of black beard on one cheek and where his shirt buttons were torn away Ebony could see that the tattoo continued down his chest.

The man reached out, his forearm and hand missing, the humerus barely covered in skin. His other arm swished in the water, propelling him towards her. Ebony jumped back.

'You came! You answered my call!' cried the corpse. When he spoke, the air smelled rank and rotten, like diseased fish being roasted. 'Now you must release me.'

Although Ebony knew it was her real Uncle Cornelius and she shouldn't be afraid, she dropped the stick and stumbled back. A silent scream caught in her throat and she froze as the tattoos started to shift and move, slithering around the man's neck and throat. Then the body collapsed, turning back into a lifeless corpse. In front of her eyes it floated away against the current, vanishing into the inky dark.

Ebony ran for her life towards the cottage, shouting Old Joe's name. Only when she reached the cottage and felt his arms wrap around her did she dare to look back.

The air was eerily still.

'Whatever's the matter?' asked Joe, looking past Ebony, trying to figure it out for himself. 'You look like you've seen a ghost.'

'I th-think I have,' said Ebony. 'It was Uncle Cornelius, Aunt Ruby's husband, and he was horrible.'

'I knew I shouldn't have let you go down there by yourself.'

'I thought it was a dead body,' said Ebony barely aware of what Old Joe was saying. 'But when it raised its head …' She shuddered.

Noticing Old Joe's silence, she looked up at his face. His lips were tight and his brow furrowed but he didn't seem at all shocked by what she had said. Ebony asked, 'What is it, Joe?'

He led her inside, closing the door behind him. Only then did he speak. 'Sit down, Ebony. Tell me, did Aunt Ruby ever tell you about Connie's disappearance?'

'No. Not in depth. She finds it too upsetting.'

'When your parents disappeared their bodies were never found, but Cornelius's body was discovered floating in the water, face down. Of course, we didn't know then that your parents had travelled back in time, but there was something strange about the whole affair. The autopsy revealed that Connie had died before hitting the water, and his eyes were wide and black, frozen in fear.'

'Could he have died from a head injury? If he hit those rocks–'

'There was no head injury, internal or external, but his body was bruised and his arm torn off. When the Order's forensics woman looked him over, she found black markings all over his body. Like tattoos, but not created with ink.'

'Icarus has those now,' blurted Ebony. 'They're somehow linked to Ambrose.'

Old Joe winced. 'I think Connie's death is too.'

'You think Ambrose murdered him?'

'Maybe not personally, but I think he got someone, or something, that totally terrified your uncle to do it for him. I'll tell you my story and see what you think.'

Ebony settled herself to listen as Old Joe cleared his throat.

'I haven't told anyone this, but after Connie's body was found, I went out to sea looking for clues. It was a cold night and a storm grew out of the dark. The wind howled and waves lashed and I was drifting towards the Razor Rocks. I was only in my rowing boat, so I had to turn back.'

'A rowing boat? What were you thinking?'

Old Joe paused, stroking his beard with a big, calloused hand. Snuggling down against the cushion, Ebony waited for the rest of the story.

'As I tried to row away, one of my oars caught in something. Thinking it was kelp, I gave it a strong tug. When it surfaced, there was something clinging to it. A figure so terrifying it would make your hair stand on end.'

'Did it have a moving tattoo?'

'The very same! Frozen with fear, I watched as it slid across the oar and into the boat. I recognised your uncle's face right away, but he didn't seem to know me. He asked if I was the guardian and begged me to release him. I didn't know what he was talking about and stayed silent. That made him fierce angry. He grabbed me with his one good hand and those bony fingers tried to shake me out of my skeleton. I thought he was going to throw me overboard.'

'How did you escape?'

'I finally found my voice and said I'd ask my friend from the Order of Nine Lives about this guardian. This appeared to startle the ghost – he let go of me and dived overboard into the waves. Maybe he thought I meant Ambrose? I didn't stick around to find out. I rowed with all my might. When I reached land, I tethered my boat as quickly as I could and ran for my life. Only when I was halfway up the back field did I dare to stop and look out to sea.'

'Had it followed you?'

'No. As I'd rowed away, I could hear him crying out. Looking back, those cries seemed desperate rather than angry, but at the time I was too scared to realise that. I never went near the place again.'

'Why didn't you tell Grandpa? He was your best friend.'

'I know, but he was still distraught about losing your parents and Cornelius. I knew he'd want to go poking around the wreckage. That area has never been safe, but when I realised the Razor Rocks were cursed by Connie's ghost, I was afraid your grandpa would do something foolish and get himself killed trying to help. Since then, stories of dead souls rising in that spot discouraged anyone from venturing too closely – I think the ghost is haunting the area, waiting for you to release him or maybe for his murderer to return so he can get revenge.'

'I don't know how to release him. Maybe Aunt Ruby will have an idea – we must tell her.' Ebony sat forward excitedly.

Old Joe shook his head. 'Is now the time to reopen old wounds? What if she doesn't know and then has to live with the knowledge that her husband's soul is cursed to haunt that desolate spot?'

Uncertain, Ebony slumped back on the sofa. As she curled up under a warm duvet placed over her by Old Joe, she shivered. The old man stroked her hair, then placed several sods of turf on the fire and turned towards the stairs. 'The best thing to do right now is get some sleep and forget you've seen it at all. Your grandpa would be proud of the fine girl you've turned into,' he called after him, before heading up to bed.

Ebony snuggled down but as soon as she heard Joe's bedroom door close, her eyes sprang open. Every corner of the room seemed to come alive in the flickering flames.

In the shadows she imagined she could see the sea ghost's grimacing face. Her nose twitched, imagining the smell of rotting, diseased fish. Her ears rang with its voice – she tried covering them, but the tighter she squeezed, the louder his plea echoed.

You came! You answered my call! Now, you must release me.

As the words played over and over in her mind, she vowed to help him – as guardian, she must find a way.

Just after midnight, Ebony woke with a start. It took a moment for her eyes to adjust, the glowing fire providing barely enough light for her to recognise where she was. Then it all came rushing back – the Shadowlands, almost drowning, the ghost and Old Joe's cottage. On the roof rain splattered, thick and heavy, and gusts of wind wailed around the chimney and down into the flue. A screech of tyres sounded outside, followed by a sprinkling of pebbles, as a motorbike screamed to a halt. She realised that the sound of its approach must have been what woke her up.

Icarus Bean.

Figuring he must be too weak to use the Shadowlands and uncertain how he would react to being sent to help her, Ebony flattened herself down and pretended to be asleep. As Icarus hammered on the door, she hid her face under the covers.

'All right, all right,' called Old Joe as the knocking continued. 'I'm an old man and I'm slow!'

As Old Joe opened the door, Icarus stomped in, water dripping off his leathers.

'Where is the little fool?' Spotting Ebony on the sofa, Icarus strode over. 'Don't bother pretending to be asleep,' he said, snatching the covers off her face and sprinkling her with raindrops, 'that knocking would have woken the dead!'

Ebony opened one eye. Icarus's hair stuck out in all directions where he'd yanked off his helmet and his eyes were as black as storm clouds. He was sodden, puddles forming on the floor around him.

'Hey,' said Old Joe, moving closer, 'we speak with respect in my house.'

'Oh, really?' said Icarus, eyeballing the old man.

Old Joe stood his ground, his forehead crinkling as he surveyed Icarus's face. Ebony noticed that Icarus's shoulders were hunched as though giant boulders were crushing them.

'Are you OK, Icarus?' Old Joe asked. 'You look a little … strange.'

'I'm fine,' snapped Icarus, rubbing his eyes. 'Tired. It was a long journey in this torrent – especially after being kidnapped in my sleep by your aunt!' He threw Ebony a look of disgust before dashing outside again, as though suddenly remembering something. The rain was pelting down, loud as marbles as it hit the ground. Stomping back in, he held up a dripping wet cage.

'Winston!' cried Ebony. It seemed odd for Icarus to bring him, but she was grateful to have her best friend join her. 'Thank you, Uncle.'

He shoved the cage into her hands. 'Ruby said you're to keep Winston with you at all times from now on. Pets are going missing at an alarming rate. The Deus-Umbra is hungry.'

Feeling Winston shudder, Ebony took him out of his cage and hugged him close. Soaking wet, he smelled of drains, but Ebony didn't care.

'I'll keep you with me always from now on. I missed you,' she said.

Winston tried to squeak in reply but his throat was hoarse and it came out as a cough. Wrapping him up in the folds of Old Joe's fleece dressing gown, Ebony returned to the sofa and tucked the quilt around them both. Icarus removed his leathers and settled in the armchair next to the fire. His mouth curved downwards and his brow sagged as he warmed his hands.

'Will you give me a few minutes with Ebony alone?' he asked, staring into the flames.

Old Joe looked from Icarus to Ebony. When Ebony nodded, his face relaxed a little. 'Tea?' he asked.

'Perfect. Tea it is,' said Icarus, still not making eye contact.

As the old man headed for the kitchen, Icarus turned to his niece and narrowed his cold, unfriendly eyes. Ebony knew she was in big trouble.

'You all think you're so very clever, don't you?' he said. 'I told you that I didn't want any part of this. I have warned Ruby of the danger but she will not listen. She's letting sentimentality get in the way of common sense. Ambrose's power over me grows stronger each day. The other day I woke up from a trance, violently beating my fists against the wall. My hands were bruised and bleeding and yet I could not stop; it was Ambrose's doing. He means me – and those around me – harm. Dark thoughts attack me in my dreams and when I'm awake. What if he manages to take complete control while we're alone?'

'I didn't know they were going to break you out – and besides, I've shown I can look after myself,' protested Ebony. 'I found the Reflectory and I helped Chiyoko escape from the Deus-Umbra. It was me who destroyed the machine and stopped Ambrose taking my soul. You should give me some credit!'

'And if I hadn't contacted your past selves and got them to help you, you'd have been dead back in April. What are you playing at, Ebony? A state of emergency has been called and you're messing around in the Shadowlands, making a pest of yourself and risking your life. Not to mention withholding important information.'

'I only just found out about the attack on Dublin,' said Ebony, waving her aunt's note. 'If anyone had bothered to listen to me, it wouldn't have come to this. I've been saying for weeks that we should hunt down our enemies instead of waiting to be picked off. I know Ambrose and Zach are coming for me and it's time to act. If you'd taught me how to travel in time weeks ago, my parents could have been helping us already.'

Ebony drew her legs up as close to her body as she could.

She had hoped her words would prompt Icarus into action, but instead, his scowl deepened. He scratched at his neck, revealing a tiny spike of black flicking in and out of his collar. In Ebony's vision of the future the marking had covered his face – last time she had seen it, it only went to his elbow. It was already taking over his body, but what did that mean? She had seen the state of the real Uncle Cornelius – was Icarus destined for a similar fate? Rubbing his chin, worry lines creasing his forehead, Icarus seemed to age before Ebony's eyes.

'We don't care about your being related to Ambrose,' said Ebony. 'It doesn't matter. And I've seen footage of you meeting him and know that he forced that mark on you. But what I don't understand is how he proved to you that you were adopted.'

'Rufus remembered me arriving in the family as a baby – Ruby was too young – but it was Ambrose who revealed to him that we were related. He claimed that different families took us in and although having a brother was never mentioned, he was older and, therefore, remembered flashes of the time before we were adopted. But he was too young to remember my name or any specific details – and I remembered nothing. When he became the judge he was able to find out who I was and he kept that knowledge to himself until he could use it to his advantage. I thought he might have been lying to your parents so I suggested a meeting; I thought I was going there to prove him wrong and I was sure I could escape before he sprang any trap he might have planned. But when he showed me the adoption papers that he copied and sent to Mrs O'Hara so that the Order would stop trusting me, I realised he was telling the truth. It hit me harder than I expected. And then ... well, you say you saw what happened next.'

'The man from the Order – you didn't kill him. You fought back.'

'But I also didn't save him – and I have to live with the guilt. That's partly why I took so long to come back – after what happened I went back to the past again to try once more to convince your parents to return, but to no avail. Especially once they spotted how I'd been marked.'

Hearing the lull in conversation, Old Joe popped his head out of the kitchen, but Ebony waved him away, certain he'd listen in anyway.

'You have no idea how my dreams torture me, Ebony. How my blood burns. I'm trying to fight it but I don't know how. What if I lose control again – when I'm with you?' He swallowed, his Adam's apple bobbing violently. 'What if the vision Mrs O'Hara showed us comes true and you die because of me? You saw me call for your death!'

'It's a chance I'm willing to take,' replied Ebony. She bit her lip as Icarus bunched his hair in his fists and she reached for his hand. As she took hold, there was a flash of light and she was transported back to the scene from Mrs O'Hara's puppet show. The haunted people, Shadow Walkers with whips, Icarus calling for her death. Their hands still joined, Icarus could see it too. He looked at Ebony and, his grip tightening, she saw murder flash in his eyes. Yanking his hand from hers, the scene fell away. They were back in Old Joe's cottage.

'You see,' growled Icarus. 'I'm cursed.'

'There's hope if we work together!' cried Ebony. 'We can't let Ambrose beat us – not after we've been through so much together. You said yourself I'd be dead already if it wasn't for you. And I've made some progress.'

Heart racing, Ebony informed Icarus of all her recent findings: the vision of Zach and Ambrose contacting the Deus-Umbra, locating the *Samphire* shipwreck and Seamus's mask. The words tumbled out so fast her thoughts could barely keep up. As she revealed the ghostly sighting of the real Uncle Cornelius and Old Joe's theory that he was haunting the Razor Rocks, Old Joe came in with a tray of tea and biscuits.

'I've seen the ghost too,' said Old Joe.

Icarus looked up, the flickering flames of the fire dancing shadows across his skin. Even in the warm glow, his lips looked pale.

'I thought we couldn't have ghosts in the Order,' said Ebony. As she spoke, Icarus scratched at his arm. His sleeve lifted, and Ebony saw the tattoo peeping out. It twisted and squirmed, like it was trying to break free. 'I thought that because we're reincarnated it wasn't possible. We live, we die, we reincarnate – until we reach our Destiny or fail nine times. That's it.'

'That's what I thought too – but clearly we were both

wrong. Connie's ghost has proved otherwise. I can't explain it but you saw the state of his soul in the Reflectory,' replied Icarus. 'There's got to be a reason.'

'He spoke about needing to be released,' added Ebony. 'Part of his soul must be trapped somehow. As guardian, I will have to find a way to help him.'

'We have more pressing matters right now, Ebony,' said Icarus. He lifted his forearm as the mark twisted its way out of his shirt sleeve, stretching over the tendons in his hand. His face darkened and his eyes glowed red for an instant. When the mark stopped moving, Icarus unclenched his jaw and looked Ebony in the eye. 'Do you still trust me?'

'I do. But there's something I want to do before we go back to Dublin,' she replied. Ignoring Icarus's groan, she continued. 'Seamus's illness is linked to his missing mask. It's out at the Razor Rocks, embedded in the sand. Seamus won't get better without it and we need a full team – Seamus included – to take on Ambrose. Will you help me get it back?'

Eyes flaring, Icarus looked from Ebony to Old Joe, then nodded, tight-lipped. As Ebony explained where she had seen the mask, Old Joe blew on his mug of tea and Winston squirmed on her lap.

'OK,' replied Icarus. 'Joe – do you know the fisherman that found Ebony? The one that fishes the Razor Rocks?'

'I do,' replied Old Joe, scratching at his chin. 'Dennis the Anchor's his name. He's not a bad sort. Cantankerous but reliable.'

'Good,' replied Icarus. 'Can you call him and ask him if we can take a trip out tomorrow? I'll pay the going rate, of course.'

'What, now?' asked Ebony, checking the clock on the wall. It was 1.30 a.m.

'Not a chance,' said Old Joe. 'He's an early riser and an early sleeper – the tide starts coming in at 7 a.m. tomorrow, bringing the fish with it, so he'll have to be in deep water by then. He'll be out with the curlews. Wait at the pier at 5 a.m. – but you'll be going alone. That girl's had enough of a fright. She's staying put.'

'No, I want to go!' protested Ebony. 'I promised I'd help Seamus.'

'5 a.m.? That's the middle of the night!' said Icarus at the same time.

'To you, maybe, but that's your only chance,' said Joe, ignoring Ebony's protest. 'Dennis is not much for socialising and believes strangers are bad luck on his boat – but catch him unawares and it's worth a try.'

'What if he won't take me?'

'Us!' said Ebony.

'Me,' replied Icarus.

Old Joe shrugged. 'That's the luck of the draw.'

'Fine,' said Icarus, turning back towards the fire.

'Will you stay here tonight, instead of the cottage?' asked Old Joe. 'Ebony has the sofa and you can take the floor. I'd give you my bed, but if I get down, I'll never get back up.'

'Sure, I'll make camp here,' said Icarus, pouring his tea and taking a sip. 'But I won't stay long. The Order will come looking for me once they can free up some men. They think I'm working with Ambrose, so I'll be high on their "most wanted" list.'

Pulling up the covers, Ebony yawned. But inside, her mind raced – how could she convince Icarus to show her how to time travel in the Shadowlands? Icarus shivered and moved closer to the fire. His inner clothes were dry but rumpled, and they smelled of sweat. His shoulder bones jutted out and the veins on his neck were visible, creating a menacing silhouette like a storybook witch's. Handing him two pillows and several thick blankets, Old Joe said, 'Get some sleep. A fresh day, a fresh start.'

'I very much doubt it,' said Icarus, his voice flat.

Ebony watched as Icarus folded one blanket and laid it on the rug in front of the fire, then wrapped the other around his shoulders. Throwing the pillow down, he cocooned himself in his makeshift bed, gripping one arm tightly as he closed his eyes; it was the arm that bore the tattoo. As Old Joe got up to leave, Ebony snuggled down, even though she knew she wouldn't be able to sleep. Waiting until she heard Icarus's snores rising from his cocoon, she crept around him and stoked the fire, positioning three sods of turf on top of the glowing coals. Returning to the sofa, she cuddled Winston, watching the dancing flames.

An hour and lots of fidgeting later, unable to get the

tattooed corpse out of her mind, an idea hit. Icarus could refuse to let her accompany him on the boat, but there was another way that she could help: whatever had happened to the real Uncle Cornelius, part of his soul was in the Reflectory – she had seen it with her own eyes in the Emergency Room.

And hadn't she released other souls from Ambrose's power before?

The last time she'd been in the Reflectory she'd discovered the plug in her grandpa's neck and freed him, but it had been after she'd left the Emergency Room, so she hadn't had a chance to check her uncle's soul. If she returned, maybe she would be able to release him like she had the others.

The Reflectory was her domain; it was where she belonged and no one could stop her going there.

30

Ebony scribbled a note explaining where she was going and left it next to Icarus. Then, pulling on her runners and coat, and grabbing her rucksack and Old Joe's torch, she tucked Winston into her trouser pocket and crept to the front door. Gently tugging open the door and sneaking outside, she headed straight for the woods. Even though she had been told that the doorway to the Reflectory could be opened from anywhere, she felt that returning to the copse where she had previously accessed it would give her the best chance of success. The light from the torch jiggled up and down, making the ferns and foliage around her seem to shudder and shake. It was like a scene from a horror film, setting Ebony's nerves on edge as her feet pounded the tarmac. It would never have bothered her before; Old Joe was right – the city was getting under her skin.

Water splashed from muddy puddles up her legs as she raced along. After a moment, she switched off the torch. Listening, to make sure she hadn't been followed, she continued for a while in the dark. She had grown up in these parts and, despite the torrential rain and overcast sky, her eyes adjusted to the night quickly. When she was certain she was alone, she clicked the light back on and hurried. The rain eased off and above the woods the clouds were beginning to clear. Panting and holding her side to ease a stitch, Ebony slowed to a march. Stepping off the path into the undergrowth for the final part of the ascent, briars caught on her trousers and jacket and tore at her skin, but she pushed on. Soon the rain stopped completely and Ebony was standing in a copse of oak trees overlooking the sea, the shining moon turning her skin bluish.

Winston popped his head out as she got to work. *This is important*, she thought. *Believe that I am true of heart.* Taking off her amulet and wrapping it around the stem of the bronze rose, she held the items up in the glare of the moon and closed her eyes. When nothing happened, she tried to think of the happiest thoughts she could – fishing for lobster with her grandpa, cuddling with Winston – and a sense of peace enveloped her. The rose began to burn blue, sparks spluttering from its centre, and a sprinkling of dust glimmered in the air. The centre of the rose glowed brightly for a split second, and Ebony stood firm. The petals chimed like bells and unfurled, each displaying a series of symbols and markings that slid onto the ground, forming a strange web-like structure made up of different-coloured lights and beams. As they began to blink out, Ebony held her breath. There was a rumbling and the stone Ebony was waiting for pushed up out of the ground, the mahogany door in its centre.

Wasting no time, Ebony inserted her grandpa's medal into the peep hole, and when the glowing crescent-moon-shaped hole appeared in its centre, she inserted the amulet. She pushed open the door and removed the amulet and medal before stepping through and taking a deep breath. The door had disappeared from view, but reaching out she could feel it in front of her. On the floor, the black rose that would allow her to open the door from the inside glistened, but it was small and she was afraid it would be difficult to spot from far away. Taking the whip she had borrowed out of her rucksack, she laid it on the ground so it ran the width of the door. She lifted Winston out, put him on the ground and she pointed.

'It'll make it easier to find the exit when we need it. Now, let's get to the Emergency Room.'

Winston nodded and scampered ahead. As she stepped into the magical glittering world, the gentle breeze warmed Ebony's heart, filling it with possibilities. But her mind was wary. The last time she visited the Reflectory she had trapped a Shadow Walker inside. She had hoped the magic there would expel it, and her aunt had agreed when they'd discussed it, but she couldn't be certain. Following Winston, Ebony headed past the array of lush trees and blooming flowers, towards the nothingness where visions of memories crept out of the mist and swatted at her. Ducking and avoiding these, and fighting the haziness that grew in her mind as she wandered deeper into the Reflectory, Ebony searched for the rows of luminous souls sitting in front of their bright-bulbed mirrors, preparing for their next life. Spotting the bulbs glowing up ahead, Winston quickened his pace.

'I don't know how you're so smart, Winston, but I'd be lost without you,' said Ebony.

But before they reached the souls, Ebony's shoe stuck to something tacky on the ground. Lifting her foot up, she saw black goo stretching from the sole. Thinking nothing of it, she carried on, but after a few steps, an agonising burning sensation ripped through her hand. Realising that it meant the Shadow Walker was nearby, Ebony gripped her wrist to stem the pain and staggered on. Winston stopped, his fur on end. Ebony gave him an encouraging nod, even though they had to be on their guard.

Stepping into another pile of goo, she checked around. Noticing Winston was waiting near another black mark on the floor up ahead, her heart almost stopped. Reaching down, she traced around it with her fingers: it was the shape of a skull. She looked around and realised there were more, and not only that, there were also skull-shaped holes in the glittering mist. The Shadow Walker was causing damage and she would have to get it out of there.

Hearing a crashing nearby, Ebony snatched up Winston and ducked down behind one of the mirrors. Peeping out, she saw a furious Shadow Walker the width of a barrel, with short legs and knuckles almost grazing the ground.

His stumpy teeth bared and drool dripping from his lips, he roared and lashed out, trying to swipe at the soul of a young woman gazing serenely into her mirror. Heart pounding, Ebony clamped her hand over her mouth, but when the creature's chunky fist passed right through the soul, leaving it undamaged, she relaxed. Clearly the creature couldn't harm the souls themselves. The Shadow Walker roared and beat its chest before trying again; starved of its fun for so long in the Reflectory, it was baying for blood. It lumbered on – and it was coming her way.

Holding her wrist as tightly as she could to stop the pain, Ebony held her breath as she planned her next move. She knew from experience that her gun would be useless against the creature, and if she fired it, she would be expelled, just like Zach had been on her first visit here when he attempted to shoot her. The Reflectory was a place of regeneration and didn't like violence. Letting the Shadow Walker attack her was her only chance; it would be worth a few bruises to get the creature out of there. Stopping a few metres away, the Shadow Walker sniffed the air, its nostrils bubbling and rumbling as it took a deep whiff – it must have caught her scent. She watched its chunky, calloused fingers curling and uncurling. Leaping out, Ebony faced the Shadow Walker and roared at the top of her voice, 'Here I am!'

The Shadow Walker cackled wildly and thumped its way towards her. Lifting its thick forearms, it roared at her, yellow spit flying. Winston bared his teeth and hissed and Ebony held her breath. The next thing she knew, she was being lifted into the air by the waistband of her trousers. She could smell the Shadow Walker's rotten breath as she dangled. Crossing her fingers, she hoped her plan would work. With a flick of its wrist, the creature flung Ebony through the air. She landed with a thump – thankfully, not on top of Winston – and groaned in pain. A squeal from Winston made her look up: the Shadow Walker was glowing. A crackling sound filled Ebony's ears as its body splintered and shattered, then exploded. Hot air blasted Ebony's face and the pain in her hand died away. The Shadow Walker was gone.

Scrambling to her feet, Ebony motioned for Winston to lead on. They made their way quickly towards the Emergency Room in the distance, its name flashing in red neon above the huge doorway.

Inside, the Emergency Room looked the same as she'd left it. The real Uncle Cornelius's dull yellow form was perched on its seat, covered in scars and fissures. Above his head was his mirror and beside him smashed pieces of porcelain: the remains of the replica that Zach and Ambrose had used when they were trying to trick Ebony into thinking Zach's mum was still there. It had been Winston who had discovered that deception and she was thankful to have him with her this time too. But there was no time for sentimentality: this was her chance to help Aunt Ruby's husband.

Moving closer, Ebony examined the marks on his face. It was the first time she had looked closely at the damage. The scars visible on his face and neck matched the tattoo she'd seen on the sea ghost. Tentatively, she peeped inside his shirt. The soul was covered in a swirling black tattoo, only the part of it on his face and neck had hardened and lost its colour, turning into something resembling scar tissue.

Hands trembling, Ebony checked the back of his neck, feeling around until her fingers hit against something small, round and smooth. It was exactly what she'd been hoping to find. As she had suspected, Ambrose had inserted one of his plugs that let him steal the soul's regenerative power. But looking at the state the soul was in, she guessed that it didn't have much energy left to give. Hoping it would survive her intervention, and feeling a little guilty that she hadn't thought to do this the last time she was there, Ebony pulled the plug out. The second it was free, the soul inhaled loudly and jerked upright. Trembling, Connie's eyes opened and he spoke in a dry, cracked voice: 'Are you the guardian? Are you here to release me?'

Ebony looked deep into his eyes. 'Yes. I've released you.'

His face broke into a smile and, as he slumped back into his chair, movement showed in the mirror above his head. As a single bulb lit up at the top of his mirror, indistinguishable shapes began to form in its reflective surface. The image became clearer, and a single lantern could be seen hanging in the prow of a boat, waves rippling up ahead. As the boat lifted and tilted on a wave, Ebony saw the name on its side: it was the *Samphire* – she must be seeing her uncle's last memory. Suddenly, a figure emerged out of the shadows: Ambrose. His mouth moved wildly, spit flying, and then Shadow Walkers began to appear. Two, then four, then six in total. Ambrose pointed and the Shadow Walkers closed in, arms outstretched. Then everything went shaky, then black. A dark comet flew out of the mirror, forcing Ebony to duck. She watched it smash against the wall and disappear. Old Joe was right: Ambrose was responsible for Connie's death.

Ebony addressed the soul. 'You can go now. And I promise, when I get back to Dublin, I'll avenge your murder. Ambrose has done enough damage to this family.'

The soul's face slackened and Connie's eyes closed as he returned to his previous state, quiet and inert. But his soul didn't disappear, nor did the marks on his skin. Disheartened, Ebony turned from her uncle, examining the plug in her hand. It was shiny red with a black skull on it, the same as those she'd found on the other souls. Closing her fingers around it, she tucked it into her pocket – she hadn't kept the others last time: she'd been in too much of a rush. But maybe it would come in useful later; perhaps she could figure out a way to use it to lead her to Ambrose.

Leaving the Emergency Room and heading straight for the exit, Ebony was stopped in her tracks by a strange, howling wind. She hadn't heard it in the Reflectory before and it made her skin crawl.

'Wait – what's that, Winston?'

Winston stopped and listened also, the fur on his body standing on end. As Ebony followed the noise, Winston waved his paws to try to stop her. But Ebony continued. The sound led to a strange mirror. All of its light bulbs were switched off and an empty chair sat in front of it. It was at the end of a row, pushed away from the other mirrors. In its centre was a black spot the size of a dinner plate; it looked like the surface was tarnished. Had it been there before? She definitely hadn't noticed it, but she'd been so focused on her mission, she could have easily missed it. Following her gaze, Winston raised his right paw and began to jump up and down on the spot, but it was too late; Ebony's inquisitive nature drew her in.

'I don't know what this is, Winston, but I don't like it.'

Moving closer, she reached out and touched the cool glass. As her hand slid down, she felt a gust of wind and discovered that the spot was, in fact, a hole, with a howling wind swirling and spinning inside. She stared into its depths – there was only darkness. It was like staring into the blackest night imaginable.

Then the hole started to grow. In its centre, the face of Ambrose appeared. His grey eyes were so close she could see flecks of black in his irises. He grinned at her.

'You seem to forget that I can locate you whenever I want,' he said. 'I thought I'd come and see what mischief you were up to.'

Before she could reply, he began to push his head through the hole. Ebony stepped back and gasped. This was how Ambrose was accessing the Reflectory – she had to stop him!

On the floor, Winston squealed loudly. Uncertain what to do, Ebony paused, racking her brain for a way to destroy the mirror. As Ambrose's hand appeared, curling around the edges and stretching the hole to make way for more of his body to push through, she knew she had to act. Dropping her rucksack on the floor, she crouched to rummage through it, trying to find something to shatter the glass. Winston rushed over and peered in.

When Ebony's hand brushed something cold and metal, she had an idea. 'Although the doorways aren't the same,' she said, pulling out her bronze rose, 'and I don't know how Ambrose managed to open his in the first place, I hope this works.'

As soon as she lifted the rose, the petals started to glow and, from the centre, sparks spluttered.

'This looks like a good sign, Winston.'

Wrapping her amulet around the stem of the rose, she held it at arm's length, pointing the heart of the rose towards the black hole. The sparks grew in number and size, fizzing like a sparkler. Winston dodged the sparks and scrambled up Ebony's leg where he clung on and watched. Holding her arm steady, Ebony closed her eyes and pictured the hole closing. Hearing a squeak from Winston and feeling his claws prick into her thigh, she opened her eyes. A blue beam from the centre of the rose had connected with the outside of the black hole, making it glow brightly. In the centre, Ambrose's face glared at her.

'It's too late, Ebony,' he said. 'I've taken the city, and now I'll take you.'

'No,' said Ebony firmly, her eyebrows creasing into a V shape.

Ambrose's face cracked into a grin as he forced one arm through the hole. Winston jumped from Ebony's leg, heading straight for the mirror; his teeth connecting with a finger, he bit down hard. Ambrose roared but didn't pull back.

Dangling, Winston kept his teeth locked. A droplet of blood dripped from Ambrose's finger onto Winston's face.

Lifting the rose higher, Ebony tightened the muscles in her arm as she concentrated harder. *Please close. Help me, sky world, please!*

The rose lit up like sheet lightning, then the familiar chimes that always accompanied the rose's magic began to sound. As the noise magnified, the blue beam changed colour, darkening to purple, and the hole began to shrink.

Ambrose's eyes widened for an instant and his smile faltered. 'You're not strong enough,' he mocked.

But Ebony stood her ground. The beam turned red then orange then green, and with each colour change, the hole grew smaller. Ambrose withdrew his head so his face was no longer visible, but his arm remained, with Winston dangling from it and several drops of blood on the ground below. The hole continued to shrink. It closed around Ambrose's arm, his shirt sleeve bunching with the pressure. Ebony stared, not sure what to do. If Ambrose didn't pull his arm out, would it be chopped off? Would he be trapped in the mirror? Letting go, Winston dropped to the ground, panting, and Ebony bent down and grabbed him, then jumped back out of Ambrose's reach. Holding Winston close, she watched the arm. Just as she thought Ambrose wouldn't be able to get free, he yanked his arm back through. The hole blinked a kaleidoscope of colours, then disappeared.

The glass in the mirror was once again whole, a pure sheet

of silver reflecting her image back at her. Dropping the rose to her side, and shifting Winston to her shoulder, Ebony ran her fingers over the surface. It was cold and smooth; the doorway was closed. Taking out her gun and lifting it above her head, she hit the glass as hard as she could. A web of cracks covered the mirror. Ebony hit it again for good measure and the surface shattered.

'That should stop him getting back in and he won't be able to damage any more souls. But you heard him: he's taken the city. We'd better go get my parents – and quick.'

As they raced to the exit, the world around them soon transformed back to shimmering mist and moments later the whip appeared. Using it as a guide, Ebony located the black rose and twisted it firmly to make the door appear. Then, she pushed her grandpa's medal into the peephole, followed by the amulet. As the door sprang open, she quickly dashed through, careful to bring her precious objects with her. Once outside, she looked around for any sign of their enemies. Under the moonlight, all was still. Satisfied that they were safe, for now, Ebony quickly closed the door; lifting the bronze rose high in the air, she let it work its magic once more.

As the doorway to the Reflectory vanished, Ebony secured her precious items in her rucksack and, Winston in her sleeve, took off through the scrub. Arriving back at the cottage, drenched with sweat, she saw that Icarus's bike was gone. She snuck inside and found his blankets and pillow in a messy pile. The clock showed 5.30 a.m. Exhausted, too tired to even remove her runners or change her clothes, Ebony flopped onto the sofa, Winston still in her sleeve, and fell fast asleep.

32

It seemed to Ebony like she had only been asleep for minutes when Old Joe touched her shoulder, waking her with a start. But when she checked the clock, she saw that she'd been asleep for hours. Joe held out a steaming mug of tea and the air smelled of frying eggs. The fire had died out hours ago. Sitting up, she found Winston sleeping near her feet. Outside, the rain was once again torrential; it hammered against the rooftop and tinkled in the chimney. Water oozed in under the front door, soaking the mat, and every breath, even Winston's, could be seen in the cold, damp air.

'Is Icarus at sea in this?' asked Ebony. 'If so, he's wasting his time; the swells will be too high for him to dive down in this weather.'

Old Joe nodded. 'His bike's gone. I'm guessing he rode it to the pier. I can't believe I didn't wake up. I usually jump at the slightest noise. You didn't hear him either?'

Ebony took the tea and sipped it. The hot liquid slipped down her throat, warming her insides. She let the steam warm her face. 'I wasn't here. I went into the Reflectory.'

'You did what?' shouted Old Joe, making Winston jump. 'I

promised your aunt I'd keep you out of trouble but you can't help yourself – you go looking for it!'

Ebony shrugged. 'I'm safe and sound. In fact, I got rid of the Shadow Walker that was trapped in there and I managed to make contact with Connie – only I'm not sure I managed to release his soul. But guess what? I found how Ambrose was getting inside the Reflectory and closed it up.'

Her words sinking in, Old Joe rubbed his chin. 'Wait – what did you say about the sea ghost?'

'I visited his soul and checked him over. Ambrose was holding his soul in stasis – he had the same type of plug inserted into his neck as the rest of the souls – but there's more going on and I think it's to do with his mark.'

Ebony removed the plug from her rucksack and held it in her palm, the sign of the Shadow Walkers clearly visible. 'When I removed this, he showed me how he died. You were right – it was Ambrose and his Shadow Walkers. Although his soul didn't disappear, I'm hoping he can now pass through to whatever fate awaits. He's suffered enough.'

'It sounds like you've done good work,' said Joe, 'but you have to be more careful, do you hear?' He handed her a newspaper. 'I thought you might want to read this while I finish the eggs.'

Winston's nose twitched, detecting the whiff of breakfast cooking. Waking, he stretched and yawned, sticking out his pink tongue. Clambering over to Ebony's lap, he sat on his hind legs so they could read the news together.

CURFEW ISSUED – DUBLIN UNDER SIEGE

As yet more bodies turn up and shadow-like figures attack the city, the residents of Dublin have been ordered to stay inside. The number of bodies found bearing the dreaded skull – now nicknamed the 'death mark' – has reached double figures and security forces confirm that the north side of the city is suffering most. A man calling himself Commander Ambrose has signed a declaration claiming control of the area and warned that this is only the tip of the iceberg. As a result, special forces have been called in to help. While emergency services struggle to deal with the current situation, these highly trained soldiers have taken to the streets. Until the situation is stabilised, the advice from the authorities is stay inside!

Folding the paper and setting it aside, Ebony shoved the blankets away. Old Joe returned with a plate of food and Ebony frowned as she took it. Balancing an egg on top of a slice of toast, she took a bite.

'We can't wait any longer,' she said, her mouth full. 'When Icarus gets back, we have to–'

The front door flew open and Icarus stormed in. Ebony jumped, almost dropping her breakfast.

'We have to what?' he asked, teeth chattering. He was

dripping wet, hair stuck to his head and his face tinged with green – it must have been a bumpy voyage. 'Discuss why you ran off to the Reflectory without waking me?'

'Sorry,' replied Ebony, looking for the mask but unable to see it anywhere. 'I thought you might stop me but I had to go. Did you find the mask?'

'Yes, despite that ghost of yours doing its best to hinder me – your description was spot on. But we have to be straight with each other about everything from now on.' When Ebony nodded, he continued. 'You did well to spot the mask. It took me a couple of tries – you were right, the currents there are treacherous – but I managed to snag it on my second attempt. When I got back to shore I sent it to Mrs O'Hara by King Vulture.'

'I hope the mask helps Seamus to wake up,' said Ebony. 'But Connie's ghost … I released his soul hours ago – I hoped he would be at rest.'

'It was Connie for sure. I'd recognise him anywhere, even with his face disfigured. He tried to stop me getting back in the boat and, failing, sank to the depths.'

'I don't know what else to do!' said Ebony, scrunching her forehead. Quickly, she described her visit to the Reflectory and showed Icarus the plug. Connie's memory flashed in her mind. 'Wait – what if his mark ties him to Ambrose and he can't go to his rest while Ambrose is alive? Maybe I have to bring Ambrose to justice for him?' Waving the newspaper, she added, 'At least Ambrose should be easy enough to find – look!'

She handed the newspaper over. Icarus read quickly and took a moment to think things through.

'Things are worse than I thought. You were right: despite the risk, you need to convince your parents to return, and quickly. I will show you how to get to them. Do you still have the memento mori Ruby gave you?'

As Ebony set her food down to search through her rucksack for the photograph, Winston dived on an egg and lapped up the yolk. Noticing that her mother hadn't faded any further, Ebony showed the picture to Icarus and then placed it in her pocket. Finally, she zipped and shouldered her bag, which still contained her gun, her rose and the medallion, and swallowed hard. She was unexpectedly nervous now that the time had come. Meeting her parents – what would she say? There was no time to ponder it; Icarus was on his feet, heading towards the back door.

Outside, the rain had eased to a light shower, the black clouds having passed overhead. As Winston made to follow, Icarus clapped his hands in quick succession in front of the rat's nose, making him halt. 'You're not invited. The Shadowlands are no place for you.'

'But Aunt Ruby said I had to keep him with me at all times.'

'Not on this occasion – I'm making the call and your aunt isn't here.' Turning to Old Joe, Icarus added, 'We'll return to Dublin, so if you don't hear from Ruby via King Vulture in the next few hours – our timing might be a bit off – let her know where we went and that we could be in trouble. She'll want to be informed.'

As Ebony followed Icarus outside, she felt Winston clamber up her leg and drop into one of her pockets. She gently tapped it, cautioning him to stay still. If Icarus spotted him, he would make him stay – but she needed Winston by her side. Joining Icarus in the shadow of a large sycamore, she found herself searching the nearby shore.

Impatiently, Icarus clapped his hands. 'We don't have time for daydreaming. Concentrate!' He pointed Ebony towards the deepest shadow. 'And make sure you have the photograph handy.'

Taking it from her pocket, Ebony clasped the photo and closed her eyes. Entering the Shadowlands took more concentration than she had expected because her mind was racing. Taking slow, deep breaths, she held her amulet with her free hand, allowing herself to be enveloped by a cool, airy sensation. As she imagined becoming part of the shadows, morphing into them, they began to shimmer and merge. Breathing even more slowly, Ebony let the shadows wrap around her. But each time she nearly passed through, something jolted her out.

'Focus!' urged Icarus, his voice distorting as he passed easily into the other realm. 'Your wandering thoughts are blocking your ability to pass through.'

Slowly, the outline of the ragged shoreline faded. The world turned dark for an instant as everything lost its colour.

Ebony allowed the darkness around her to expand, steadying herself for the moment the world felt like it was dropping away. Seconds later she was beside Icarus, her surroundings grainy and in shades of grey. Checking her hands and body had turned fully sketch-like, Ebony took one last big breath then looked to Icarus for direction. He wasted no time. Dropping to his knees, he scored a line across, adding the direction lines at the end.

'Holding an object from the time is the best way to travel. You can add the date in Roman numerals too, but with both of us concentrating on the photograph, there should be no need for that,' he explained.

Ebony waited, watching him. No wonder she'd gone wrong before – she hadn't considered using an item from the time period, even though it had been in her rucksack all along. She'd been so close with the dates, though – if only she'd known to use Roman numerals. Realising Icarus had taken hold of one end of the scored line, tearing it up from the ground, Ebony gripped the other end. Soon, she was leaping onto the billowing ripples, riding the shadows back in time.

As the rippling stopped and a ribbon of colour cascaded its way towards them, Ebony held her hand over the pocket containing Winston. Crossing her fingers as she flew off the end, she sailed up into the air next to Icarus, hoping with all her might that they'd arrive at 23 Mercury Lane and in the desired year. Landing with a thump, Ebony's face hurt and her stomach felt like it had been pummelled by a professional boxer. Unable to breathe properly, she realised she was face down on hard, cold ground. Managing to move her fingers, she found the pocket Winston was in; he nudged her with his nose to let her know he was safe. But had they landed where they'd expected to?

Climbing to her feet and staggering forward on unstable legs, Ebony heard a squelch. Under the faint glow of a gas-lit street lamp, she didn't need to check what she'd stood in – from the way it smelled she guessed there had been horses in the vicinity. The air was cold and damp and as she edged away from the manure, trying to make sense of her surroundings, she could also smell rotten vegetables, smoke and overflowing drains. She was in a wide, dark street but the air was murky.

Fog wrapped around the street lamps, creating an eerie amber glow; it was so thick, she couldn't make out the buildings.

A sudden loud clamour sounded to her right. Ebony jumped onto the pavement as a pair of horses emerged from the mist, heads bobbing and nostrils steaming as their hooves pounded the ground, dragging a carriage behind them. The man driving them flicked his whip and shouted, his back straight as he tipped his elegant top hat at Ebony.

'We did it,' Ebony said under her breath. 'We've gone back to the past.'

But where was Icarus and how had they managed to get separated? He'd been right there when she'd jumped.

A cough sounded and Ebony saw a figure emerge from the fog. She could tell by its shape and size that it was a man.

'Icarus?' called Ebony, squinting into the fog. 'Is that you?'

But the man was too squat and broad. His suit was tattered and filthy. Not knowing where to run and with visibility poor, Ebony stayed rooted to the spot. The man walked up to her and leaned in, grinning. His teeth were as yellow as a Shadow Walker's and his face was smudged with dirt. His eyes were shaded by the brim of his hat so she couldn't make them out. He held a red-and-white-striped cane in his right hand, topped with a brass fist. Tapping the cane on the ground, his awful grin spread wider and wider.

'What do we have here, then?' said the man. 'Are you lost?'

'No,' said Ebony, trying to keep her voice from wavering. 'I'm waiting for someone. My uncle.'

'Is that right?' said the man, looking around. 'A young girl like you shouldn't be alone on the streets on a night like this.'

'My uncle won't be long.'

'Really? How interesting.'

The man stepped forward and Ebony stepped back until she was pressed against a wrought-iron railing. There was a grating sound as the man tugged on the fist at the top of the cane – it came away, revealing a long, sharp blade. Extending the blade, the man showed it to Ebony. The amber light gave it a rusty tinge, like dried blood. Feeling Winston struggle in her pocket, she tried to force him to stay there by placing her hand over the top. But seconds later his furry body pushed past and scampered down her leg.

'How about you hand over that strange bag of yours?' the man said.

Clinging to the rucksack straps over her shoulders, Ebony shook her head. 'I'm sorry, I can't.'

'Full of treasure, is it?'

He slid the blade under one of the straps.

'No!' she cried. 'You can't have it.'

Squealing, Winston pounced on the thief's ankle and bit hard and the blade clattered to the ground. The man cried out and shook his leg. Winston flew through the air, his cheeks pulled back and his paws spread as he disappeared into the fog. Listening for his landing, Ebony held her breath, but the fog sucked up any noise. Not knowing whether her best friend was safe or not, Ebony looked around for an escape.

But the thief wasn't giving up that easily. Gathering himself, he snatched up the blade and held it to Ebony's cheek. The tip pressed into her flesh.

'Now, about that bag.'

Not knowing what else to do, Ebony screamed.

'What's going on over there?' called a voice. It was distorted in the murk, but deep and gruff.

'Icarus!' cried Ebony. 'Icarus, over here!'

Out of the fog came the figure of a man, his stride fast and determined, heading straight towards them, a pistol held high. As the figure approached, Ebony realised that, once again, it wasn't Icarus.

'Leave her alone or I'll shoot!' said the man.

The thief eyed the pistol carefully, threw Ebony a disgruntled look, then sheathed his blade and backed away, disappearing into the fog.

Ebony looked at her rescuer. Up close, the man was tall, thin and well groomed, with a black moustache and piercing blue eyes. With a jolt, she realised she was staring into the face of Rufus Smart.

'Father?' she choked.

She watched as his expression switched from concern to disbelief.

'Ebony?' he said, grabbing her by the elbow and surveying her clothes. 'Is that really you? Are you here alone?'

Her legs giving way, Ebony saw stars in the air around her. She began to crumple, but her father grabbed her round the waist, supporting her until she was able to stand on her own again. Winston reappeared, eyes bulging and his mouth wide open, panting. Ebony bent down and reached out for him but he dodged her grip and clambered into her sleeve instead. His heart hammered against her wrist.

Taking Ebony's face in his hands, Rufus looked deep into his daughter's eyes. 'I can't believe you're here,' he said, eyes glistening and lips trembling.

Feeling her own eyes sting, Ebony blinked hard and nodded. Rufus pulled her into a warm hug and she secretly wiped a tear on his sleeve. Taking slow, deep breaths, Ebony tried to make sense of the situation. Where was Icarus – had he abandoned her? With Dublin at war, the Order wouldn't have time to look for him. Maybe now he'd got her here he'd taken his chance to run, hoping to prevent Mrs O'Hara's vision from coming true.

'Let's get you inside, where it's safe,' said Rufus, looking around cautiously. 'Come on!'

Ebony's blood thundered in her temples. His arm still around her waist to steady her, her father led her along the street. Moments later, they reached a familiar set of steps and a brass door-knocker. It was 23 Mercury Lane. Before they could climb the steps, a yell rang out. 'Inside!' roared Icarus, loud and clear, as he rounded the corner at the far end of the street at top speed. 'Shadow Walkers were following us. I tried to ditch them but they're not far behind!'

Ebony's heart thumped at the sound of his voice. Instinctively, she reached inside her rucksack for her gun, making a silent promise to never doubt her uncle again. As Icarus neared, his eyes and hair wild, three huge Shadow Walkers followed him around the corner. Even from this distance, in the fog, Ebony could see their bloodthirsty eyes and snarling mouths – but their pace was slow, their bulk hindering their advance. Rufus was quick to act: he pulled Ebony up the steps, opened the door and pushed her inside.

'Ivy! We're under attack!' he shouted, before ducking into the living room.

He returned seconds later with a bow and positioned himself on the top step. Ebony followed him back outside, her gun raised. The bow her father was using was the same as the one Seamus had used in the battle with the Shadow Walkers outside the Order's headquarters a few months ago; as Rufus stretched the string, a green arrow appeared. He released the arrow and Ebony held her breath as it sailed through the air, then punched straight into the chest of one of the oncoming creatures. Behind her she could hear footsteps coming down the stairs, but she was too busy watching Icarus to turn around.

'Look out Icarus,' she cried as one of the creatures reached for him.

Hearing her cry, Icarus glanced over his shoulder, then darted left as Ebony aimed right. She pulled the trigger, hitting the Shadow Walker and shattering it into a thousand blobs of black goo.

'Good shot!' cried Rufus.

As Icarus raced up the steps and ducked into the hallway, Rufus fired another arrow, taking down the last Shadow Walker. He strode into the hallway pushing Ebony before him, then slammed the door shut and locked and bolted it in several places.

'What happened to you?' asked Ebony, turning to her uncle.

'We were followed,' replied Icarus, gasping for breath. Sweat dripped from his forehead and he looked unnaturally white. 'I realised at the last minute so I changed the location in my mind. I'm sorry – there was no time to explain. I lost some of them, but these ones were hard to shake off.'

'Well, we've sorted them for now,' said Rufus, propping the bow against the wall and rubbing his hands together. 'I'm impressed by your shooting skills, Ebony.'

'Thanks,' she said, pleased with the praise, 'but they'll soon re-form. We don't have much time.'

'Ebony's right,' said a voice that made Ebony's heart clatter against her rib cage; it sounded exactly like her own. Her mother was standing at the bottom of the stairs staring at her with a tentative smile. Then she stepped forward and took Ebony in a fierce hug. 'You have no idea how I have longed for this moment,' she whispered. Then, taking a step back, she cleared her throat and said, 'I assume you're here for a reason, so let's talk. Come.'

Rufus lit a trio of candles in a brass holder to illuminate the gloom of the hallway and strode towards the kitchen, his wife in tow. Ebony could hear Icarus's ragged breathing behind her. She still felt guilty for thinking he had abandoned her.

As her father and mother turned through the kitchen door, Ebony paused – now things were calmer, nerves began to hit. She was unsure what to do. Should she call them by name or use Mother and Father?

'What will I say to them?' she asked Icarus.

'Whatever it takes to convince them to return,' he said. 'But hurry – those Shadow Walkers will soon re-form and find us.'

'Maybe you should try again.'

'They won't listen to me. They no longer trust me – and anyway, before I left last time I wasn't exactly friendly. This is down to you.'

Edging forwards, Ebony passed into the warm glow of the kitchen.

As her eyes adjusted to the blinding cluster of candles in the middle of the table, Ebony saw her mother and father seated side by side, rigid as sticks. Despite the tight bun, Ebony could tell from the waves trying to escape that her mother had a head of thick curls. Her heart skipped and she felt a smile spread across her face.

Glancing at each other first, their faces full of shadows in the flickering candlelight, Rufus and Ivy settled their gaze on Ebony. But their expressions betrayed their nerves and no one moved. Striding in, Icarus bumped into Ebony, knocking her against the table. The candlesticks rocked, making the shadows grow and dance.

'I know you don't really know each other,' he said, pulling out a chair opposite her mother and motioning for Ebony to sit, 'but we don't have time for niceties, so let's get this conversation started.'

Icarus sat and then nodded to Ebony to begin. As she settled in the chair and folded her arms on the table, Winston clambered out and squeaked. Ivy coughed, eyeing her husband.

Ebony tried to push Winston back inside, in case his presence angered Icarus, but he refused to budge.

'I see you're like your grandpa,' said Rufus, nodding towards Winston, 'but vermin should not be on the table.'

It was the opposite of what Ebony had expected. Her grandpa was always rescuing strays, wild or domestic. Squirrels, crows, hedgehogs, even a pine marten, had graced their kitchen for recovery at one time. She had expected her father to share the same love for animals.

'He's a pet, not vermin,' said Ebony. 'And he's cleaned regularly.'

But her grandpa had also taught her that being open-minded and accepting of other people got you a long way, so she swallowed any further argument. Opening her sleeve wide, Ebony let Winston crawl back inside and, reluctantly, dropped her arm to her lap.

A slamming noise sounded from under the sink, making Ebony jump. The door rattled and shook violently as something crashed against it on the other side. There was a vicious roar, followed by what sounded like a series of deep scratches: something huge and angry was trying to claw its way out.

'Mulligan?' she asked, looking to her parents for an answer.

'Yes. Recently caught, before our Victorian selves disappeared and we took their place. Not yet trained, so we suggest you steer clear.'

'If you can obey orders, for once,' commented Icarus.

Inside, Ebony's stomach twisted into knots and she threw Icarus an annoyed look. As she glared at him, the mark on his face grew and twisted, and he winced, trying to hide the pain.

'Why have you returned, Icarus, bringing danger to our door? And why bring Ebony with you?' said Rufus. 'We made it quite clear we didn't want to see you again and that we weren't coming back with you. It's too risky.'

'But you must. Ebony told me about the weapon you're building – and we need it. Ambrose has captured Dublin and he won't stop there. He intends to take over the world and make everyone worship the Deus-Umbra while he steals the power of reincarnation for himself.'

Rufus gasped. 'He's captured the city? What's he playing at? He's jeopardising the future of the Order!'

'That's the idea,' said Icarus.

'His? Or yours? After all, you share the same blood.'

Looking at her uncle, Ebony saw the hurt flicker in his eyes, even though he fought to hide it. She understood her father's caution, but Icarus couldn't help what family he was born into – surely his actions were a better indicator of his worth?

As Icarus turned his face away, Ebony saw the tattoo on his neck stretch and twist. She could tell it was causing him pain; the muscles along his jaw tightened as he fought the urge to cry out.

'We needed *The Book of Learning* to power the weapon,'

said Rufus. 'Without it we have no way to make it work and without it there is nothing we can–'

'Coward,' interrupted Icarus, his voice bitter and cold.

As the two men glared at each other, Ebony studied her mother, who so far had remained silent. Closer up, the flickering flames turned her face ghost-like, her eyes shining unnaturally. Dry patches of skin showed between her fingers and along her jawline, raw and seeping, and black half-moons under her eyes betrayed a severe lack of sleep.

She's sick, thought Ebony. Turning to her father she said, 'But I know you want to help. Otherwise why would you continue to work on the weapon, which is of no use to you here?'

Rufus answered, 'That was your mother's idea. We travelled back to this time out of fear of Ambrose and we knew we could never go back or he would kill us. But it almost destroyed us to leave you behind and your mother couldn't resist occasionally returning to the present to make sure you were OK. Once a year, she risked her life to get a glimpse of you. Then, the last time, she arrived at Oddley Cove just in time to see you on a ship fighting off a dragon and a demon.'

Ebony's stomach flipped; they hadn't really abandoned her after all.

Ivy took up the story. 'Unfortunately, I had no way to get to you or I would have come to help, no matter the consequences. As it was, I waited to make sure you were OK, but I also realised that you hadn't been able to totally defeat the demon and it would undoubtedly return. So we decided to start work on the weapon again, in the hope that this time we could perfect it. And to do that we would have to contact the future – there was no other way for us to get *The Book of Learning*. So we sent the memento mori to where we knew you would get it.'

'And then Icarus arrived and told us that the book had been destroyed,' added Rufus. 'We did research alternative power sources, but to no avail. The truth is, getting the weapon to work was the only way we could help you.'

'If you come back with us, I'll get you the power you need.'

Her parents stared at her. 'How?' said Rufus. 'I've already told you, the weapon is useless without *The Book of Learning*. There is no way to power it.'

'I can go back in time right now and retrieve *The Book of Learning* from the past. Icarus can accompany you to the future and I'll bring it to you there. It'll be quicker that way.'

'Ebony, that's a crazy idea,' said Icarus. 'You've only ever travelled in time once – I can't possibly allow you to attempt such a hazardous journey on your own.'

Rufus shot Icarus an angry look. 'Keep out of this. How do we even know what side you're on?'

'I'm willing to try,' said Ebony, ignoring her father's outburst. 'What have we got to lose?'

'It might be our only chance,' said Ivy.

Rising from his seat and slamming his fist on the table, Icarus glared at Ebony's parents. 'You would put your daughter

– our guardian – at such risk?' he shouted. His eyes swirled and blackened, his shoulders hunching. As he slammed his fist again, a deep, inhuman roar sounded in his throat and a sliver of the black mark poked out from under his jumper. Tendril-like, it slithered its way up his neck and around his throat where it gripped tightly. 'Argh!' cried Icarus. 'Make it stop.'

Ebony reached out to help, but her mother caught her hand and held it fast.

'Stop! You don't know if it will infect you too,' she said.

'I think you have to be marked by Ambrose's device,' Ebony explained, staring into Ivy's red-rimmed eyes. 'I know you're wary of Icarus,' she continued, 'but I can vouch for him. I need all of you to work together so we can sort this out.'

Ebony watched as Icarus gritted his teeth and fought against the pain. Gripping the back of his neck tightly, he closed his eyes and took deep, ragged breaths. After a few moments, his jaw relaxed and his hand dropped to his side. Satisfied the pain had gone and Icarus had regained control, Ebony pressed on. 'We also have another problem. Aunt Ruby's husband is haunting the Razor Rocks where your boat went down.'

Ivy and Rufus looked at each other. 'Connie?'

'Ambrose murdered him when you escaped and although his body was recovered he's still haunting the area.'

'We didn't even know he was hurt,' said Rufus, his face darkening. 'We had no idea.'

'Dead, not hurt,' said Icarus.

'We weren't even in the boat – it was a decoy,' continued Rufus, looking at Ebony. 'Connie was meant to sink the boat with several items on it that would link it to us – including a photograph of you – so even if the wreck was found without our bodies people would assume we had been on board. Then he was to make his way back to land by dinghy and tell everyone he'd seen us head out earlier that day.'

'After meeting his ghost, I visited his soul in the Reflectory. I hoped I'd released him, but Icarus saw him still haunting the area of the wreckage. I think we have to destroy Ambrose or at least bring him to justice, to set him free. You have to help him by helping us. After all, he died assisting you! And besides, even if you can't make the weapon work, we need all the manpower we can muster. Dublin is at war; your family and friends within the Order are fighting for their lives right now – how can you hide here and let them all die?'

Ivy and Rufus exchanged glances. Ivy put her face in her hands as a coughing fit began. Her throat crackled and croaked with each cough. After a moment, the cough subsided and Ivy laid a hand on her husband's arm. 'Ebony's right, we should help.'

'We can't do that without returning to that time,' said Rufus, 'which we are not going to do. If Ebony does get the book, then she needs to bring it here, not to the future.'

Ivy turned to her husband. 'Rufus, you've heard what they said. Ambrose is winning. Even without the weapon maybe we can help the Order. If Ebony is willing to trust Icarus, then so am I – why will you not go back?'

'Because,' cried Rufus, his face crumpling, 'if we do it might kill you.'

35

Ebony looked at her parents in stunned silence. Ivy burst into a hacking cough, her lungs heaving. It looked like she was trying to say something, but the coughing wouldn't stop. As her face turned puce, her eyes watering, Rufus placed his arm around her shoulders, holding her until the fit subsided.

Then he looked straight at Ebony. 'As you can see, your mother is too sick to travel. The energy it takes to make the journey is too great. Such an effort could kill her. I will not take the risk of losing her – I've already lost enough.'

Ebony turned to her mother. 'But whatever's wrong with you could probably be treated if you come with us. You know how much more advanced medicine is in our time. And if Icarus helps you make the journey, I'm sure you'd make it back OK.'

Ivy looked at her husband and Ebony spotted a glimmer of hope. Her mother had come around to the idea – her father was the challenge.

'You have to come back,' said Ebony, resting her hand on her father's arm. 'It's the only way for her to get well. And I'll get you *The Book of Learning* if you do, like I promised.'

'And if you fail?' asked Rufus.

'Then we'll all die anyway,' said Icarus. 'Ebony's on her last life so it will affect nothing in the grand scheme of things. You're making excuses for your own cowardice.'

Rufus rose to his feet and moved around the table until the two men stood eyeball to eyeball. Icarus seemed to grow by inches as he pushed his face close to Rufus, the mark around his throat climbing up around his chin. Staring at it in horror, Rufus gave Icarus a shove, forcing him to stagger backwards.

'Back off, Icarus. That mark means you could be under Ambrose's control. How can I trust you with our lives?'

'You're a fool Rufus. If I was working with Ambrose I would have killed you the moment I saw you.' He reached into a coat pocket and pulled out a gun to prove his point.

'Stop it, both of you!' cried Ebony jumping up.

Breathing heavily, Rufus glared at Icarus. 'She's right. We're being foolish. Let's talk this through.'

Then Ebony cried out as a searing pain shot through her hand. As Icarus and Rufus both turned to look at her, something moved in the corner of the room behind them. A pair of red eyes glowed and Winston squealed as a roar sounded from underneath the sink. As the Shadow Walker lunged from the shadows Ebony moved fast. She grabbed her gun and fired, splattering the creature into gooey pieces. As she did, Icarus lifted his gun and pointed it straight at her. For a split second her heart stopped, but he fired over her shoulder, blasting a Shadow Walker that had appeared behind her in the head. The second creature also exploded.

As the noise of Icarus's shot died away Ebony heard her father gasp, 'Ivy!'

A third creature had appeared behind Ivy. She stood facing it, unarmed. Its eyes gleamed as it lifted its arm to strike. As Ivy cried out, Ebony took aim but hesitated, afraid of hitting her mother. Then, a third shot rang out and the Shadow Walker exploded. Icarus stepped forward, gun in hand. The mark had now claimed his cheek, and his eyes were dark, but Ebony could see he was fighting the effects.

'As you can see, it's no longer safe here either,' he said. 'We must leave. And quickly.'

Rufus looked like he was about to argue but Ivy placed a hand on his arm. 'Rufus, please. He's right. We can't hide here any longer. We must return with Icarus and do what we can to help. I know you're worried about me, but I want to take the risk and if you don't agree to it, I'll go anyway. I won't let our daughter face this alone any longer.'

Rufus sighed. 'I'll get the weapon, then we'll go. It's safe upstairs, let me go and fetch it.'

As he left the room, Ebony decided to ask another question that was nagging at her. Pulling the photograph out of her pocket, she laid it flat on the table. In the weakened candlelight, it was difficult to see Ivy at all in the image. 'Do you know why you're fading in this picture?' she asked her mother.

But it was Icarus who spoke up. 'That photo shows the connection between the two eras. Her image is fading because of her ill health. If she doesn't return soon, she'll never be able to. Time is of the essence.'

Rufus returned a moment later with a large gun in his arms. Gleaming and sleek, the D-STRUCTOR looked out of place in the gloomy surroundings. Curious, Ebony reached out and ran her finger along the weapon; it was cold and smooth. It didn't look particularly powerful, but she had to hope.

Watching Ebony, Ivy smiled. 'We're ready – but what do we do now?' Her wheezing chest and the bags under her eyes betrayed her exhaustion.

'Don't worry, Ivy. I'll do all the hard work. You'll just have to take my hand and I'll get you back,' said Icarus. A look of relief passed over her face.

'How do we know you won't take us straight to Ambrose?' said Rufus, his eyes on the writhing tattoo. 'How do we know it's not a trick? We've been here years without any trouble from the Shadow Walkers and then you come along and …'

Icarus glared at Rufus. His eyes glowed red for an instant, then returned to normal, only dull and lacklustre. Ebony put her hand on his shoulder in support but he shook it off.

'I understand,' he said through gritted teeth, 'your misgivings. They match my own. I can promise you that I'm not tricking you. I only want to help. I just saved your wife's life. But this thing,' he pulled at the skin on his neck, as though trying to wrench it off, 'this I cannot control. We have to go now, before it takes over completely. Or those Shadow Walkers re-form.'

'And Ebony?' asked Rufus, fear showing in his eyes.

'I'll get you the book and meet you back in Mercury Lane in my time,' she replied.

Icarus glared at her. 'You're determined to do this, aren't you? No matter the risk.'

'Yes. It's the only chance we have of getting the weapon to work. Without it we can't win. There's no other way.'

'But if you do this, don't you risk changing history?' asked Rufus.

'No – once we're successful, I'll return it to the exact spot I took it from, a moment later, so nothing will change.'

'It sounds to me like Ebony knows what she's doing,' said Ivy. 'Let's see her off safely and then go.'

'There's one more thing,' said Icarus to Ebony. 'When I've delivered your parents back to our time, I'm going to disappear. I can feel the power of this mark growing and if it allows Ambrose to gain full control of me I'm a danger to the Order.'

'With us, you'll stay stronger,' protested Ebony. 'We'll help you fight it.'

'I don't want to risk it. It's getting close to my birth moon and so the danger could be greater. We do this on my terms or not at all.'

Knowing better than to argue further – she needed him

to return her parents and they couldn't fail having come this far – Ebony agreed.

'Now, what time do you want to return to?' asked Icarus. 'In case I need to find you.'

Ignoring the flash of red in his eyes, the twitch in his forehead as the mark flowered onto his temple, Ebony took a deep breath. Noticing one of the Shadow Walkers had already begun to re-form, she decided quickly.

'The beginning,' she said. 'When *The Book of Learning* was first forged. Where it all began.'

'Are you sure?' asked Icarus, his face creasing. 'You don't have an object from then – it will take a lot of strength to get back that far.'

Ebony nodded. It was when the book would be at its most powerful. 'I'm going back to the year 856.'

As they prepared to leave, Ebony hugged her parents, trying to keep her fears from showing on her face. What if she failed to retrieve *The Book of Learning*? Or the weapon didn't help even if she did succeed? What if her mother didn't make it or Icarus couldn't fight Ambrose's influence long enough to get them back safely? On her shoulder, Winston shifted his weight, clinging tightly to her curls. She stroked his head, his warm fur giving her courage. Rufus raised an eyebrow at Winston.

'He's coming with me,' said Ebony, shifting him to her pocket where it was safer. 'I want him by my side.'

Ebony stared hard at the deepest shadows and imagined merging with them. Icarus had already passed through, and Ebony breathed slowly, trying to keep calm and minimise distractions. As she glanced up at her parents, her mum's eyes filled with tears and Rufus waved, his jaw clenched. Steadying her breath and concentrating on her task, Ebony held tight to the straps of her rucksack and passed through into the world of grey smudges and lines. Icarus was already preparing for her departure.

'Please, be careful, Uncle,' said Ebony.

He smiled, his eyes wrinkling slightly, and nodded. Just as quickly, the smile disappeared and the sullen look returned. The arrow scored and Roman numerals added – DCCCLVI – Icarus helped Ebony rip up the ground and give it a strong shake. As the ripples began, Ebony watched, securing an image of what her first past self had looked like when *The Book of Learning* had shown her to Ebony before – her own face but wearing a white tunic, a gold band of ivy on her head – then leapt onto the third ripple. As she did so she turned, shouting, 'Take care of my parents and yourself,' but Icarus was already gone.

Closing her eyes, Ebony hoped that everything would be fine. Not wanting to end up in the wrong place or time, she focused her mind on her past self. Pushing into a seated position, concentrating like never before, she rode the shadows back through time. The journey was smooth but lengthy; her bones and flesh felt like they were trying to burst from her skin and her head felt like it was being pummelled with rocks on the inside. She tried not to let her worries in, but the longer she travelled, the harder it became. *It's never going to end*, thought Ebony, *I'm not strong enough.*

Holding the image of her past self fast in her mind, imagining the texture of the white robe, the weight of the gold band in her hair, Ebony squeezed her eyes as tightly as she could, trying to ignore the thudding in her brain. Soon, she was flying through the air. Landing with a thud, on her feet this time, her legs turned to jelly but she managed to stay upright. Although she was a little disoriented, the headache quickly ebbed, her bones and flesh settling back comfortably inside her body.

It was daytime. Judging by the sun, it was late afternoon. Around her, the land was wild: hills covered in trees, dusty paths leading through waist-length undergrowth. Bird song rang out and a smell of burning timber filled the air. Looking around for clues as to where they were, Ebony spotted a wisp of smoke rising up from behind a hill.

'Smoke means people, so that's where we'll go,' she said.

With Winston on her shoulder, her rucksack on her back and her gun in her pocket, Ebony began the steep climb.

By the time she made it over the top of the hill, it was almost dark. Ebony stumbled her way along the rocky path until she could see down into a small, early medieval settlement in a valley below with lots of wooden huts and a larger building that looked like a hall. It was deathly quiet, and from inside the huts, fires could be seen flickering as people prepared for bed. An outdoor fire burned in the dirt, not far from the hall. It provided enough light for Ebony to see the settlement clearly.

'What should we do now, Winston?'

Winston blinked and shrugged his shoulders, looking

towards the village. Suddenly, his ears flattened and his tail waved angrily. Ebony followed his gaze.

Ambrose had stepped into the light from the fire, flanked by armed men. They gathered around the blaze, warming their hands with the flames, in heated discussion. Had he followed her from the future and somehow found the settlement first? Or was this a past incarnation? There was only one way to find out.

Clambering towards a huge boulder halfway down the hill, Ebony made a steady and quiet descent, careful not to disturb any of the small stones. Her legs wobbled as she got closer to the men and her nerves began to fray. She paused as the door to the hall opened and a girl with black curls and a gold crown of ivy appeared.

'That's the first ever me!' whispered Ebony to Winston. 'She'll know where to find the book.'

As the girl crossed towards the fire, Ebony's heart thumped against her rib cage. But Ambrose welcomed her with a warm hug and Ebony relaxed.

'This isn't our Ambrose. I think we should get closer, but we should try to avoid detection. They'll never have seen clothes like these before and I don't know what sort of reception we'd get.'

On her shoulder, Winston squirmed. He tugged on her hair, but Ebony ignored his protest and continued to climb down. The path was uneven, so it wasn't easy and Winston clung on as Ebony crept along. Underfoot, a flurry of rocks dislodged and bounced down the hillside. Ebony shrank down, holding her breath. Her past self looked up but the men continued their conversation undisturbed. Moving Winston to her pocket, Ebony kept going. Soon the huts were within reach and she crouched down, hoping the darkness would conceal her. She watched as Ambrose and his men parted ways, the armed guards returning to the hall and Ambrose heading to one of the wooden huts. The girl followed Ambrose, trailing behind.

Ebony stayed completely still, but as the girl reached the hut, she turned towards Ebony, smiled and beckoned, before hurrying inside.

'What do you think, Winston?' whispered Ebony. 'Is it safe?'

When he gave a reassuring squeak, she crept across the open ground, unnoticed, and paused outside the hut. Hearing voices inside, she listened.

'Have you thought about my proposal?' asked Ambrose. 'You know we are in a time of terrible strife. Some of our people are trying to access the sky world without its permission. Two of the guardians have already been killed – we must end this war between our kind and unite our people. You are the person to lead us.'

'The sky world chooses its leaders,' replied her past self. 'I am thankful for your guidance but I believe it will protect the rest of us.'

The legends she'd learned from *The Book of Learning*

clicking into place, Ebony realised she had returned to the time before their mutual soul was bestowed the honour and responsibility of being sole guardian, when there had been nine guardians who could enter the Reflectory.

'Spoken like the true and wise girl you are,' replied Ambrose. 'Your parents would be very proud of you.'

'Thank you. I owe it all to you. And now, I think it is time.'

The voices stopped and the door was wrenched open, making Ebony jump. Face to face with her past self, Ebony waited to see what would happen next, poised to run just in case. When the girl smiled warmly, Ebony relaxed.

'Welcome. We have been expecting you,' said her past self. '*The Book of Learning* told me you were coming.'

As Ebony stepped inside, the door closed behind her. Winston stayed hidden in her pocket, completely still.

'So it is true: our selves really can contact us from the future,' said Ambrose, looking her up and down, his eyes taking in her rucksack before settling on her face. '*The Book of Learning* foretold it, but I must admit, I doubted it would really happen.'

Instinctively, Ebony held onto her rucksack straps. Inspecting Ambrose closely, she saw that he had the same grey hair, only it flowed loosely, instead of being slicked back in a V. He wore a white robe and furs around his shoulders. As he smiled in greeting, Ebony relaxed; this definitely wasn't Ambrose from her own time – but could she trust him? Uncertain what else to do, she nodded, one eye on the girl.

Stepping forward, her past self took hold of Ebony's hands. 'Don't worry,' she said. 'We will not hurt you. This is Ambrose. I have been in his care since my parents died. He is helping me reunite our people. I believe that without him we'll always be at war and the Reflectory will be infiltrated.'

'If you rely on him, the war will never end,' said Ebony.

'What a strange thing to say,' said Ambrose, looking shocked and hurt. 'I only have the Order's best interests at heart. And with my adopted daughter's help, I intend to restore peace among our kind.'

Moving to his side, the past Ebony Smart took hold of both of his hands and looked him in the eye. 'Forgive her, Ambrose. She does not know our ways and we do not know what terrible sufferings she has endured. You always tell me to be honourable and kind.'

Ambrose smiled at her affectionately. 'Of course. You are right.' Turning to Ebony, he said, 'We know why you have come. You want the book – am I right?'

'Yes. May I have it?'

'Of course,' replied Ambrose. 'But first we should eat and let you rest.'

A squeak sounded from Ebony's pocket and Winston popped his head out. Ambrose chuckled and reached forward to give Winston a stroke. Instinctively, Winston cowered, but Ambrose was gentle. Looking around, he grabbed a loaf of nearby bread, tore off a small piece and handed it to Winston. The rat took it in his jaws and dropped back into Ebony's pocket. She could feel him jiggling as he ate.

'Come,' Ambrose said, gesturing to the table of food, 'you must be weary.'

But Ebony shook her head. 'I must hurry. Terrible things are happening in the future. I have to get home as quickly as I can.'

'Then let me lead the way,' said her past self.

Ambrose motioned for Ebony to follow her. 'After you.'

As they stepped out into the night, relief washed over Ebony. She was going to get the book and put things right.

Inside the hall, fiery beacons flickered around the sides, creating a warm glow. Ebony followed her past self along a narrow aisle, bench seating on either side like in a church, towards a silver chest sitting on a raised plinth beside an armed guard. The chest was covered in engravings. Ebony's heart skipped: they were identical to the markings on *The Book of Learning*.

The guard straightened as the two girls approached. Taking a key from a pouch hung around her waist, the original Ebony Smart motioned for the guard to leave. When he had gone, she unlocked the chest and opened the lid. The sides fell open, revealing *The Book of Learning* on a plump purple cushion. Seeing the ornate silver casing, Ebony felt tears well in her eyes. She stepped forward, hand outstretched, but her past self moved in front of her.

'The book told me to warn you that you must return it to this time when you are finished. Do you swear to do so?'

'I swear,' said Ebony.

'Then it is yours,' replied the girl and she lifted it and handed it over.

The casing felt cool and deliciously familiar in Ebony's hand.

'Go,' said the girl. 'Complete your mission and return the book. The Order's destiny is in your hands.'

Ambrose clapped his hands and two guards appeared. Ebony watched warily, but her worries were soon put to rest as he spoke.

'Escort this girl to wherever she needs to go and then report back to me.'

'Thank you,' said Ebony, backing away.

'Stay safe,' warned her past self.

Heeding her words, Ebony headed straight for the hill, flanked by her protectors. Her heart beat wildly, partly with the effort of walking so fast, but also with pride. With the book in her possession, she was certain they would be able to defeat their enemies and restore peace once again.

When they reached the outskirts, the guards paused and looked back towards the village.

'Is everything OK?' asked Ebony, following their gaze.

While she was distracted, one of them snatched the book from her grasp. Startled, she opened her mouth to call for help, but the other guard shoved a piece of cloth in her mouth, gagging her, then yanked her arms behind her back. He tugged off her rucksack and tied her wrists with rope. The guards dragged Ebony towards a small, dimly lit hut at the edge of the village. They chuckled as they shoved her into a corner and bound her ankles.

Struggling to break free, Ebony wondered how had she been so foolish as to let herself be duped? Her joy at seeing the book again had clouded her instincts and now she risked failing everyone. Without the book, her parents wouldn't be able to power the weapon and Ambrose would win. She looked around her, seeking a way to escape.

'There's no way out,' said Ambrose, suddenly appearing in the doorway.

He nodded at the guards and they bowed, handed the book and rucksack to him and left. Ebony heard them shuffling, standing guard outside the door. Now they were alone, Ambrose's demeanour changed. His eyes narrowed and his expression soured as he set the book on the table and began rummaging through her bag.

'It is time to talk on my terms, Ebony Smart from the future.' Ambrose came forward and crouched in front of her. 'If you scream the guards will kill anyone who comes to help.'

He pulled the gag from her mouth, then held up her bronze rose and mahogany medal. 'I recognise this rose as a copy of the one our guardians use to get into the Reflectory, but I don't know how they do it and you're going to tell me.'

Ebony shook her head. 'Never.'

'Oh, really? Let me see if I can persuade you.'

Laying the objects next to *The Book of Learning* and lunging forward, Ambrose grabbed at Ebony's trouser pocket. Realising he was going for Winston, she squirmed, trying to protect her friend. But tied up as she was, her efforts were useless. In seconds, Ambrose had Winston by the scruff of his neck, dangling in the air. His teeth snapping, Winston tried to bite his captor, but he couldn't reach. Kicking out her legs, Ebony caught Ambrose on the ankle. He gasped and, with his free hand, slapped her across the face.

'One more stunt like that and your rat is wolf bait,' he threatened.

Lifting Winston higher, Ambrose jabbed a finger into his stomach. The rat squealed and Ebony fought to break free, even though she knew the bindings held her fast.

'Tell me what I want to know. The Order does not know how to use the power it has. But I have great plans. The power should be mine. This is my destiny – I have known this since I was a small boy – and you have no right to stand in my way.'

'No! I know you from the future. Right now, you still have seven guardians, but soon there will be only one – and as the future holder of that responsibility, I refuse to give you any information that will help you.'

'And yet, without realising it, you already have!'

Seeing Ebony's confused look, Ambrose laughed and continued, 'I did not know if I was on the right path, but it seems that my plan will work after all. I've invested a lot of time in gaining your predecessor's trust, becoming like a father to her, all the while stirring up unrest and encouraging the ordinary people of this world to despise the Order and their power. I had hoped that, with all the other guardians dead in this lifetime, the sky world would make her the one true guardian. Then, because she trusts me above all others, she will reveal her secrets to me. However, since you are here, getting you to talk will be quicker. You might even have saved her life. Perhaps a little force will offer some encouragement?'

Shaking Winston until his eyes rolled and teeth rattled, Ambrose looked directly at Ebony. 'You will tell me.'

'Never,' she said again, her heart pounding in her chest.

'Have it your way,' said Ambrose, stuffing the gag back in her mouth and drawing a knife from his tunic. 'Perhaps you'll change your mind when I take one of your friend's limbs – how long do you think a rat can survive with three legs?'

Ebony struggled and cried out, her scream muffled. At the same time, grunts and groans sounded outside. The door burst open as Ambrose raised the knife, ready to strike, and Ebony's past self rushed in, flanked by four men.

'What is the meaning of this, my dear?' asked Ambrose, turning. Outside, his guards were on the ground, crumpled up in pain.

'That is what I have come to ask you. I saw you send off my future self, and I watched her go, wishing her well. Imagine my surprise when I saw your guards turn on her and drag her to this hut. Why is she your prisoner?'

'She is not what she seems. I believe she has come from the future to inflict harm. She has no intention of leaving, but instead will stay to spread lies and fear among us – you heard what she said earlier about me being the cause of war.'

Ebony struggled against the bindings, burning her wrists and ankles.

'That is not what the book showed me,' replied the girl. 'I believe you are acting in good faith, but you have made a mistake. If she was a threat, the book would never have told me to help her. It is wrong to detain her.'

'But I only have your best interests at heart! We must keep this girl prisoner and find out her plans so we can protect ourselves if more people from the future come.'

'I do not want to argue with you,' replied the girl. 'But I must do as the book decreed. Set her free.'

Two of her men stepped forward. One retrieved the knife from Ambrose, while the other took Winston and set him on the floor. Then, with a nod from their leader, they each grabbed one of Ambrose's arms – taken by surprise, he didn't put up a struggle. Meanwhile, one of the remaining men untied Ebony and removed her gag, while the other kept an eye on Ambrose's two guards outside. As soon as Ebony was free, she snatched up Winston and held him close, one eye on Ambrose and the other on *The Book of Learning*. Ambrose struggled against his captors but together the men were too strong. Ambrose's shoulders slumped, as though defeated, but Ebony could almost see his mind racing – was he going to show his true colours or continue the deceit?

As the men escorted him to the door, he pleaded. 'You're making a terrible mistake. I am only trying to protect you. You cannot trust her.'

'I am sorry,' said the girl. 'Please forgive me.'

Waiting until Ambrose and his guards had been taken away, she reached out to Winston, an entranced look on her face.

'Look after him – he is the key to a better future.' She pointed to the rose and medal. 'Are these yours?' When Ebony nodded, she carefully repacked the rucksack and handed it over, followed by *The Book of Learning*, then backed away. 'Now, go. Don't worry, you will be safe. I will hold Ambrose until first light.'

'Will you be OK?'

'Ambrose will forgive me. He understands the importance of maintaining peace within the Order.'

As Ebony took the book, her mind raced – how much could she tell her past self without changing history?

'I have to tell you something,' she started.

But the girl held up her hand and shook her head. 'You must tell me nothing – giving me information to change my own future could cause untold harm. Allow my destiny to find me. Now, go – complete your own.'

Moving to the doorway, Ebony checked outside. The coast was clear. The night was still dark but the outdoor fire gave her enough light to find her way. Mustering her courage, she took off at a sprint, running as fast as she could towards the shadows, not daring to look back. Reaching the edge of the village, Ebony lifted Winston onto her shoulder and took out *The Book of Learning*.

'I can't believe we got it,' she said. 'Now, let's go home.'

But a shimmer of glitter lifted from the book's cool, silver casing.

'Winston, look. It wants to tell me something.'

There was no sign of anyone following, so she wasted no time in opening it. Using the special fingerprint combination, the book sprang open. The pages were completely blank. Realising that by going back in time it was like opening a new book, she stroked the inside cover and waited. Moments later, letters appeared.

The Order of Nine Lives bids you welcome. You may enter.

On the page to the right, a drawing of a closed eye appeared, like the first time, along with a list of dates. The book juddered and the pages fluttered as hundreds of voices called her name.

Ebony. Ebony.

There were cries and screams also, wailing and keening as a squall of wind whipped around her. Remembering this from the first time she had opened the book, Ebony took a deep breath and waited for it to settle on two blank pages.

'Show me where Ambrose and Zach are hiding,' cried Ebony. 'I need your help.'

The wind stopped, and the voices died away as the book settled.

Ebony reached out. As her hand connected with the book, she was transported to a dark room in front of a shrine she recognised – the one she had seen Zach and Ambrose use to contact the Deus-Umbra. Turning, she came face to face with the demon. It looked angry, its wings coiled around its body. It looked Ebony in the eye and roared, forcing her to step back.

'I told you,' said a voice Ebony recognised – Ambrose. But it sounded like it was coming from where she was standing. She quickly realised what was happening. *The Book of Learning* was allowing her to see through Ambrose's eyes. 'I will release you when we get what we need: Ebony and the rat.'

Wondering what Winston had to do with it, she waited, hoping for more answers. The Deus-Umbra snapped its jaws and tried to lurch forward, but Ambrose simply tutted and looked down. In his hand was the small control she had seen in her earlier vision. When he pressed the button, it clicked. The demon roared and Ambrose chuckled, looking at the demon's leg. Something glowed around its ankle – the thin, silver chain – and the creature began to jerk and shudder, screaming in pain. Ambrose clicked the control again and the Deus-Umbra stopped wailing.

Ambrose moved around the demon and Ebony saw a set of glass lift doors that seemed very out of place in the dark, oppressive room. He pressed the button and, as the doors slid open, stepped inside. Footsteps followed him; Ebony guessed they belonged to Zach Stone. As the glass doors closed, Ebony saw the reflection in them and gasped.

Ambrose's cold eyes were staring back and beside him stood Zach.

There was a low hum, like an army of insects, as the lift rose. Through the glass she could just make out a wall of earth and writhing bugs. Like her Hideout, they were underground. Beside her, Zach's reflection grimaced in disgust. An involuntary shiver ran through her. Soon a finger of light poked in and, looking up, she saw a sliver of sky above.

Where are you? she wondered, willing the book to let her remain a little longer.

As though hearing her, Ambrose frowned. He looked at Zach, then back to his reflection. Trying to keep her thoughts quiet, Ebony waited, watching carefully. As the lift finally came eye-level with the light, Ebony watched a face appear. It was a small, sharp-toothed, grinning cat, carved from wood and painted bright orange, with green around its wide, staring eyes. As the lift rose higher, a larger version of the creature appeared carved above it and, on top, a majestic-looking eagle with a hooked yellow beak and wings edged with giant snakes. It was a totem pole. It looked Aztec, but that didn't make any sense. Behind it was red dirt backed by shrubs. Ebony tried to figure out where they were.

As the lift stopped, the colours of the totem pole glowed brightly and an array of sounds filtered in. Ebony listened intently. She could hear water splashing, a strange barking and a distant roar. None of it made any sense. Suddenly, a flock of flamingos strode into view, their pink legs bent backwards and their round eyes unblinking.

I know where they are! thought Ebony.

Instantly, Ambrose's voice sounded in her head. 'GET OUT!' it yelled.

Expelled from Ambrose's brain, Ebony found herself panting on the ground. The book was covered in dust, the image of the totem pole frozen on its pages.

'Did you see?' asked Ebony.

Winston shook his head.

'They're in the zoo,' said Ebony, snatching up the book and clambering to her feet. 'That's where they're hiding the Deus-Umbra. We'd better get home.'

Leaping into Ebony's trouser pocket, Winston's body trembled as she tucked the book into her other side pocket. Breathing deeply, she merged with the shadows. Scoring the earth and date, she tugged at the earth and, when the ripples showed, started her journey forward in time. However, they had only been riding for seconds when a screech sounded from above. Looking up, afraid that it might be the Deus-Umbra, Ebony's stomach relaxed as she saw a King Vulture swooping overhead, one set of claws bunched like a fist. As the giant bird released its claws, a piece of paper fluttered down and Ebony snatched it out of the air.

GO WITH THE KING VULTURE the message read in big capital letters, with Aunt Ruby's signature below.

As the vulture swooped down towards her, Ebony raised one arm and grabbed hold of the thick, ribbed claws, happy to let the messenger take her wherever she needed to be.

Moments later Ebony landed on solid ground. The sky was grey, choked with dust, forcing her to shield her eyes while they adjusted. Around her, the streets were eerily silent. There was no sign of the special forces that the newspaper report had mentioned. Buses and cars littered the roads, abandoned, upturned and burning. Shop fronts were smashed, their contents spilling onto the pavement. A girl snuck by, her face covered with a scarf, and disappeared through one of the broken windows. A group of rainbow lorikeets chattered on the surviving windowsills of the tallest buildings, alongside pigeons and sparrows, a strange shot of colour and noise in the gloom. It took Ebony a moment to recognise her surroundings. Squinting through the dust, she could hardly believe it was Dublin.

She realised she was on Burgh Quay, at one end of O'Connell Bridge. The bridge's ornate streetlights lay smashed and battered on the ground and its balustrades were crumbling. Ebony checked the Spire in the distance. She could see it had already fallen, cutting through the GPO – on the other side of the bridge, under the O'Connell monument, the construction of a stage had already begun. But it was not yet complete, so there was still time to stop what she had seen in the vision of the future from happening.

Scanning the area once more, Ebony tightened her rucksack straps and tried to figure out where she should go. Heading to the zoo alone would be a mistake. She had expected Aunt Ruby to be waiting but there was no sign of her and most ordinary people were obviously obeying the curfew, scared for their lives.

'But where's the Order?' she said aloud.

As her voice echoed in the air, pain shot through her head and her brain throbbed. It pulsed violently as though about to explode. As she felt cold fingers probing, she realised Zach was trying to read her mind. *Hello, Ebony*, echoed his voice in her head. Balling her fists, she fought his intrusion. But she could feel him inside her, like a parasite, sucking at her thoughts. Gun ready, Ebony looked left and right – he usually read her mind when he was nearby. *You might as well give up – you know we'll find you.* Realising he was trying to pinpoint her exact location, she squeezed her eyes shut and fought back. Unexpectedly, she saw a flash of his thoughts – dark and murderous – and a glimpse of the world through his eyes. Armed Shadow Walkers stood on either side of him.

Look around so I can see where you are, willed Ebony. As though sensing the intrusion, Zach left her mind and the pain ended. A hand on her shoulder made Ebony spin round, gun lifted. It was Aunt Ruby.

'Ebony, thank goodness. You've been gone for days – we were beginning to lose hope!'

'I'm fine.' She lowered her gun. 'I got *The Book of Learning* from the past. Did my parents return safely?'

'Yes. Icarus brought them back. But things have reached crisis point. We have to act before Ambrose takes complete control,' said Aunt Ruby, leading Ebony across the road. 'Mercury Lane was attacked and so was HQ. Seamus saw the battle coming so we went underground. That's why I sent the King Vulture to find you and bring you here, instead of Mercury Lane.'

'Seamus is better?'

Aunt Ruby nodded. 'The mask worked. You saved him. And what's more, since his illness his skills are much improved – his connection to the demon seems to have given him extra powers.'

Stopping at a coffee shop with boarded-up windows, Aunt Ruby checked no one was watching, opened the door and guided Ebony inside. Without windows, it was dark and cool. Closing the door and sparking up her lighter, Aunt Ruby led the way down two flights of stairs, filling Ebony in as their feet clattered on the tiled floor.

'We've been working on the weapon, but we need a plan. Up until now the Order has managed to keep Ambrose distracted and most of the ordinary citizens of Dublin safe. But that can't last: we're losing people to wounds and capture. We must locate our enemies and attack, but we have to be careful; without enough manpower, we only have stealth and wit to rely on.'

'Zach tried to read my mind and I fought back. I could tell he's in the city,' said Ebony, 'but I couldn't see his exact location. And Ambrose is hiding the Deus-Umbra in the zoo. They've been under our noses all along.'

'That explains the exotic animals running around the place,' replied her aunt. 'But if Zach is so near, we must be extremely careful.'

Winston popped his head out of Ebony's pocket and squeaked, and Aunt Ruby looked relieved to see him. Reaching a door at the bottom of the stairs, Ruby gave a special knock. Several clunks sounded before the door opened, bright light gushing out. Uncle Cornelius stepped aside, letting Ebony pass. Inside, her parents and Mulligan were among those waiting. Relieved to see her mother had survived the journey, Ebony rushed over and gave her a hug.

Pulling out *The Book of Learning*, she held it high for everyone to see. It glinted under the strip lights as everyone gasped. Next to where Ebony was standing, the gun was laid out on a large table in the centre of the room, hooked up to a machine the size of a cereal box and a monitor. Around the walls were boxes of coffee filters, takeaway cups and plastic spoons stacked floor to ceiling. In one corner, tucked between two towers of boxes, Chiyoko was busy at a computer screen. Seeing Ebony, she smiled broadly. Ebony smiled back, then looked around the room, frowning.

'I know it looks shabby, but that was the plan,' explained Rufus. 'We needed somewhere they'd never think of looking for us.'

'Let's get to work. Do you want the book open or closed?' asked Ebony.

Before she could even try the fingerprint combination, Rufus took the book, handling it like a delicate egg, and positioned it in a dock on the machine. Flicking a switch, everyone watched and waited.

'Let's hope this works,' he said. 'Your aunt has helped us with some modifications that should make it charge more quickly and efficiently. She has also helped us incorporate some technology that has been developed since we left, so we no longer need any other source than *The Book of Learning* to fully charge the weapon. It's amazing how much things have changed in such a short time.'

Aunt Ruby was already checking the monitor and Ebony watched as *The Book of Learning* trembled. It glowed in its dock, sending a blue fizz of sparks along the wires. The gun lit up like a flare, rumbling thunderously. On a small LED screen on one side of the weapon, an icon of an empty battery started to fill.

'It's working,' said Ivy, her voice croaking.

The pain in her hand suddenly flaring, Ebony sensed Shadow Walkers nearby. She needed to get up to speed as quickly as she could.

'How is Icarus?' asked Ebony.

Aunt Ruby stopped what she was doing and the room fell silent. 'He was in incredible pain and finding it hard to keep his emotions in check. Worried he'd lose control and hurt one of us, he left as soon as he got back. We haven't seen him since. But someone has been eagerly awaiting your return.'

Aunt Ruby pointed to a door leading to an adjoining room that Ebony hadn't noticed. As Ivy opened it, Ebony rushed inside to find Drinkwater, Miss Malone, and the rest of the O'Haras busy at work.

'Seamus! You're better!' cried Ebony.

Mrs O'Hara and Seamus were seated in front of a huge white screen, gathering puppets, their masks at their feet.

'Thanks to you,' said Seamus, his skin glowing with health. 'I remember everything about when I was possessed. I could hear you but I couldn't stop it. But Ambrose made a serious mistake. When he forced the Deus-Umbra to take possession of my body, it worked both ways – I could feel the demon, sense its thoughts. And it let me learn a bit about Ambrose's plans. That's how we knew in advance about the attacks on Mercury Lane and headquarters. I assume your aunt has already told you about them?'

When Ebony nodded, he continued, 'It meant we were able to evacuate before they arrived so most of the Order is still safe. I could also sense the demon's weakness – it still hasn't regained its full strength since our last battle, but with Ambrose's help, it is growing stronger. Part of me can still sense it. And since I got the mask back and my soul returned to my body, my Shadow Custodian powers have increased – it must be the demon's influence. I'm ready to fight.'

A blast of light and heat from the other room silenced everyone and they crowded through the doorway to see what had happened. As the heat faded, Ebony looked at the gun on the table and saw that the little battery was already full. The weapon was charged to maximum capacity.

'Is it ready?' asked Mr O'Hara.

'It is,' replied Rufus, lifting the gun, a determined look on his face. 'But from our previous tests we know that we only have five shots before it will need charging again. And we can't be sure how much damage it will actually do to a fully fledged demon.'

'No matter, it's our best hope. It's time to fight,' said O'Hara. 'The rest of the Order is stationed in groups around the city – after the attack on HQ, we thought it would be best to split up but stay on high alert.' He lifted his mobile. 'They're all on standby, awaiting our command. We just need a plan.'

'Ebony has located Ambrose; he is in the zoo with the Deus-Umbra,' said Aunt Ruby. 'And Zach's in the city some-where, although the streets outside seem quiet.'

'Then our focus,' said Mr O'Hara, 'must be to get to the zoo, take out the demon and stop Ambrose, using whatever means necessary. As Seamus told you, the demon's still in a weakened state, so this is our best chance to take it down permanently. If we're going to do this, we need to do it now.'

A murmur of agreement spread around the room.

O'Hara continued, 'I propose that we use our people to create a distraction and draw the Shadow Walkers away from the zoo so Ambrose will be left with less protection. That's when we seize our chance.'

'What about Zach?' asked Ebony. 'It's quiet but, knowing him, he's probably somewhere nearby.'

'Does he have an army with him?'

Ebony shook her head. 'From what I could see, just a few Shadow Walkers.'

'Then we continue with our plan.'

'The quays are the quickest route to the zoo from here,' said Aunt Ruby.

Mr O'Hara nodded. 'Agreed. We'll cross O'Connell Bridge and head straight for the zoo. We'll travel on foot; that will give our people enough time to start drawing the Shadow Walkers away. Drinkwater, Malone: it's up to you to monitor this area.' He circled the bridge area with one finger. 'You will have one group with you – Drinkwater, call the group in St Stephen's Green and tell them to leave now and meet us here. Your aim is to help us get safely away and then make sure we're not followed by Zach and his Shadow Walkers. Stay in contact with the rest of the Order. My wife and Seamus will assist you from here.'

'Yes, sir,' said Drinkwater and Malone in unison.

'Ebony, Ruby, Mulligan, Uncle Cornelius and Rufus: our focus is reaching the zoo to take Ambrose by surprise. Rufus, you'll take the D-STRUCTOR.'

As Rufus unhooked the charged gun, Mrs O'Hara and Seamus returned to the other room and positioned themselves in front of their screen, wearing their masks.

'What about us?' asked Ivy, Chiyoko by her side.

'Ivy, you're too sick, and Chiyoko, we need you to hack into the city's CCTV so you can help your mother and Seamus direct their help where it is needed. You both stay here.'

As though backing up his words, Ivy was racked with a fit of coughing, bending over in pain. When it subsided, Ebony saw the disappointment on her mother's face, but she was far too sick to fight.

'Let's do this,' said Ebony. 'Let's end this once and for all.'

The room became a flurry of activity as Drinkwater, Mr O'Hara, Miss Malone and Aunt Ruby contacted the rest of the Order to convey the overall plan. Once everything had been explained, Mr O'Hara clapped his hands to get everyone's attention and announced, 'We're all set. Everyone know what they're doing?' A murmur of agreement rumbled around the room. 'Then let's take half an hour to prepare. That will allow the others to start drawing the Shadow Walkers away.'

As the people in the room began to chatter in groups, Ebony took the opportunity to speak to her mother. 'You'll be useful here.'

'I came back to fight. To put things right, after all this time. With the Order, with you.'

'You've done what you can by completing the weapon.

When we win this battle,' said Ebony, 'there'll be plenty of time for everything else.'

Her mum shrugged and, not knowing what else to say – they didn't want to admit that if things didn't go according to plan, they might never see each other again – they sat together and chatted about more normal times, like Ebony's life in Oddley Cove, her move to Dublin and her best friend, Winston. It felt strange, yet good.

After half an hour had passed, Mr O'Hara gathered everyone round. 'It's time. Get your weapons.'

Chiyoko returned to her computer as everyone who was going armed themselves. Ebony pulled *The Book of Learning* from its dock and put it in her pocket. Mulligan and Uncle Cornelius headed up the stairs, their muscles bulging and sharp claws out. Aunt Ruby was close behind. Gun ready, Winston in her pocket, Ebony followed. Under her breath she muttered, 'Ambrose, Zach – we're ready for you.'

As she stepped outside, Ebony searched the horizon. The group from St Stephen's Green were waiting, weapons ready, but all was still quiet. Beside her, Mr O'Hara surveyed the locality. Not even a breath of wind whispered along the Liffey.

'I don't like it,' Ebony whispered to her aunt as a twinge of pain shot through her hand.

'Neither do I,' replied Aunt Ruby, 'but we need to stick to the plan.'

The rest of their group crept out onto the street and, with the wildcats and Mr O'Hara leading, they headed across the bridge, weapons ready. The silence unnerving, Ebony stayed close to her aunt. As they neared the half-built stage, a surge of pain attacked Ebony's hand and she doubled over. Everyone paused.

'Shadow Walkers?' asked Aunt Ruby.

Ebony nodded, teeth gritted. She couldn't let the pain beat her. As another shot of pain ran through her hand, Ebony cried out. The others surrounded her with guns poised, waiting for their guardian to recover. At the same time, a loud and familiar crack of a whip sounded from O'Connell Street. Looking up, Ebony saw Zach and his Shadow Walkers emerge from a street close to the GPO. She forced herself upright and glared in his direction. As Zach's eyes connected with Ebony's, she saw them light up with triumph and a lump formed in her throat. Every inch of her wanted to attack him and get her revenge once and for all but she kept her cool and awaited O'Hara's command.

'Stick to the plan! Hurry!' cried O'Hara, and everyone obeyed, the wildcats leading, their heads swivelling left and right, searching for more of the enemy. As they turned left onto the quays, they hadn't got far when a number of Shadow Walkers appeared up ahead, blocking their way. *Zach must have had more Shadow Walkers with him than I realised*, thought Ebony. Everyone screeched to a halt as the Shadow Walkers used their cutlasses and huge spiked metal balls to hit out at anything in their way. Parked cars were tossed aside, lamp posts and bins were smashed.

'What now?' asked Miss Malone. 'Do we go back?'

Aunt Ruby checked behind them and shook her head. 'Zach and his Shadow Walkers are behind us so there's no way back. They have us hemmed in but the others will hold them off. We'll have to fight our way through.'

'There's too many of them for us to do this on our own. I'll call for more back-up,' said Mr O'Hara.

Peering back, Ebony saw that Zach was close behind. His Shadow Walkers were multiplying – and fast. As Mr O'Hara radioed for extra help, the Order split into two groups and stood back to back, facing the oncoming enemy in both directions. Although her priority was to reach the zoo, Ebony relished the opportunity to face her grandpa's murderer. Her hand still screamed with pain but she gritted her teeth, trying to ignore it; she couldn't let it distract her. As her aunt and the wildcats readied for battle by Ebony's side, Zach's voice rang in her head: *This is it, Ebony Smart. Prepare to give us the gift of your soul.*

There was a momentary pause before Zach pointed his arm straight at her and screamed, 'Bring me the girl and her rat. Kill the rest!'

Bursting into action, the Shadow Walkers rushed forward on both sides, baying for blood, the noise thunderous as they charged. Mulligan and Uncle Cornelius sprang forward first, leaping through the air with their claws out, their powerful hind legs propelling them at top speed. The humans followed and the sound of weapons firing, metal clanking against metal, and cries filled the air. Heading straight for Zach, firing at every Shadow Walker she could see, Ebony's arm felt like it was on fire, but she gritted her teeth and ignored the pain.

There was a cry as Uncle Cornelius swiped a Shadow Walker high into the air. As he ran on through the ranks, two more Shadow Walkers sailed backwards and crashed down on top of their comrades. Ebony fired at an oncoming Shadow Walker to slow it down and Mulligan leapt in. Grabbing the creature by its throat with his teeth, the wildcat shook it like a rag doll. Within moments, several Shadow Walkers were put out of action, but three of the Order's people had been crushed underfoot. The Order was putting up a good fight, but as quickly as they could destroy their enemies, they were re-forming.

Ebony scanned for Zach Stone. At that moment, a roar from the Shadow Walkers went up as the Deus-Umbra swooped down inches above the battle. *You have no chance now.* Zach's thought flashed through her mind and Ebony lifted her weapon, more determined than ever to prove him wrong. Remembering Ambrose's words – *I will release you when we get what we need: Ebony and the rat* – she checked on Winston. He was rolled in a ball in her pocket, shivering but unharmed. As Ebony planned her next move, Uncle Cornelius soared over her head, grabbing a Shadow Walker she hadn't spotted by the throat and pinning him to the ground. Realising how lucky she'd just been, Ebony went to shoot it but Uncle Cornelius was in the way. Noticing her predicament, Drinkwater ran closer for a better shot.

'Shoot!' Ebony shouted.

Drinkwater crouched down near a wall and, lifting his gun, took aim. His bullet hit the Shadow Walker in the heart, making it flash, crackle, then explode. A screech rang out and the Deus-Umbra streaked across the sky in the distance, its wings pulled back as it ripped through the air.

'It's searching for you,' said Aunt Ruby, joining Ebony. 'Try to stay hidden in the crowd.'

As the fighting raged, Ebony and the others were ma-noeuvred onto the wooden boardwalk that ran alongside the river.

'They're trying to trap us,' yelled Aunt Ruby. 'Push back!'

While Uncle Cornelius was fending off a particularly large Shadow Walker, the Deus-Umbra snatched a man from the ground and carried him high into the air. The demon occupied, Ebony surveyed the current situation. Mulligan was holding off two Shadow Walkers with his thrashing jaws and claws, and Aunt Ruby had just taken out another couple with a single shot. Meanwhile, Mr O'Hara was on a Shadow Walker's shoulders, his arms locked around its neck as it flailed about, trying to dislodge him. Zach was in the middle of the fray, his electric whip fizzing. Ebony took aim at him, but Miss Malone lurched into the way as she grappled with a Shadow Walker trying to steal her bow. Pulling back the string, an arrow appearing instantly, she fired into the creature's stomach at point-blank range. It dropped to the ground and Miss Malone staggered backwards. But Zach was gone.

Where are you? thought Ebony.

Behind you, came his immediate reply.

Surprised, Ebony spun round. Zach was a few metres away. He laughed and his face darkened, shimmered and re-formed. As he snapped his whip against the ground, a bolt of lightning shot out, heading straight for her. She dodged to the side, firing at him as she did. The bullet skimmed his shoulder and red blossomed on his white top. Zach touched his finger to the blood and his eyes turned completely black. Growling fiercely, he threw himself at her, wrapping her in a vice-like grip and shoving her against the walkway's railings. She could see the intense hatred in his eyes as, using his weight to pin her, he lifted the whip and squeezed it against her throat, burning her flesh.

Grabbing his wrists, Ebony fought hard, relieving the pressure on her windpipe. Over Zach's shoulder, she spotted a pack of grey wolves creeping along the walkway towards them, tongues lolling between their sharp teeth. The smell of blood must have attracted them. Kicking him hard in the shin, Ebony used the momentary release of pressure as he flinched backwards to push Zach towards the wolves but, startled, they leapt over the wall onto the road. Zach lashed out again, but this time Ebony ducked. He bared his teeth and laughed, a sound that was less than human; she watched his face turn shadowy for just an instant, his eyes turning to red pinpricks. Fear gripped her stomach. Was he changing into a Shadow Walker? She gave him a hard, unexpected punch in the gut and he stumbled backwards.

Her vision was momentarily obscured as Uncle Cornelius leapt between them, swiping at a Shadow Walker with his curved, bloodied claws. Then Mulligan's huge snout appeared, his sharp teeth sinking into the Shadow Walker's arm and dragging him backwards. When they moved away Zach had once again disappeared from view. Meanwhile, more of the Order appeared from Ebony's right, led by the blonde security woman Ebony recognised from outside O'Hara's office when the Shadow Walkers had infiltrated the cemetery entrance. Ebony felt a wave of relief flood through the tired fighters locked in battle. Bows, crossbows and guns in hand, the additional fighters fired wildly at the enemy, bringing a new surge of energy to the Order's side.

Heading towards where she had last seen Zach, Ebony stopped in her tracks as five creatures sprang up in front of her. They were completely black and without faces, and Ebony's breath caught in her throat. Raising her gun, she moved to fire, but Aunt Ruby jumped in her way.

'They're Mrs O'Hara's puppets! Don't shoot!'

Realising her mistake, Ebony stepped aside. As the shadow puppets reached the battle, she watched as they seemed to grow in size and bulk. As a group, they leaned in, picked up a Shadow Walker and lobbed it through the air; the creature flew high into the sky, then crashed to the ground, impaled on a snapped lamp post. Hearing a rumble of marching feet over the cries and clashing weapons, Ebony followed the noise: more fierce puppets were joining the fight.

A scream sounded from the bridge, and Ebony looked towards it. Her mother and Chiyoko were running as fast as their legs could carry them, the Deus-Umbra on their tail.

'Look out!' screamed Ebony, alerting her father nearby.

He followed her gaze, then pointed the D-STRUCTOR at the creature and took aim. Ivy and Chiyoko ducked as they ran, but the Deus-Umbra swerved and the beam missed, although it gave the pair a chance to escape. They dodged through the fighting and wove their way towards Ebony.

'What are you doing here?' asked Ebony, looking at her mother and Chiyoko in turn. 'You're too sick to fight, and you're meant to be helping your mother and Seamus. Go back to the coffee shop!'

'We saw on the CCTV that you were in trouble so we came to help,' replied Ivy.

'Please go back!' pleaded Ebony.

But there was no way back, as the Deus-Umbra landed on the walkway in front of them. It moved closer with slow, careful steps, its fangs bared and dripping saliva. The demon glared at Ebony.

'You leave her alone,' said Ivy, stepping in front of her daughter.

The demon continued towards them but Ivy stood her ground. As she lifted her bow, it swatted her sideways and she tumbled over the railing. She just managed to catch hold of the edge and clung on. Ebony screamed and fired her gun twice in quick succession, but the shots bounced off the demon, leaving it unharmed.

Then Chiyoko opened her mouth and sang. The noise was deafening and pure; it reminded Ebony of the cry of the Silent Peregrine that had driven off the demon the last time they fought. The Deus-Umbra covered its ears and bent at the waist, twisting and turning as if the sound was causing it pain. A cacophony of noise blew up around them as flocks of pigeons, gulls, lorikeets, ducks and sparrows suddenly appeared. King Vultures swooped from the horizon. Birds answered Chiyoko's call from miles around, filling the sky. From every direction, Ebony watched more birds appear – curlews with their long, curved beaks, low-flying guillemots and hordes of geese in V formations – flocking around Chiyoko to protect her as she continued her strange, melancholic song. The demon launched itself skywards with a roar and the birds followed.

'They won't stop it, but they might create a distraction for a while,' said Chiyoko, finally stopping.

As Ebony watched, the army of birds pursued the demon, attacking with beaks and claws. Shrieking with annoyance, the Deus-Umbra lashed out. Dozens of corpses hit the ground, the bird's necks and wings twisted at odd angles.

A cry from behind returned Ebony's attention to the ground. 'Ebony, help.'

Spotting her mother's hand clinging to the railing, Ebony raced over and grabbed hold. She tried to pull Ivy up, but her mother seemed incredibly heavy. Ebony peered past her towards the water to see if her foot was caught in something and gasped: a Shadow Walker was clamped onto her mother's leg.

40

'Leave her alone,' shouted Ebony, still trying to haul her mother up. Chiyoko joined in, but the weight was too much. The creature clung on, refusing to let go. Ivy began to cough, her body shuddering with the effort. Noticing the struggle, Aunt Ruby rushed to their aid, dodging fists and feet and weapons as she made her way to them. With her help, on the count of three, they hauled Ivy upwards. At the same time, she kicked and kicked the Shadow Walker's arm until it released its grip on her, tumbling into the water.

'That was a close one,' said Ivy, as they began to pull her over the railing and back onto the walkway.

A hand appeared, grasping the lowest part of the railing, followed by the Shadow Walker's head. It emerged roaring, green phlegm flying in all directions, as it dragged its bulk over the side and onto the boardwalk. Ebony yanked her mother backwards as the creature struck out, but the blow caught Aunt Ruby in the face. Its next blow landed in her stomach and Aunt Ruby bent over, winded. Ebony went to fire at it but the creature grabbed Aunt Ruby, its fingers curling round her throat and lifting her onto her toes, blocking Ebony's shot. Gurgling, Ruby swung in its grip, her eyes wide and bulging. Then the Deus-Umbra streaked overhead, its shadow momentarily blocking out the light and distracting the Shadow Walker. As it loosened its grip on Ruby, she wrenched herself free. Mulligan soared through the air, knocking the creature over the side of the bridge. They both plummeted into the water below. Looking over the side, Ebony saw Mulligan swimming along the Liffey, looking for somewhere to climb out.

Meanwhile the Deus-Umbra circled above, the number of birds attacking it reduced to a handful. Many had tired, while others had been frightened off, killed or injured. Only the biggest birds remained and the Deus-Umbra no longer seemed bothered by their pecks and scratches.

'Can you do that again, Chiyoko?' asked Ebony.

She shook her head. 'I called all the birds I could.'

'Then we need my father.'

Spotting him on the road above, she raced towards him. She tripped and felt Winston slip from her pocket, but to her relief, Aunt Ruby, who was close behind her, noticed and snatched him up. Knowing Winston was safe, Ebony pushed on.

'You need to shoot the demon,' she yelled, as she approached her father.

'I've already missed once,' he replied, training the D-STRUCTOR. 'I can't afford to waste any more of the charge. Can you hold off the Shadow Walkers so that I can concentrate?'

Ruby and Ebony turned to face their opponents and Rufus took his chance. He tracked the demon as it swept through the sky, aimed carefully and fired. The laser shot out and hit the Deus-Umbra, holding it static in the air for a moment. It shivered as it lit up and screeched in pain as a gash opened in its flesh but, as the beam faded, the effects proved momentary and a white scar formed over the wound. The demon screeched, then plummeted towards them. Spying Winston perched on Aunt Ruby's shoulder, the demon swerved. Before anyone realised what was happening, it had grabbed Aunt Ruby by the waist and swooped back up, high as the clouds, Aunt Ruby dangling from its claws. Winston squealed as they rose into the air and Ebony saw Aunt Ruby tuck him into a pocket. As Rufus aimed to fire again, Ebony stopped him.

'No! What if you hit Aunt Ruby or Winston, or the creature drops them?' She watched as the demon turned from the battle and soared off into the distance. 'It's heading for the zoo. We have to go after them, now.'

But despite her positive words, her heart sank as the Deus-Umbra disappeared from sight. Even though she had known Ambrose wanted Winston, she had failed to protect him. Frowning, she watched as the demon grew smaller and smaller, until it was just a dot in the distance.

Now are you ready to play, Ebony Smart? Zach's voice filled her mind.

Ebony began to run in the direction of the zoo, shooting at the Shadow Walkers around her. She burst out the far side of the battle and raced on. Fast and hard, her feet pounded the pavement. A screech of tyres rang out and Ebony turned to see Drinkwater at the wheel of an armoured vehicle; beside him, Mr O'Hara waved for Ebony to get in as it pulled to a stop. The door slid open, revealing Chiyoko and her parents already inside. Rufus stuck out his head.

'Come on, Ebony!' he yelled.

Looking back, Ebony could see that more of the Order had arrived and the puppets manned by Seamus and Mrs O'Hara were going strong. She spotted the wildcats and Miss Malone in the thick of battle. She didn't want to leave them, but she had to rescue Aunt Ruby and Winston. Ducking as a Shadow Walker that had followed her swiped at her with its cutlass, she wasted no more time and ran for the open door. As she leapt into the vehicle, the Shadow Walker tried to follow; her father yanked the door closed just in time. As they pulled away, the Shadow Walker roared, attracting the others. Ivy handed Ebony some fresh ammunition.

'In case you're low,' she said.

'I thought you were meant to hold the fort at the bridge, Drinkwater?' asked Ebony, concerned for those left behind.

'With Ruby gone, you're a man down. It's better I come with you,' he replied.

'Will we get through?' she asked, indicating the devastation along the road up ahead.

'We have to,' said Drinkwater, speeding up.

Without warning, a Shadow Walker leaped in front of the

car. It roared, lifting its arm and thrusting its cutlass towards the windscreen. Drinkwater swerved, but others appeared, blocking the way, their screeches deafening and their eyes glowing brighter. The tyres spun as Drinkwater floored the accelerator and the car burst through the mob, the smell of burning rubber filling the air. A traffic cone hurtled towards the vehicle and bounced off the back.

As they sped along the quays in the direction of the Phoenix Park and Dublin Zoo, dodging shattered glass, discarded cars and debris, Ebony and Chiyoko looked out of the back window. The Shadow Walkers had been left behind but Mulligan and Uncle Cornelius were pounding the pavement, their jowls wobbling and tongues lolling as they raced behind.

'Let the wildcats in,' yelled Ebony.

At the touch of a button, the back of the vehicle opened. Drinkwater slowed a little so they could catch up and Uncle Cornelius took a giant leap, landing in the back with a thud, quickly followed by Mulligan. As they drove on, Drinkwater dodged the debris expertly, weaving left and right; they soon left the river behind and the gates to the Phoenix Park came into view. Drinkwater yanked the wheel to the right, turning into the park, and raced down the centre of the road, the vehicle thumping up and down as he drove straight across a small, grassy roundabout. They hadn't quite reached the zoo entrance when a pair of large, angry-looking rhinos blocked their way. Screeching to a halt, Drinkwater pressed a button that opened all the doors, and they watched, waiting to see what the animals would do. Nose dipped and horns pointing their way, the biggest pawed and snorted, its piggy eyes staring at the vehicle. After a moment, it stopped pawing and Ivy let out a sigh. But then Chiyoko screamed – the rhino was charging!

Everyone jumped out of the vehicle and ran to the right, zigzagging in case the rhino decided to chase them. They raced through the bushes and into the green space beyond. There was a loud crunch as the rhino hit the armoured car, but no one stopped to check the damage. They ran for their lives, keeping the trees to their left. Reaching two gentle giraffes grazing on the top leaves of a tall tree, their jaws munching and grinding, the group slowed and passed by quietly, none of them taller than the giraffes' knees. Crossing a small side road, Mr O'Hara waved everyone to a stop.

They hunkered down and listened. All was silent. Crouching low, they continued along a pathway lined with trees that were usually filled with squirrels and small birds. As they reached the octagonal-shaped teahouse, they ducked behind the building and peered through the windows. All around, there were signs of struggle – discarded weapons, splatters of blood and trampled grass, but thankfully no bodies. At the entrance to the zoo up ahead, the turnstiles were smashed but there was no sign of life. It seemed like the Order's members assigned to this task had achieved their goal and drawn off any Shadow Walkers guarding the entrance to the zoo. All was clear.

41

As the group stepped into the entrance of the zoo, weapons ready, an empty lake stretched out in front of them. It was eerily quiet. Across the way, on their island, the usually noisy crested macaques stared out, blinking, not making a sound. Even the babies were still.

'They must sense the Deus-Umbra nearby,' said Ebony. Opening *The Book of Learning*, she showed the others the image frozen to the page.

'We're looking for some kind of entrance underground near this totem pole. The ground around it was dry earth, but I couldn't see anything else that would give us any clues.'

'How do you know that's where the demon's taken them?' asked Mr O'Hara.

'Because that's where Ambrose has been hiding. And that's where his soul-swapping machine must be.'

Drinkwater fidgeted with his gun. 'I thought you destroyed that.'

'I did. But Zach told me they still want my soul so they must have made another.'

'Then why didn't he just get the Deus-Umbra to take you?'

asked Chiyoko.

'For some reason, he also wants Winston. My aunt just happened to get in the way. And by taking them, he knew I'd follow,' replied Ebony.

Closing the book, she tucked it back into the pocket where Winston often hid. His absence stung. *We must hurry*, she thought, as Zach's laughter rang in her mind. An uncomfortable silence fell as the group studied the map of the zoo on the board at the entrance. There was no sign of a totem pole marked anywhere. They had no choice but to search the grounds.

'Do we stay together or split up?' asked Rufus.

'We'll be safer together,' said Drinkwater.

'Let's go that way,' said Ebony, trying to sound confident as she turned left, her gun poised.

Uncle Cornelius and Mulligan paused as a low growl filled the air. Above their heads, a broken electric fence crackled; it reminded Ebony of Zach's whip and she felt her heart blacken. *If they dare harm a single hair on Winston's or Aunt Ruby's head*, she thought.

The growl came from a lion still trapped in its enclosure. It was standing on a rock halfway up a hilly verge, head lifted and tail swishing angrily, sending its call up to the sky. Seemingly understanding, the two wildcats replied, their voices melancholy. The lion growled and lay down, its head on its paws.

'It looks scared,' said Chiyoko, studying its submissive pose.

Keeping their footsteps quiet, the group pushed on, their eyes on the smashed windows, broken cages and empty enclosures. But there was no sign of a totem pole anywhere. As they veered to the right, a pair of snow-white leopards appeared on the path. They were huge, with piercing yellow eyes. Although they were beautiful, their teeth and claws were deadly. Ebony and the others paused, while Uncle Cornelius and Mulligan pushed their way to the front, eyeing the big cats warily. The wildcats began to growl, lifting their cheeks to show their teeth in warning. But the leopards refused to back off. Ebony saw the muscles on both the wildcats' shoulders quiver and quake. The leopards crouched lower, their ears flat and teeth showing.

'Are they hungry or trying to escape?' asked Chiyoko.

'I don't know, but we have to get past,' replied Ebony.

The leopards moved first, leaping forward, but Uncle Cornelius and Mulligan were quick to respond, defending their group. Their bodies met in mid-air, jaws wide and snarling, claws extended. As they tumbled to the ground, the animals split apart and circled each other warily. Spots of blood splattered their coats and the ground as their growls rang in the air. Suddenly, one of the leopards sprang forward, trying to grab Mulligan by his throat, but he leaped into the air and landed behind it, twisting and biting its flank. The leopard struggled and managed to shake Mulligan loose. Hurt, it crouched low, crimson spilling over its beautiful white coat, and backed away from the wildcats, calling its mate.

The other leopard responded, bounding away from Uncle Cornelius and joining its companion, baring its teeth. In response, Mulligan and Uncle Cornelius faced the pair, making threatening noises. They all crouched low, watching each other warily. The onlookers held their breath as the big cats stared each other down. Without warning, Mulligan pounced, roaring, and the two leopards fled. Sprinting around Ebony and the others, they raced off along the path that led to the entrance.

Checking on Mulligan and Uncle Cornelius in turn, Ebony could see that their wounds were minor and not life-threatening. There was no time to bandage them and the group pushed on, eyes and ears alert. Soon, they came across a huge fake black tree with wires overhead for orangutans to cross. Rufus waved for the group to pause.

'This could be it,' he said. 'It's got plenty of dirt.'

Ebony scanned the ground. There was no totem pole in sight. Only more trees and bamboo. The hiss of a nearby water-filter system made Ebony jump. Knowing this was no time for nerves, she continued, the others following, quiet and solemn. Spotting a walkway up to some animal cages, Ebony called out. 'Wait, I have an idea!'

As the others stopped, she raced up the slope and, from her vantage point, scanned the grounds. Her hand began to hurt, the pain sharp. Looking around for the cause, Ebony spied Zach making his way through the zoo with six Shadow Walkers. He was following their route, which she hoped meant they'd chosen the right way. But it also meant they had little time to find their destination while Zach knew exactly where he was going, which gave him an advantage. As the two injured snow leopards raced by Zach, he watched them for a moment, a smile on his lips. Ebony shuddered. She lifted her gun and aimed; even though she knew she was too far away to hit him, it felt good. Chest clenching, she lowered the gun and raced down to tell the others to hurry. There was still plenty of ground to cover and they couldn't risk Zach catching up to them – otherwise, Ambrose would have more support.

They all broke into a run, racing along walkways lined with bamboo and a number of seemingly empty pens. Soon Ebony heard the sound of waves. Reaching a water enclosure, she watched as three sea lions swam back and forth, graceful in the rippling water. Spotting movement above the water line, they propelled themselves out onto land one by one and began barking.

'Ssh,' commanded Ebony, 'you'll give our position away.'

But the sea lions kept barking, their noise echoing in the quiet zoo. Ebony realised she'd heard that noise before – it was when *The Book of Learning* had showed her the totem pole. They were close! Moving on quickly, they passed the glass tank for underwater viewing.

Stepping into an open space, Ebony spotted the totem pole in front of her, the two cats and eagle staring in her direction.

'We've found it,' said Ebony. 'But where's the lift?'

Searching around frantically, she spied the jawbone of a whale on a mound of earth, only metres away. Tucking her gun into her pocket and creeping up to it, she positioned her back to the jawbone and crouched down, imagining herself rising from the earth. It was exactly the same angle as what she'd seen. This was where the lift opened – but how?

Before she could find a switch or button to call the lift, there was a noise behind her. Turning, she saw the jaw bone had lifted off the ground and the Deus-Umbra was underneath, looking out at her from behind glass doors. As the doors parted she turned to run, but the Deus-Umbra was too fast, snatching Ebony and dragging her inside. Before the others could help her, the doors snapped shut and they sank into the earth, and Ebony's heart felt like it might explode as the demon's saliva dripped down her spine.

42

The large underground room was lit with a red lamp. Aunt Ruby was tied to a chair in the corner to the left of the lift, mouth covered with duct tape, and Winston was trapped in a Perspex box with holes – it looked like something the zoo might use for observing a sick animal. Ebony tried to make a dash for the box but the Deus-Umbra yanked her backwards, pulling her off her feet, and dragged her along the ground, dropping her at Ambrose's feet.

Snatching her up like she weighed no more than a feather, Ambrose pulled her across to the far side of the room where Icarus Bean was slumped in a chair, a cage-like contraption on his head, attached to a series of wires. Horrified, Ebony stared at him in disbelief – how had he got there? Was Ambrose completely in control of him now? Icarus's head lolled to one side, his closed eyelids twitching, drool escaping the corner of his mouth. The dark mark now covered half of his face; as she watched, it twisted and coiled. There was another chair of the same design and, in-between, a machine with two levers and four buttons. It looked similar to Ambrose's earlier soul-swapping device, only more sophisticated. Ebony struggled, trying to wriggle free, but Ambrose easily overpowered her. In seconds, he had removed her rucksack, throwing it across the room. Then he forced her into the empty chair, securing her with leather straps that cut into her wrists and ankles. Unable to break free, Ebony stared across the room at her aunt.

Working quickly, Ambrose forced a second wired contraption down onto Ebony's head. Each strip of metal on it had small spikes inside, making her scalp bleed. Looking on, Aunt Ruby struggled, trying to say something, but the tape made her words indecipherable.

The lift began to hum and Ebony's hand throbbed: she knew what was coming. Moments later, the lift arrived, two Shadow Walkers staring out of the glass doors. Ebony could see bodies squashed in behind them and held her breath.

The Shadow Walkers parted to let Zach through, a sneer on his face. In one hand he held the D-STRUCTOR, and behind him, he dragged Rufus by the hair. As he dropped Rufus face down, the Shadow Walkers, armed with their captives' weapons, shoved Chiyoko, Mr O'Hara and Drinkwater against the wall to the right of the lift. One of the Shadow Walkers reached out and dragged Rufus to join the others; he struggled upright, bruised and battered. Her mother and the wildcats were missing; Ebony crossed her fingers, hoping they were safe.

'Glad you could join us,' said Ambrose.

As he turned away, Zach shot him a look of triumph.

'Let the others go,' yelled Ebony, knowing it was a useless plea but hoping it might buy her some time. 'You have me now.'

'The others are worthless, true, but I want them to see their precious guardian defeated. And this one? He's worth more to me than you know,' said Ambrose, picking up Winston's box and giving it a shake. Winston bounced around inside like a ball. Placing him down closer to Ebony, so she could get a good look, Ambrose chuckled as Winston staggered, dizzy and sore. 'You should have minded him more carefully. After all, he was a gift from the sky world.'

Ebony felt her face fall and Zach chuckled as Ambrose continued, 'Didn't you realise? Even though he's so smart and rather long-lived for his type of vermin? He's the one that will choose the next guardian. And now you've given him to me.'

'What?' cried Ebony, looking at Winston.

Ambrose strode across to Aunt Ruby and ripped away the duct tape. 'I'll leave you to explain this one. Oh, this is going to be good.'

Aunt Ruby's eyes begged forgiveness as she spoke. 'You know how there are always one hundred Nine Lives families, and to keep the balance, preventing us from being wiped out, replacements need to be chosen when a family passes through to Ultimation or Obliteration? They undergo a transformation and Nine Lives souls are implanted in their bodies?'

Ebony nodded, trying to figure out what this had to do with her pet rat.

'As sole guardian, your replacement has to be exceptional. When the sky world reduced the trust to a single guardian, it decided to enlist help with choosing the next one. It had to be someone or something unbiased that could never gain from the sky world's power, so they decided to use an animal. That's Winston's role; having seen your capabilities, he can ensure they're present in the next choice.'

'How do you know this?' asked Ebony.

'A recent vision from Mrs O'Hara showed me Winston's future. I didn't know whether or not to tell you – you were under so much pressure already. I'd always known Winston was special – only I hadn't realised just how special.'

'Zach was able to read her mind,' said Ambrose. 'So if this attempt to swap your soul fails, we'll keep him. And I'll use a little persuasion to make sure my choice becomes his. This rat may be special, but he'll never be able to withstand my torture. Either way, I win.'

Looking pleased with his plan, Ambrose glared at Zach. 'Get on with it. I want the power of reincarnation. Now!'

Zach grinned at Ebony as he leaned in. 'Soon we'll have the power of eternal life,' he said. 'You might have killed my mother, Ebony, but as you can see,' he gestured at Icarus, 'there are other bodies we can use. Now that my father answers to us, he's the perfect candidate. So how do you like our new guardian?'

Keeping the D-STRUCTOR in one hand, Zach pushed a lever halfway down with the other, and the machine started to emit a whirring noise. He let go and pushed the button below it, which flashed yellow. Ebony felt a tingling sensation run through her body. Beside her, Icarus's cheeks were reddening and sweat beaded on his forehead, turning his fringe sticky. He opened his glassy eyes, barely conscious.

Taking hold of the other lever, Zach pushed it and the whirring noise doubled. He pushed the button underneath the second lever and it turned green. Ebony felt an icy wave rush through her veins and limbs, setting her teeth on edge and making her legs shake.

'Zach, no!' Ebony rasped, gritting her teeth through the pain. 'You heard him. Ambrose wants the power of reincarnation for himself. He's using you!'

From the way his eyes narrowed, Ebony knew she had hit a nerve. Incensed, he shoved both levers to full capacity and, against her will, Ebony screamed. Her blood turned to ice, her arms and legs turning numb. If she survived, what would happen to her soul? And if she died, what would happen to Winston?

The Deus-Umbra leaned over Ebony, its eyes full of menace as it sniffed the length of her body, leaving a trail of stinking drool. As the machine started to suck the soul from her body, Ebony concentrated on trying to stay conscious. Her eyes flickering to Winston, his paws pressed against the glass and shivering, she felt tears drip down her cheeks.

'You're nothing but a coward, demon,' yelled Aunt Ruby.

The creature looked at her, fury in its eyes.

'You're nothing but Ambrose's puppet. Once he has what he wants, you'll be his slave forever. Don't you realise that?'

The Deus-Umbra looked to Ambrose and roared, lifting his wings out wide.

'He won't ever release you,' continued Ruby, as Ebony fought the effects of the machine. 'You've lived too long, seen too much to not know this.'

The demon glanced at Ebony, then moved towards Ambrose, pointing at the anklet with its spiked claws. But something stopped him in his tracks. Ambrose held up the control and clicked it, making the Deus-Umbra writhe and roar. Watching, Zach and Ambrose chuckled.

'And now we have this,' said Zach, holding up the D-STRUCTOR. 'So even if you manage to get that thing off your leg, we can still kill you, demon.'

The Deus-Umbra continued to roar in pain, its wings flapping uncontrollably.

'You should kill Ambrose before he becomes too powerful to stop,' goaded Ruby.

Ambrose shook his head. 'I am already too powerful, Ruby,' he said. 'Your words hold no threat for me.'

Deciding his point had been made, Ambrose clicked the control button again. The second the pain stopped, the demon growled and lunged forward.

'No!' roared Ambrose, clicking once more.

At the same time, Zach fired the D-STRUCTOR at the Deus-Umbra, his eyes fuelled with hate. The demon lit up and juddered. As it crashed to the floor, its outstretched claws wrapped around the wires attaching Ebony and Icarus to the machine and ripped them away with one almighty pull. Sparks flew and Ebony felt her scalp rip as the contraption on her head came away. Icarus gasped, his body jerking, and Ebony felt the icy assault stop: the machine was now inactive. Checking on the demon, Ebony watched as the large hole in its gut covered with scar tissue, but it seemed to take longer to heal this time.

'Stupid creature,' screamed Ambrose.

Ebony expected the demon to leap up – the gun had barely slowed it when her father hit it – but this time it stayed motionless. The weapon seemed to have injured it more severely this time. But there were now only two shots left.

While the others were distracted, Ebony took slow, deep breaths, regaining her energy. As Zach and Ambrose worked to fix the machine, Ebony saw the rest of her group exchange glances and mouth silent words behind the Shadow Walkers' backs. Assuming their captives were subdued, the creatures were too busy watching the Deus-Umbra and Ambrose to notice. Quietly, O'Hara, Chiyoko and Drinkwater climbed to their feet. Next to Ebony, Icarus Bean wriggled and writhed. The mark on his face twitched and slithered, and Icarus gritted his jaw. His eyes switched from pure black to his usual grey. Catching Ebony's eyes, she saw hatred flash through them.

'Icarus, we must work together,' said Ebony. 'You can still fight them.'

Zach and Ambrose both chuckled as they continued to focus on fixing the machine.

'It's pointless, Ebony,' said Ambrose. 'Icarus is with us now. It's all over.'

'Please, Uncle,' Ebony pleaded, 'don't let them win. Not after all we've been through.'

Staring at Ebony, eyes hard and cold, Icarus's lips lifted into a sneer.

At that moment, Drinkwater, O'Hara and Chiyoko leapt into action. Chiyoko snatched a Shadow Walker's cutlass, taking it by surprise, and thrust the sword into its chest. As the creature roared, clutching its wound as it staggered back, the other Shadow Walker tried to grab Chiyoko and, seeing his chance, Drinkwater snatched his own gun from the creature's hand and fired into its stomach at point-blank range. It exploded into tiny lumps of black goo, the weapons it was holding clattering to the ground. O'Hara snatched them up. Keeping a gun for himself, he handed another to Chiyoko. Rufus, however, was nowhere to be seen, and although she twisted her head as far as she could, Ebony could not find him.

With the Shadow Walkers out of action, Drinkwater charged towards Ambrose, not daring to shoot in case he hit Ebony by mistake. Hearing his approach, Ambrose turned from the machine and threw a punch that connected with

Drinkwater's jaw and sent him flying. At the same time, Mr O'Hara and Chiyoko managed to cut Aunt Ruby free before snatching up Ebony's rucksack. Ruby's circulation had been restricted for so long, she struggled to stand, but with O'Hara's help, she eventually managed and grasped the gun he offered her. Weapons lifted, they turned their backs to the lift and faced their enemy.

'Let the others go,' said Aunt Ruby.

Zach and Ambrose seemed strangely unworried by their reversal in fortune. Zach shook his head and laughed. Feeling something loosening the straps on her feet, Ebony fought to stop herself looking down and drawing attention to the fact. On the floor nearby, she saw the Deus-Umbra open one eye, then close it again and realised it was faking unconsciousness.

'This is your chance to show me your loyalty, brother, by making sure the guardian stays put,' Ambrose said to Icarus, unsheathing a knife from his belt and holding it out.

Taking it, Icarus slowly stood up from his chair, eyeing everyone in turn. His movements were cautious. As his gaze fell on Ebony, she held her breath. His eyes flashed grey and black in quick succession – an internal battle clearly visible – and his knuckles turned white as he gripped the knife, moving closer. When Ambrose turned to reattach the wires to Ebony's head, Icarus pounced. He grabbed Ambrose around the neck, dragging him backwards and twisting him away from Ebony. Then, with two quick slashes, he cut the straps around her wrists. Ambrose cried out with rage and butted the back of his head into Icarus's face. Already weak from fighting Ambrose's hold over him, Icarus was knocked to the dusty ground.

Before Ebony could move, Zach snatched a gun from his belt and pressed it to her head. 'Lower your weapons, all of you,' he called out.

Everyone did as he requested. Zach's laughter was deep and dark, resonating like the skin of a drum as he looked to Ambrose for direction.

'How pathetic,' said Ambrose, standing his ground. 'What were you going to do? Even if you got out of here, how far did you think you would get? You seem to have forgotten, we have a demon. And now that we have this as well,' he said, nodding towards the D-STRUCTOR, which Zach was clutching, 'you have no way to defeat it or us.'

Suddenly, Rufus jumped up from behind Ebony's chair and snatched the gun Zach was holding to Ebony's head, at the same time knocking him backwards. As Zach toppled, Ebony jumped over him and grabbed the box that held Winston. Ambrose lunged towards her but Icarus leapt up, throwing himself between Ebony and Ambrose. Meanwhile, Rufus wrestled the D-STRUCTOR from Zach's grip and joined the others, who had raised their weapons once more, but hadn't fired for fear of hitting Ebony, Icarus or both.

'Come now, Icarus,' said Ambrose. He lifted one hand and placed it on his brother's forehead, staring intently into his eyes. 'You know I can control you. You will do as I say. Be a good brother and put her back in the chair.'

The black mark on Icarus's cheek swirled and grew, stretching higher and wider across his face. His body trembling, he turned towards her, gritting his teeth against the pain. Ebony watched his eyes turn black and vacant. As Icarus reached forward, the veins and sinews in his arms pulsating, her legs wobbled; there was nowhere for her to run. She was trapped.

'No!' cried Aunt Ruby, frustration edging her voice.

But instead of thrusting Ebony back into the chair, Icarus whirled around, pushed Ambrose backwards and pulled her across the room to join the others. Ebony's hand throbbed as black shapes began to grow in the corners of the room. Within seconds, several Shadow Walkers appeared, with more starting to form behind them. Knowing they would have no chance against so many Shadow Walkers in such a small space, Ebony and the others backed into the lift.

'You can't fight me forever, brother,' said Ambrose, shaking his head, a smile playing on his lips.

As his words died on his lips, Icarus pressed the button and the lift doors closed. Moments later, they were heading back up above ground, the sound of Ambrose's laughter ringing out below.

'What do we do now?' asked Chiyoko, handing Ebony her rucksack. 'Ambrose and Zach don't even seem worried that we just escaped.'

'They will keep coming after me and Winston,' replied Ebony, 'so we must stand and fight.'

43

As the outside light trickled into the lift, Icarus started to moan. It was a deep, hollow sound, like a wild animal caught in a snare. He gripped his hair and cried out. Aunt Ruby stayed by his side but the others flattened themselves against the glass to keep their distance. Ebony was certain everyone would hear her heart bouncing against her rib cage. She could see the fear on the others' faces.

When the lift drew level with the ground outside, Ebony hit the button and everyone tumbled out. The wildcats were waiting, guarding her mother. She was lying on the ground, unconscious but beginning to stir; Rufus raced over to check on her. Icarus fell to his knees, covering his ears as though trying to block out a terrible sound. As Aunt Ruby went to put her arm around his shoulder, he hit out at her and roared, his eyes turning red and fiery, his face almost completely covered by the mark. Ebony shot at the lift control so the others couldn't follow, but it was a futile act.

Seconds later a rumble sounded from underground and the earth shook. The Deus-Umbra burst from the earth, smashing through the totem pole, sending splintered wood and rocks in all directions. Drinkwater cried out as a large stone hit him on the head. Chiyoko and Ebony dropped to the ground and huddled together, making themselves as small as possible. When the pummelling ended, Ebony looked up to see Zach and Ambrose being set down by the demon. Mr O'Hara fired his gun in their direction, but they dodged the shot and as Ambrose returned fire, Zach sent his whip cracking through the air towards Ebony.

Diving to the right, Ebony was too slow to avoid it; the whip sizzled as it wrapped around her middle, the smell of burning cloth filling the air. The pain was excruciating and stars danced in front of her eyes as Zach pulled her towards him. The others raised their guns, but Zach yanked his whip back and ducked out of the way. A roar rang out and Uncle Cornelius sailed through the air, swatting Zach. He flew backwards and landed with a crunch, moaning. But he was quickly back on his feet, ready to fight. He lifted his whip again, but a loud screech rang out from above, full of rage. All eyes turned to the sky.

The Deus-Umbra was hovering above them, choosing its prey. But that wasn't their only concern: Ambrose had obviously called for back-up. All around, Shadow Walkers were appearing, their eyes hot with rage. Next to Ebony, Chiyoko screamed and the Deus-Umbra replied with shrieks that filled the air as it dived towards them. Staggering to his feet, Drinkwater started to fire at the Shadow Walkers.

'Attack!' he yelled.

Responding immediately, O'Hara and Aunt Ruby leapt into battle, the wildcats by their side. Meanwhile, Chiyoko and Ebony ducked out of the demon's way just in time. There was a flash of light as Zach's whip, which had been aimed at Ebony, accidentally hit the Deus-Umbra on the nose, scorching a red, bleeding wound. The demon halted mid-air, its eyes blazing. This time, it dived for Zach.

Tipping back his head and reaching his arms into the air, Zach roared. He seemed to grow in size and bulk, his skin darkening and his features swirling and re-forming. When he opened his eyes, they were searing red. Whatever change was happening to him, it was out of control. As the Deus-Umbra closed in at top speed, Zach tried to snatch it out of the sky, but his increased strength wasn't enough. The Deus-Umbra hit him in the stomach and, lifting him from the ground, raced along at top speed, slamming him into a nearby brick wall. Zach grabbed onto the creature's leg, but the demon twisted back and scratched at Zach's face with its claws. Bloodied, Zach slumped down and the Deus-Umbra lifted into the air. It swooped again, this time aiming for Aunt Ruby.

'Kill them all, except for Ebony and the rat!' cried Ambrose, control in hand. 'Capture those two and bring Icarus. We'll return to the city. The people can be her judge and jury.'

Ebony shuddered, Mrs O'Hara's vision playing in her mind; it could still come true. Afraid for their own lives, the people would call for her blood.

As the Deus-Umbra plummeted, Rufus fired, hitting it in the chest. The demon screeched, its wings flapping angrily as the force of the weapon's charge held it in mid-air. The whole of its chest turned white and the demon screeched at the top of its lungs, but the sound was weaker than before. It was clearly in pain.

Looking to see how the others were faring, Ebony spotted her mother pushing herself into a sitting position. Ivy pointed to something glinting on the ground at the demon's feet. It was the silver anklet. It must have snapped off during the fight with Zach.

'Demon,' cried Ebony, pointing, 'it's time for you to take revenge on your captors.'

The Deus-Umbra threw back its head and screeched triumphantly. Pulling back its wings, it dived straight at Ambrose. His face turning pale, Ambrose tried clicking the control but nothing happened. When that failed, he raised his gun and fired over and over, but the bullets bounced off the demon's flesh. Incensed, the Deus-Umbra swooped, forcing Ambrose to duck as its claws reached for him, slashing holes in the back of his shirt and drawing blood.

Eyes wide, Ambrose straightened and pleaded, 'I can make people worship you again! I am the one who originally freed you! The one who fed you and kept you safe!'

'You deceived me, chained me, treated me like your slave, and for that you shall pay,' roared the demon.

'I can see now that what I did was wrong. We can work

together, as equals. Imagine what we could achieve.'

In reply, the demon turned in mid-air. 'You will never be my equal, *human*.' It dived at top speed, and as Ambrose turned to run, snatched him up in its claws, wrenching him from the ground. Ambrose wriggled and kicked as blood trickled down his neck.

As the demon rose, it shook Ambrose wildly from side to side. Then it shot high up into the clouds. Ebony saw something falling from the sky and the demon weaving in and out of the clouds. Its claws were now empty. Ebony turned away as a sickening crunch signalled Ambrose's end.

One by one, the Shadow Walkers started to melt back into the shadows. For a moment Ebony wondered why, but then she remembered that the creatures had been trapped in the Shadowlands until Ambrose had made them into an army. Their ability to remain in the real world must have ended with his death. But she knew it wouldn't be so easy to get rid of Zach and the demon.

Searching for the Deus-Umbra, Ebony saw it in the distance, turning back towards them. Yet hope filled her heart. She knew that the vision Mrs O'Hara had shown her could no longer come true: Ambrose was dead and the demon was no longer supporting her enemies. Zach was alone.

Catching a movement in the corner of her eye, Ebony turned but a flash of light blinded her as Zach's whip cracked against the ground somewhere nearby. As her eyes cleared, she saw that he had grabbed Ambrose's gun and was running away, his gait slow and lumbering, like that of a Shadow Walker. She sprinted after him, but he turned and flicked his whip towards her once more. Another flash of light, snake-like this time, cut across her path but she leapt over it and raised her gun, preparing to shoot. But before she could pull the trigger, she felt something huge and hairy slam into her as a loud shot rang out. The next instant, she was on the ground, flattened by something extremely heavy.

Then she heard a scream and, even though the sound was muffled to Ebony, trapped under the huge body, she recognised the voice. It was Aunt Ruby. But why was she screaming?

Pushing and shoving to break free, Ebony's nostrils stung from the scent of damp fur and blood. No matter how much she tried, she couldn't get the beast off. Heart pounding, hoping her gut instinct was wrong, Ebony tried again. Voices sounded, and she felt the weight lifted off her as the body was rolled to one side. Uncle Cornelius, his face creased and dark, pulled Ebony to her feet as Aunt Ruby sank to her knees and wailed. All around, animals cried out as though they shared her sorrow. Ebony stepped forward, hand to her mouth, sobs rising in her chest.

'Mulligan,' she cried.

Dropping to her knees, she put her arms around his neck and unleashed her sobs into his fur. Stroking and hugging him, Ebony spotted a bloody hole in his side, red drenching his fur. Mulligan had saved her from Zach's bullet, sacrificing his own life for hers. Rage took over and Ebony jumped to her feet.

'After him!' yelled Ebony, pointing in the direction she had last seen Zach. But it was no use. He was gone.

Heart aching, and not quite able to comprehend the loss of Mulligan, Ebony rejoined the fighting, leaving her aunt and Uncle Cornelius to mourn. Her mother was on her feet now, hands shading her eyes as she searched the sky for the demon. Suddenly, the Deus-Umbra appeared and it was diving fast, claws out and wings peeled back. Nostrils steaming, the demon was heading straight for Rufus.

'Father, watch out,' screamed Ebony.

Rufus lifted the D-STRUCTOR and fired as the others looked on; they all knew it was their last shot, their last chance to destroy the demon. Hit in the chest by the weapon's beam, the demon glowed and roared, stopping in its tracks. Ebony hoped that it had been weakened enough for the weapon to finish its work this time. After a few seconds, the demon plunged to the ground, a deep wound visible in its chest that showed no sign of healing.

'You did it,' cried Ebony, rushing to her father to give him a hug.

But a gasp from Ivy stopped her. Spinning round, she saw the demon slowly climbing to its feet, its breath ragged but its strength clearly returning.

An idea struck her: it was their last hope. Kneeling, Ebony took her bronze rose from her rucksack and held it high. Eyes on the Deus-Umbra, she filled her mind with the happiest thoughts possible, just like when she needed to open the Reflectory. The rose sparked and chimed, spurring Ebony on. Squeezing her eyes shut, she concentrated as hard as she could, picturing her grandpa's face and Winston's twitching nose. Feeling a shudder ripple through her arm, she opened her eyes: a blue beam shot out of the rose, hitting the Deus-Umbra in its chest wound. The wound grew until a hole appeared in the demon's body and its agonised screech filled the sky.

Ebony held the rose steady and a second hole appeared. Vibrations buzzed up her arms, like shock waves, and she felt her energy flowing from her, but she held firm. The Deus-Umbra screamed and roared, but Ebony didn't waver. The holes continued to multiply and Ebony felt herself weakening. Stars danced in front of her eyes but she held fast.

The holes expanded, tearing through the Deus-Umbra's body. They grew and joined, until Ebony could see the blue sky beaming through it. Eventually, only the demon's outline remained, and it flashed like a neon sign in the air. Then what remained of the Deus-Umbra exploded. As the sky lit up with the blast, the beam from the rose disappeared and Ebony collapsed to the ground, completely drained. She felt the world tilt and turn black.

44

The afternoon glow crept slowly along the ground towards Ebony, making the grass shine.

'Give her some air,' said Aunt Ruby gently.

Everyone shuffled back, far enough to provide her with breathing space but close enough to keep watch. Although the deaths of Ambrose and the Deus-Umbra had ended the battle, they were still wary. The Shadow Walkers had melted away into the shadows, but Zach could still be nearby. Drinkwater was particularly alert; he stood beside the group, gun lifted in case the enemy returned.

Icarus Bean, his face no longer showing any sign of the mark Ambrose had inflicted upon him, placed Winston on Ebony's chest, next to the bronze rose clasped in her fingers. Winston tapped one paw gently near her quiet heart, hoping for a response. In the gentle glow of the sun's sinking rays, Ebony's pale skin took on a golden hue that made her look almost angelic.

'She's alive,' confirmed Aunt Ruby, checking Ebony's pulse. 'But barely.'

Gulping down her sorrow and trying not to cry, she looked

up at the group. A single tear dropped from Winston's eye onto the bronze rose. As it landed, the rose shimmered with a silver mist, moon-bright sparks exploding from the petals. Jumping back, Winston's paw caught in the locket around Ebony's neck. Losing his footing, he tumbled from Ebony's chest to the ground, snapping the chain with his weight. The amulet and its chain slipped from her neck. Diving straight for it, Winston snatched it up in his jaws. As he righted himself, a blue beam shot out of the amulet, firing straight into the heart of the rose. As it made impact, a series of tinkling bells began to chime, filling the air with a sweet yet melancholic song.

'Look!' cried Ivy, pointing to the rose.

As it glowed, the bronze petals began to unfurl. One by one, each peeled back, revealing glowing blue symbols and codes that slipped onto the ground like teardrops. The shapes lengthened on the ground, forming an intricate blanket of coloured beams. As everyone stared, mouths open and breathing fast, the petals began to change colour and soften.

'What's happening?' asked Chiyoko.

'The rose. It's turning back into its original form,' said Aunt Ruby, her violet eyes sparkling. 'But that means the sky world must think she no longer needs it …' Her voice choked.

'You mean … she's dying?' asked Rufus.

On hearing this, Uncle Cornelius tipped back his head and gave a gut-wrenching howl from somewhere deep and dark. His cry rang out across the zoo, filling the air with sadness.

Chiyoko cuddled against her father and Rufus pulled Ivy into his arms in a tight hug. Drinkwater lowered his gun and turned to look at Ebony, sorrow clouding his features.

A pained squeal sounded from the ground. Winston leapt up from where he had fallen and sprang back towards his perch on her chest. But before he touched her body, the rose sparked and he bounced back to the grass. An invisible force was obstructing his way. Rubbing his eyes and grinding his teeth, he tried again and again. Each time, he hit against something invisible and bounced back to the ground. Eventually, panting, he stopped.

Aunt Ruby reached out her hand cautiously; nothing barred her way. Unobstructed, she stroked Ebony's cheek, making gentle soothing noises, but when she picked up Winston and tried to lift him onto Ebony's chest, she felt resistance and her hand could not continue.

'I don't know why this is happening,' she whispered, putting him gently back on the ground, 'but I think it's time for you to say goodbye, little friend.'

He blinked twice. Slowly. And shook his head, lifting his right paw.

Picking up the amulet, she wound it around his neck, the delicate silver moon dangling below his throat like a pendulum, sparkling in the sunlight. Seeing his heart pounding in his chest, Aunt Ruby smiled. 'This belongs to you now. You know what you have to do. The honour of finding the next guardian has fallen to you. Ebony would be proud.'

All eyes turned to Ebony as her mouth opened and her eyelids fluttered. She licked her dry lips and colour flushed her cheeks.

'She's waking up,' cried Ivy.

Winston went to move forward, but stopped, shoulders slumped, his eyes dull and listless as he watched. As Ebony stirred, everyone fell silent. Opening her eyes, she pushed herself to a seated position. Her skin was dewy and her eyes bright, as though she had been in a deep sleep and was waking refreshed and rested.

'Ebony, you did it. The demon is gone,' said Ivy.

Taking her daughter's hand, she began to cough. Ebony looked her way and smiled, but her eyes were glassy. Her skin shimmered as she surveyed her surroundings and colourful lights appeared, clustering all around her. Realising where she was, Ebony shook her head as though trying to clear her thoughts. 'What happened? Is everyone OK?'

'It all worked out just fine,' said Rufus, reaching forward to stroke his daughter's face.

As he made contact, a cluster of glitter exploded around them. Ebony's skin adopted a strange luminosity, her body straightening and strengthening. The silver mist expanded, grey sparkles filling the air.

'Winston!' cried Ebony, spying him on the ground nearby.

She reached for him but something invisible stopped her. Looking at her family, her face crumpled with worry. As the mists continued to grow, glittering and swirling around them, Ivy stopped coughing. It took a moment for Ebony to formulate her words.

'Why can't I reach Winston?' she asked. 'What's happening?'

As Uncle Cornelius whimpered, images of the battle came rushing back into Ebony's mind, the horrors playing through her mind in technicolour, burning way too brightly. But she also remembered Ambrose's words: Winston would choose the next guardian. Slipping *The Book of Learning* from her pocket, she opened it one last time. On the page, an image formed. It was Winston, handing the amulet up to a reaching hand. But only the arm could be seen. There was no clue as to who the next guardian would be.

On the ground, Winston was shaking, his fur on end. He wrapped his stumpy tail around his body in a hug, his eyes glistening as he watched. Feeling a weird sensation, Ebony looked down at her hand. As she opened her palm, the mark of the Shadow Walkers lifted off, the eye holes on the skull closing up; turning into a petal, it fluttered up into the sky. Looking closely at her hand, Ebony realised she was fading. Just like passing through to the Shadowlands, only this time, it was different.

A rustling sound came from all around and giggles rose and fell on the air. A girl in a white robe appeared from the shadow of a fern and walked towards them. Behind her came a girl with furs around her shoulders. Around them, colourful lights danced. Next, the cowgirl appeared, glowing slightly as she stepped out from behind a tree trunk. She smiled at Ebony and pointed to where the pirate incarnation was beginning to form, creating more colourful, shimmering lights. Ebony's heart skipped as each of her past lives appeared. The girls stood behind Ebony and, holding hands, they lifted their voices in song. Their lights converged above Ebony's head, flickering like lost stars.

'You've done it,' said Icarus. 'By destroying the Deus-Umbra and Ambrose, it seems you've achieved your destiny. The battle has ended and the Order can regroup. For now, there will be peace.'

'But Zach's still out there. We have to go after him.'

'And we will – but there is nothing more you can do.' He gestured at the others. 'It's in our hands now.'

'But what if he creates another soul-swapping machine?'

'That's for the next guardian to deal with,' answered Aunt Ruby, her face wet with tears. 'You've saved the Order. Your reward is Ultimation.'

Ebony took a long, deep breath.

'I have to return *The Book of Learning*,' she said, her voice barely audible and her body almost transparent.

'Don't worry, I'll do that,' said Icarus, gently taking it from her hand. 'The book will help me. Hush now. Stop fighting it.'

'But I don't want to leave Winston,' Ebony added in a whisper.

Blinking rapidly, Winston lifted his paw and waved. Ebony waved back, tears flowing down her cheeks.

The coloured lights flickered and joined. A chuckle sounded and, as a tiny spark shot across the dazzling array of colours, her Uncle Connie appeared, beckoning. And next to him was Grandpa Tobias, his kindly eyes smiling. Like Icarus, Connie's mark had now completely disappeared, along with any disfigurement: he looked strong and healthy. Aunt Ruby's eyes filled with tears. She stepped forward and held out her hand. Her husband reached out also – although they couldn't touch, they held their palms close together, their eyes dancing.

'You released him,' said Ivy. 'Thank you, Ebony.'

Her parents moved to Aunt Ruby's side and Rufus slipped an arm around her waist to steady her. He lifted his other hand to wave at his daughter, his farewell catching in his throat. As tears streamed down Ivy's cheeks, she waved also, a sad smile on her lips.

Ebony smiled back, tears dripping down her cheeks too, as she joined her uncle and grandpa and all her past selves. Everyone held their breath as Grandpa Tobias leaned in and kissed Ebony on the top of her head. And then they faded in a shimmer of light, leaving behind only air and sunshine, a rustle in the tree tops and a hint of silvery glitter on the grass. The gentlest song could be heard on the cool September breeze, like dragonflies and bells, moonbeams and ocean waves: the sound of the universe coming to claim its guardian.

Winston gripped the amulet tightly, his body quivering. Eyes red and his face blotchy, Icarus placed *The Book of*

Learning in his pocket before reaching down for Winston. 'Come here, little man,' he said.

But Winston was bouncing on the spot, pointing to the sky, where a single black petal spun and danced in the breeze. As Aunt Ruby reached out to grab it, the petal swirled by and landed at Winston's feet.

Winston leaned in and took a deep sniff.

It smelled of *Ebonius Tobinius* roses, the Atlantic and thick black curls.

The amulet safely secured around his neck, Winston scurried up onto Icarus's palm and settled on his shoulder. Although his heart thumped, he knew he had to be brave. The Order would help him. They would grow strong again and so would he. After all, he owed it to his best friend, Ebony Smart.

Acknowledgements

Huge thanks to everyone at Mercier Press, especially Wendy Logue, for helping me bring the final part of this story to fruition; it was a long journey, but worth every minute! Also to Sarah O'Flaherty for the amazing covers, and my agent, Sallyanne Sweeney, for her continuous support every step of the way.

Susan Tomaselli, Claire Hennessy, Sinead Gleeson, Caroline Busher, Alan Early, Jackie Lynam, Cath Ryan Howard, Vanessa O'Loughlin and Ashleigh Manning, you've all been continuously wonderful in so many ways – a writer's journey is an uncertain one, so thank you for everything!

Many of these words were written or edited in the Tyrone Guthrie Centre. Thank you to all the staff for providing a great workspace, incredible food, plentiful laughs, generous support and the month's exchange to Australia – I'm deeply grateful.

Varuna Writers' House (Australia) was an incredible experience – thank you to all my new friends there who made me welcome and created the perfect environment for getting my final edits completed, with special mention to Simmone Howell and Kirsten Krauth. Also, to the Arts Council of Ireland for helping with funds for my flight down under.

A big cheer goes to the beautiful village of Schull. I moved there expecting to stay a year and forgot to leave – one visit and you'll understand why. And another cheer goes out to my writing tribe; there are too many names to mention, but you know who you are.

To my husband, an incredible human with oodles of patience and an unwavering interest in my words: you're a rock star.

And finally, to my readers and supporters – with a special mention to Nate Hoerz, who had to wait patiently for each instalment to be sent to North Carolina – thank you for everything from the bottom of my heart.